Of Snow and Scarlet

A Little Red Riding Hood Retelling

Katherine Macdonald

K Macdonald

Cover design by: Lydia V Russell
Chapter headings by: InkWolf Designs

Contents

"Children, especially attractive, well bred young ladies, should never talk to strangers, for if they should do so, they may well provide dinner for a wolf. I say "wolf," but there are various kinds of wolves. There are also those who are charming, quiet, polite, unassuming, complacent, and sweet, who pursue young women at home and in the streets. And unfortunately, it is these gentle wolves who are the most dangerous ones of all."

--Charles Perrault--

PROLOGUE

The wolf watched the girl strip bark from the tree, her red hood dusted with fresh snowflakes. She was as pretty as a porcelain doll, with milk-white skin, rosy cheeks, and thick dark hair the colour of bitter chocolate. Her hazel eyes, screwed up in concentration, were framed by long lashes.

His mother had kept a doll like that, a remnant of a childhood he knew little about.

And never would.

Mama, Mama, Mama.

A chill breeze riffled through the glade, and he caught a whiff of her scent. She smelled of vanilla and chocolate and warm bread, and his stomach rumbled with a hunger for cinnamon buns, fresh from the oven.

Behind him, he felt a similar hunger rise from the rest of the wolves, and they stirred, sniffing the air.

They would never eat another human, his father had assured him. They would never harm them, either. But the alpha had a narrow view of the word *harm*. There was no harm in chasing a small human for sport, no harm in snapping at them. And if that human fought back…

Well, then it was self-defense.

The girl stilled, as if she sensed something amiss. The wolf shrank back into the bank, his white fur blending into the snow. She lifted her dagger into the air; a pretty, jewelled thing. Unusual for a common village girl.

She whispered something under her breath. "Nobody's dinner," she said. "*Nobody's dinner.*"

He could feel a thin kind of laughter emanating from Jean, one of the other young wolves, as if he took her words as a challenge. He cast his gaze towards the alpha, waiting for permission.

The alpha gave it.

The pack lunged as one, spurting down the bank in a blur of grey, brown, blue-black. The girl screamed, abandoning her basket, and tore off through the snow. The wolves gave chase, dark paws sinking into the ground, their snarls more like howls of laughter inside the young white wolf, who held back, cowering under the weight of the boy inside, the one who hated the sound of her screams that skidded against his lungs.

There was a tug inside of him, a hard pull, less like desire and more like the feeling of iron water against his chest, the need to breathe even when you knew you would drown. The pack was running. He must too.

One of the other wolves, a dark, shaggy black creature, the colour of a lake under darkness, stopped beside him. The beta. His father.

He glanced at him, as if asking why he was pausing, at the same time almost understanding. There was a reluctance in him, too.

But he ran. He ran faster than all of them.

And the young white wolf ran too, his body moving ahead of his mind.

Since joining the pack a few months earlier, he had frequently wished for strength. Strength to topple Jean, to run for longer, to endure more.

Now he wished for the strength to break away, to rip his mind from theirs, to do anything but blindly follow.

But he did not have that power.

The wolves streamed through the woods, a blur of fang and fur, a cacophony of snarls and snaps. Hard, rancid breaths iced the air.

The girl disappeared down a snowy bank, but her scent drifted onwards, down the river. The wolves continued to run.

Only the young one held back. Something had shifted or broken. The smell was still there, falling downriver, but it was like it had been peeled away from her, although how he sensed that was beyond him.

He paused, listening. There was a quiet whimper nearby, a snuffling sound. He inched closer, and found the little girl sheltering under an uprooted tree. She'd abandoned her cloak—likely throwing it into the stream—and now cowered shivering and sobbing in the snow.

She looked up at him and let out a sharp gasp, backing up

against the tree roots.

The young wolf lowered his entire body, shuffling forward on his belly. The girl was cold, and far from the path. She'd soon freeze out there in the cold.

He thought about trying to shift back, but his mind was still more wolf than boy, and he wasn't sure he could do it. When the whole pack was in wolf form, it was harder to snap back, to return to what he was, what he used to be.

I won't hurt you. Those thoughts came clear enough. *I am a wolf, but not a monster.*

Sensing he meant her no harm, the girl timidly reached out a hand. She'd snagged her fingers fleeing from the wolves, and tiny crimson droplets speckled the snow beneath.

No harm, hmm?

He inched forward and licked her hand, a disgusting action for a human, completely normal for him as a wolf. The lines between the two had become so blurred, so quickly.

The girl let out a soft cry, and wrapped her arms around his neck, burying her face in his fur.

Through his thick skin and the stiff cold, he felt her warmth, stirred beneath the small hands balled into his fur. It had been a long time since someone had held him; although the wolves slept together for warmth, they did not hold each other like this.

He missed his human shape, and the arms of others, with a pain so deep it felt like burning.

The girl sobbed for a long time, and when she was done, he tugged on her sleeve, and led her back to safety.

1 THE WOLF GIRL

While the other village girls dreamed of flowers and princes, of meadows and sweetcakes and ribbons and balls, I forever dreamt of wolves and winter. I dreamt of dark trees and white woods, of crimson droplets in the snow, and of a quiet, warm tug inside me that I had felt that day as a girl, and never since. A feeling of danger and safety intermingled as the wolf licked my wounds and guided me safely back to the road before vanishing like a creature of mist and shadow.

I had caught flashes of him in the years that followed, months, years even between, but he had never come to me again, sticking to the shadows as if I was the one with fangs and claws.

My wolf.

Sometimes I could hear him howling, the lone white wolf, and wondered what it was he called for. I felt sometimes like howling too, like that sound was locked inside me, waiting to erupt.

"I think you've kneaded that bread enough," said my

friend Daisy, nudging my elbow.

I gave up on the dough, and turned towards her. While most of the other girls scorned me—or I scorned them, I wasn't entirely sure—due to my sharp tongue and the not insignificant rumour that my grandma was a witch and that I had inherited some of her power, Daisy had never given in to such rumours. She was as lovely as the flower for which she was named, and even when the seasons turned and she could no longer wear fresh blooms in her natural curls, she made ones of felt to weave into her braids. The white petals glowed next to the black of her hair and the brown of her skin, making her dark, honey-eyes even lovelier.

We made a strange pair. Daisy was spring and petals and pearls and amber, and I was winter and berries and glass.

I supposed I could compare myself to the jewel for which *I* was named, but although I loved the ruby-red colour of the andesine, I never felt like a jewel, something pretty and sparkling. The only thing I had in common with an andesine was that we were both hard and sharp.

A gust of wind blew the door open, and in rushed my little brother Rowan, returning from school, dragging what felt like half the forest with him in terms of leaves.

"Ro!" I hissed. "Close the door!"

He grinned sheepishly, slamming it shut behind him, and raced up the stairs, dark curls bouncing, eyes blazing. He was so wild and ordinary in the way that people expected little boys to be that no one had ever accused him of being a witch, even if his brown eyes took on a goldish glint in the light.

Our father had had eyes like that. I remembered that

much about him.

Gold eyes. A knife. The way he made Mama laugh in a minute, and curse his name in another. The bang of the door when he was gone for the last time.

Nothing else.

For months afterwards, I expected him to return. That was what he did. A soldier, Mama said, to explain his frequent absences. Away for months, years at a time, so infrequently that all my memories of him had splintered over the years.

But he always came back.

"Not this time," Mama said. "And a good thing too."

I was sure he would return to see Rowan when he was born, but he never came, and months turned into years, and years turned into understanding. There were no wars to be fought, no reason for him to be away so long, and Mama didn't mourn him.

Sometimes I wondered if she hadn't killed him herself and buried him in the woods.

I wondered what happened to consciousness after death, if it floated to the afterlife like the village priest suggested, or if it remained chained to the earth. Perhaps it never truly left the body at all, and somewhere in a shallow grave, my father's spirit moaned beneath the earth.

A dark thought. No wonder the villagers thought I was a witch.

The door banged open again, and in hurried Forrest Carter, my only other friend in the village. He thought I was a little odd too, but it never seemed to set him on edge like it did anyone else. If I ever shared a dark thought with him, he usually laughed.

"Sorry, sorry!" he said briskly as I started to hiss, closing the door behind him. "Getting mighty nippy out there."

I glared at him. "Hence why we're trying to keep it *out there.*"

Forrest laughed. He was tall and broad-shouldered, despite his slim build, with the brown hair and brown eyes of most of the village. A lot of the girls thought him very attractive, but I'd known him too long to see him as anything other than *Forrest.*

"What brings you here?"

"Why, Red, your beautiful face, of course—"

I groaned, rolling my eyes. "Buy a loaf or get out."

"I am fine for loaves, alas. I just came to tell you that there's been a wolf sighting in the forest. A few of us are heading out to see if we can trap it."

I tensed. It had been years since I had seen *my* wolf, but I couldn't shake the fear every time the hunters gunned for one that the next pelt pinned above the fireplace of Forrest's father, Russell, would be one of purest white.

"Is it... must you hunt it now, before it's even hurt anyone?"

Forrest looked at me the way he rarely did, though I knew the look from others well— like I was mad. "You want us to wait until it hurts someone? *Killed* them?"

I shouldn't have said anything. Forrest was generally cordial and open-minded. He was the only person to know of my secret hobby—a secret I hadn't even shared with Daisy—but on the subject of wolves, he would not budge.

His mother had been killed by one eight years ago, and they had never found the creature responsible. I could still remember my own mother's screams as they brought the body back to the village, and although neither of us saw the remains with our own eyes—buried under tarpaulin—I had seen the look in Forrest's face as the carriage stopped in front of him.

You did not forget a look like that. It was branded into you.

"You're right," I said swiftly, because even though I knew that my wolf wouldn't do a thing like that, I wasn't going to argue on behalf of an animal, not to someone who had lost their mother to its brother. "I'm sorry," I added. "I didn't think."

Forrest shrugged it off. "I know the rest of the village thinks you've a mean streak—"

"She does," said Daisy, as if she was glad to have something to offer the conversation. "I still love her, but she does."

I wheeled round to scowl at her while Forrest laughed. He smiled at Daisy even as his hand found mine. His rough fingers felt a little strange in mine, although I ought to have been used to them by now. "You have a kind heart, Red, deep down. Underneath all those thorns and ice."

I yanked my hand away. "I'm sure you have a good heart too," I snipped, "underneath all that *cockiness.*"

He laughed again, loud and hard, for far longer than he needed to. Then he bid us farewell and stepped out into the cold.

I wondered why he'd bothered to come in at all. He hadn't even warned us about staying inside. Perhaps he knew I wouldn't listen. I rarely did anything but my own thing.

"A bun," said Daisy.

"What?"

"You should have offered him a bun."

"Why?"

"We've made too many, and you wouldn't want him to go hungry in the woods..."

"Wouldn't I?"

Daisy narrowed her eyes. She looked about as frightening as a chipmunk, but I seized the bun on offer and marched outside regardless. The cold clawed at my skin.

"Forrest!" I hollered.

He spun on his heels, leaves blowing up around him. "What?"

I hurled the bun in his direction, hitting him squarely in the face. He just had time to grab it before it smacked the floor.

"Daisy said you should have a bun!"

"Thank you!"

"Thank her!"

I returned to the bakery, shutting the door tight behind me. Daisy stared at me.

"What?"

"You'd have more friends if you didn't throw stuff at them."

"Don't need more friends. Got you. And baked goods. What else does a girl need?"

Freedom, said the voice inside me. *From closed-mindedness, or this tiny village, I am not yet sure.*

Daisy sighed, and might have readied another lecture if it weren't for my mother appearing from the back door that led to the rest of the house.

"Andie," she said, brandishing a basket, "I want you to take these supplies to your grandma. I'm worried the first snow will be upon us soon and I don't want her to starve out there on her own."

I snorted. I doubted my grandmother had any intention of dying any time ever, let alone of starvation. She was the kind of woman who could force sustenance from a frost-ridden garden just by staring at it.

She also kept a well-stocked larder, which helped.

"Sure," I said anyway, glad of the opportunity for a walk, an excuse to leave the village behind and traipse into the wildness of the woods.

"If you leave now, you should be able to get back before dark, but please, *please* stay at hers if you don't think you'll make it back in time. Stick—"

"Stick to the path, talk to no one, watch out for wolves, and—"

"Take your cloak," said Mama. She held out the thick red cape that my grandma had made to replace the one I lost all those years ago in the woods. She forced it around my shoulders and lifted up the hood. "Don't take it off."

"Why would any sensible person do that?"

"Many things I am blessed with, but a sensible daughter is not one of them."

"Thanks, Mama."

"You're welcome." She patted my cheek. "Now be off with you."

I took a quick excursion upstairs to grab my father's knife from the bedroom I shared with Rowan. I kept it beneath the rough canvas mattress, because any memory of my father set my mother on edge. She burned his shirts when he left, gave away his favourite tankard, discarded his spare boots. She chipped him away from the house. But I wouldn't let her take the dagger, even though I knew it must have been worth a pretty penny with its silver blade and ruby hilt.

One of the few good memories I had of my father was of him giving it to me. No one else in the village would have given a child a knife, but he said a wolf should have claws, and pressed it into my palm.

He'd gone before he could teach me how to use it, but I felt its weight inside my basket every time I left the house, and it transformed my red cape into armour.

Nobody's dinner, nobody's dinner.

Dagger retrieved, I slipped outside in the chill, dense air, the cold striking against my chest. There would be a thick frost tomorrow, if not snow. I stamped my feet and rubbed my hands, finding a pair of soft kid gloves in the pockets of my cape. I pulled them on, striding up the path, past the village gates.

The village of Thornwood was located in the middle of a dense forest, hours from the nearest town. It used to be a mining village some decades before, but the tin had long since dried up. It was on a decent trade route, however, which kept it going, although our main export was now timber and fur. The woods were abundant in wildlife, but only the locals could navigate it safely. Outsiders seldom lasted long in the forests.

I knew the woods well. They had been my playground as a girl. I had climbed the large oaks and swum in the rivers and lakes, scraping knees and arms and foreheads, each tiny scar a memento, a lesson.

But when the wolves were about, I rarely strayed from the path even in the finest of weather.

The route to my grandma's was long and slow, especially as I kept stopping to pick any berries or herbs I came across, knowing that the winter might soon rob me of the chance. The crisp leaves shone bronze and copper in the faint afternoon light, giving the woods a hazy glow despite the sharpness of the wind.

But any trace of light or warmth faded the minute my eyes fell upon my grandmother's house.

It was an old, crumbling chateau, once belonging to our ancestors, the owners of the mine. But the house had drained with the tin, sucked as dry as the stone. It had all the warmth and substance of a spider-web, looking as if a strong breeze might blow it away. It was a mesh of spindly turrets and wrought iron, gargoyles rubbed smooth by age and weather. The attics were infested with birds and wildlife, and the walls creaked and groaned with time and rodents.

My grandma, Agatha De Winter, lived alone in the chateau, keeping to a few rooms on the bottom floor. In the summer, she lived in the gardens, and in the winter she holed up in the kitchen beside the hearth.

Mama did not like how far away from the rest of the village she lived, how isolated she was in the woods, but the old lady would not move. She liked her freedom, liked her space, and even though I sometimes worried that the house was not exactly stable, I understood the appeal.

No prying eyes or judging glances. No snide remarks.

The main doors to the estate were rusted and crawling with ivy, thick with brittle bark. I instead crept round to the kitchen doors, where I found Grandma bent over a large cauldron. The room smelt of chicken and thyme. Feathers coated the table, along with an assortment of herbs, spices, pickles and cured meats.

Starving, she was not.

"Grandma?"

Grandma looked up, her weathered face breaking into a smile. She was not yet sixty, but she had the look of someone very old, a wisdom to her sharp, periwinkle eyes. Every grey hair and every wrinkle held some kind of story.

"Andie!" she declared, clapping floured hands together. "Delightful to see you, my dear."

"I come bearing gifts," I declared, placing the basket down on the table. She peeled back the cloth and started unpacking the goods: a fat tallow candle, a small pot of oil, a crusty loaf and a hunk of smoked ham. She gazed at the dagger at the bottom of the basket with a mixture of both approval and displeasure; unlike my mother, Grandma approved of me keeping myself safe.

What she didn't approve of was my father, and any lingering connection I might have to him. Both she and Mama acted like Rowan and I had sprung forth of our own free will and that no man had been involved in the process at all.

Sometimes, I'd stare at myself in a looking glass and try and find some hint of this face I didn't remember, some proof of his existence in the slope of my nose or the fineness in my cheeks. I couldn't. I looked too much like Mama, and had nothing else to compare it to.

My face was my own.

Rowan though... he looked a little like someone else. I wondered if the others could see it too.

Grandma said nothing about the dagger, though, stacking away the goods in her pantry. Unlike the rest of the house, it was impeccably organised, separated into food groups and rows and rows of neatly strung herbs and jars of ointments and potions.

I stared at the impressive collection. "No wonder the villagers think you're a witch."

"Ha!" she barked.

"Grandma," I asked carefully, keeping my words low as if the cobwebs might have ears, "*are* you a witch?"

Grandma threw back her head and howled, the laugh a deep, throaty cackle that did little to dispel my suspicions. "Wouldn't that be something?"

She headed into the pantry, me trailing behind her. "Grandma! Answer the question!"

"Oh, I don't think so, dearie, it's funnier if I don't."

"You're infuriating."

"Aye, but it keeps life interesting, doesn't it? Who'd want

to be boring and ordinary?"

I stilled, thinking of the villagers and their taunts. Once, many years ago, I strolled into the graveyard on the hunt for gallyweed, a type of medicinal herb that grew well in the cool, damp conditions of the cemetery. I had hoped to get in and out before anyone saw me, picking a morning so thick with mist that the stones swirled with it. Unfortunately, Laurence Dupont, local oaf, found me rooting in the dirt, basket stuffed with herbs and jars.

"Witch!" he laughed, so loudly that his friends, lurking nearby, came over to see what was happening.

No matter that gallyweed was helpful, that it could never be used to harm. Apparently nice, normal girls did not go hunting for it in graveyards.

Grandma raised an eyebrow, as if sinking into my memory. "*You* don't want to be ordinary, surely?"

"No," I said quickly, "I just wish I didn't have to hide being weird."

"Don't, then."

"They'll run me out of the village."

"Such a loss, I'm sure."

"Mama would be sad."

"Ah," said Grandma, with something like understanding, "I suppose she would. Well, you're all always welcome here."

I glanced around at the tapestries of cobwebs that she'd long given up clearing away, and listened to the slow, strained creak of the house. "We're all right for now, Grandma."

"Hmm. Suit yourself. Pastry?"

I took one of the rolls, stuffed with raisins and dates and vanilla, and slid into a seat at the table. Grandma wittered while she stirred the broth, cleared up the feathers, and scooped out the bones from the pot once the meat had sunk from them. She gave me a small bowl to sample, and packed up a measure in a flask for the journey back.

"Unless you'd rather stay the night?" she asked.

I shook my head, thinking longingly of my warm bed beneath the eaves above the bakery, Rowan's little body curling up next to me if it got too cold.

"Best be off, then," said Grandma, taking my cloak from the back of the door. "Take care on the road. Don't—"

"Stray from the path, or talk to strangers, yes, yes, I know."

"Good." She patted my hooded head. "Off you pop then, dearie. Hurry home."

I kissed her cheek, collected my basket, and slipped down the winding path towards the bent gates.

Finn's childhood was nothing short of ordinary. He never thought himself as any different from all the other boys in the province of Voulaire where he grew up. He went to school, he learnt to read and write, he ran hoops with children down the street and climbed buildings and got into mischief. He laughed and bled and hurt as much as anyone, and if his wounds healed a little sooner than others', and if his canines were a little sharper, nobody really took notice.

The only thing remotely amiss was his father.

He wasn't around a lot, but his absence was. Finn felt it in everything, in the way his mother always cooked enough for three, in case he turned up out of the blue, in the empty chair beside the fire, in every sigh of his mother's, every glance out of the window. He felt it in the sweep of her fingers when she brushed back his black waves, her gaze speaking the words she rarely did.

You look so much like your father.

She was miserable without him, and pure joy whenever he was around. A radiance bubbled inside her, she smiled and sang and danced around the kitchen, and Finn's father smiled too, twirling her in his arms.

Then, slowly, imperceptibly, something began to shift.

Finn couldn't tell when precisely it was, or when he noticed it, but his mother started to grow tense whenever his father came around. She was curt and stiff. She stopped touching him so much. Her eyes would brim in the quiet, still evenings, and something between the pair of them thickened. Finn could not explain it, but he could feel it.

Now she was happier without him, and miserable when he was around.

One night he heard them talking after he had gone to bed.

"You are forgetting me," said his mother, her voice low and hard.

"I will never," responded his father, with the soft, cool tone he always used.

"When he comes of age, you'll never come for me again."

"As long as you want me, I will come."

Finn didn't know what she meant by 'coming of age' but the next time his father came, his parents had an argument. Finn didn't want to hear, so he crawled under the bed and stuffed his fingers in his ears.

He used to look forward to his father's visits. He'd carve him toys by hand, and sit him on his knee, and tell him stories of all the places he'd been. He taught him how to hold a dagger and tie knots, how to balance a house of cards, how to carve himself. He'd ruffle his hair and praise him and tell him he was smart and clever.

But the older he got, the less time his father seemed to

have for him. He no longer felt welcome in his lap and was apparently too old for toys.

He began to wish the visits over, so that his mother would smile again.

Soon, even his father's absence didn't summon a smile from her. It was like planting a bulb in winter. Nothing seemed to make her happy.

Shortly after his tenth birthday, Finn fell ill. One moment, he was perfectly fine, playing with his friends in an alley not far from his home. The next, a splitting headache gripped him so suddenly that for a moment, he thought he'd been hit. But there was no mark, no blood. He stumbled back into his flat half-blind, the pain in his head so intense.

His mother felt his forehead and bundled him straight into bed. He did not remember her speaking. There were hands on him and, when he dared to open his eyes, a white, pale face, but she said nothing except, "It's just a fever."

She repeated this often.

It went on for days. He thrashed in his bed, teeth set, the pain spreading from his head to the rest of him, the feeling of his body being cleaved into. Every nerve was on fire. He guzzled water, but nothing helped.

"Just a fever," his mother repeated, dousing the sweat-sodden sheets, "you just need to sweat it out."

He thought he was probably going to die, that she was just trying to comfort him, or maybe herself. He felt like his bones were breaking, like he was rotting apart, like something in him was desperately trying to claw out of his chest.

On the fourth day, he let it.

It was like ripping off a bandage, like jumping into the ice. The burning world shifted into one all hard and cold. He slipped into something like sleep, and when he woke, his fever had broken, and his mother was on the floor beside him, crying.

Her arm was slashed, the sheets were cut to ribbons, and bite marks littered the furniture.

"Mama—"

"It's all right," she said.

But nothing ever was again.

2
THE WHITE WOLF

Despite the dark halls and the grim draftiness of the chateau, I had always liked visiting Grandma, even as a child when I should have been scared of shadows, horrified of my grandma's stories about a castle where they came alive and had eyes in the dark. She told me tales of haunted forests, of kingdoms of thorns, of enchanted fairy palaces haunted by talking beasts who were really beautiful princes in disguise. She told me of wolves who were really men, or men who were really wolves, and although Mama told her to stop frightening me, the stories never did. Sometimes I felt like my human shape didn't match my soul, and it was a comfort to know I was not alone in the world.

Rowan was not so fond of them. Once, he was so scared he refused to walk home and I had to carry him all the way on my back. Apparently, the wolves couldn't get him if he was riding his sister.

"Don't let the wolves get me!" he had cried.

"Never," I said, and I took out our father's dagger. "No

wolf alive stands a chance against me!"

He laughed against my neck, and snuggled into my back.

It was a fond memory to recall, but it did little to dispel the chill that had settled into the air as I made my way home from grandma's that day, the wind thicker and colder than before. I kept to a brisk pace, my breath coming out in icy spurts.

It was a pleasant evening, despite the cold, and the rustling in the undergrowth did nothing to alarm me, at least not at first. It was likely a squirrel or a bird. Nothing to cause any kind of alarm.

It was only after half an hour that I realised the sounds hadn't let up, that the rustling of leaves only stopped when I did, and sometimes… sometimes I thought I heard breathing.

I kept moving, singing a song to quieten my pounding heart and dispel the gathering gloom.

"Once I was a maiden fair,
A crown of daisies in my hair.
To a man I gave my heart,
Thinking we would never part.
He took my love and my smile from me,
And now I sing beneath a tree."

It was possibly not the best choice, a dark, morbid song, that kissed the crisp air like a ghost swirling above a grave. I tried to think of a better one, humming a ditty about sunshine and meadows, but the words turned to felt on my tongue, unable to hold shape.

I had just turned onto the wide road when there came a

sudden snap and a painful, high-pitched yelp.

My blood ran cold.

Oh no.

I scrambled through the trees towards the noise, already knowing exactly what I would find. A vision of white and red flashed in my mind, the sound of whimpering crawling against my bones.

In a patch of leaves, its front paw clamped between the teeth of one of the hunters' traps, stood a white wolf. Blood splattered the forest floor, crimson droplets against the brown. It looked up at me with luminous eyes of ice-blue sapphire.

My wolf.

It let out a growl, low, forced, gnawing fruitlessly at the iron teeth.

"Steady, steady," I whispered, wondering what on earth I was doing. Was I honestly going to try and free a wolf?

But not just any wolf. Mine. It had saved me, once. It was only right I return the favour.

"I want to help you," I said softly. "But I need to know you're not going to attack me afterwards."

The wolf tilted its head as if it could understand me.

Foolish, foolish, I kept thinking, all the way to taking out my knife and forcing the hilt against the pressure pad.

The trap sprang free.

The wolf looked up at me, as if half surprised to find himself there at all, and scampered to the other side of the glade. I expected him to disappear, but he stayed a little distance away, licking his wounded paw.

It was still bleeding badly. An infection could end him out here, or he might starve to death before he healed, unable to hunt. A wounded animal in the forests only survived through luck.

I wished I didn't have to leave him to fend for himself. His whimpers slid against my chest.

"I can... I can help you with that," I offered, hardly knowing what I was saying, or why I supposed a wolf would listen. "There's a little hut nearby where I can wash and clean that for you."

The wolf stopped licking himself, just for a moment.

This is silly. I'm talking to a wolf like it can understand me.

But it did *seem* to understand me, just like he had understood me seven years ago, when he had guided a frightened little girl back to the path.

I wondered how old he was. He had seemed fully grown when we first met, but he didn't look old, now. Wolves rarely lived past eight years, although perhaps they might live longer if they were cared for. No way of knowing.

The wolf stood up.

"You're going to follow me?"

The wolf did nothing, not until I slowly backed out of the glade. He limped on after me, tame as a dog, not leaving my side until we reached the hut beside the lake. The sun was just starting to set, the whole place aglow with amber light, striking the silent pane of water like a glass.

The hut itself was barely visible until you were standing in front of it, nestled beneath the canopy of trees and the folds of the rock. I had discovered it several summers ago.

It must have belonged to an old woodcutter, as it was still stacked with wood, and it was this I used to try and restore it, hoping to make it something of a haven, a space of my own away from the prying eyes of the villagers.

Unfortunately, Forrest had followed me there one day, not long after I turned fourteen. I knew him, of course—I knew everyone in the village—but I knew him a little better. Our mothers had been friends, and we went to school together. Despite this, we'd never really spoken a great deal. I had some memories of being forced to play with him in our youth as our mothers prattled, but at school we largely ignored one another. The best I could say about him was that he never called me weird names, never hissed 'witch' under his breath when I passed him in the school yard, and that I'd never been tempted to pretend to hex him.

I'd found that to be one good way of dealing with the sniggering, snide remarks. One day, Laurence Dupont caught me reading a book about herbs during lunchtime, and jeered that I was looking up ingredients for a spell. He tried to take the book from me, so I snapped and said, "You know, Laurence? I *am* looking up ingredients for a spell. I'm trying to find a potion to slip into your morning milk that will make all your hair fall out..."

Laurence tried to laugh, but as luck would have it, he turned around to chuckle to his friends and slipped on a loose bit of grass.

Slipping and hair loss were two entirely different things, but it was enough to rattle him. Enough to make him wonder if I *could* place a curse on him. Enough to make him leave me alone.

And everyone else, too.

Daisy didn't move to town until the following year. I had no one. Suddenly, an ice-cold loneliness had seized me. I had always been alone, but only truly felt it back then.

The day that Forrest found me down by the lake, trying to fix the hut with the rusty tools I'd borrowed from our neighbour, I'd run away from school and felt like never going back. I hated it there. I hated the pupils and stiff room and the repetitive tasks and the old schoolmistress who never noticed how the other children behaved towards me. I dreamed of running away and becoming a herbalist in a castle in some far-off place. Perhaps I could save the life of a rich queen with my knowledge of medicinal herbs and she would reward me with a place at her court, and I could spend the rest of my days devising new remedies with like-minded people.

I don't know what he was doing there, or why he came to speak to me, but he did.

"I like your cloak," he said.

I startled. It was too warm to wear it whilst trying to fix the hut, but Mama always insisted I take it with me into the woods, a sort of good luck charm. I'd discarded it the minute I arrived.

"My grandma made it," I told him, not sure what else I was supposed to say.

"Is it supposed to ward off evil?" he asked, sounding smug. "You know, since you're supposed to be a—"

"Don't," I said.

His face fell. "Right. I'm sorry."

No one had ever apologised for calling me a witch before, and he hadn't even said the word.

I turned back to the hole in the wall I was trying to patch up, struggling to get the plank in place as I hammered it. Forrest, saying nothing, came forward to hold it while I nailed.

"What is this place?" he asked.

I shrugged. "Old woodcutter's hut, I think."

"Why are you fixing it?"

I stilled, unsure of whether or not I could trust him. Maybe this was all part of a ruse, some long joke he was playing with the other boys at school. Maybe he was waiting to trap me inside and then tell me I'd have to use my powers to escape. A couple of years ago before I pretended to hex him, Laurence had played a similar trick with some of the other boys, and trapped me in a cupboard after school.

It took my mother an hour to find me.

But… Forrest wasn't like the others, and my mother was still friends with his father, who had always been kind to me. Russell would have had his head if he did anything like that.

"I want a place to store my herbs and potions," I told him, and I pointed to the bundles and jars I'd already collected. "I'm not a witch," I explained. "I'm a herbalist."

For a moment, Forrest said nothing. "The villagers are idiots if they don't see the worth of a herbalist," he managed eventually.

"*Most* of the village are idiots."

"Can't disagree there."

In hindsight, Forrest likely didn't believe that. He'd always fitted in well with the others. He was friendly and affable and not of such intelligence that he believed himself above people.

But he was trying to cheer me up, and I appreciated that.

“Let me help you,” he continued. “Let me help you fix this place up.”

At that, I bristled. “I have nothing to trade—”

“Let me share the hut with you, then. I’d love to have a place to store my fishing gear, but I’ll let you do whatever else you like with it. And I promise not to disturb you when you’re down here. Or tell anyone about it. It can be our secret.”

I was used to secrets. I was not used to being able to share them. I decided I quite liked the idea.

“All right,” I said, after a brief pause. “I accept.”

For days and weeks afterwards, we patched it up together, stealing away into the forests in every scrap of spare time we had. Forrest borrowed better tools from his father, bartered a chest from the carpenter to store our equipment, and I used buns to bribe him into cutting our wood for us.

We worked until our fingers bled, and picked splinters from each other’s hands.

After a month, the hut was as sturdy and tight as it had ever been.

Neither of us were quite ready to finish the project yet, so we set ourselves the task of building furniture. Poor seamstress though I was, I crafted curtains for the window and painstakingly stitched a patchwork quilt and a rough mattress with a little help from Grandma. We built wonky shutters and sometimes joked about making it our proper home.

Forrest started calling me "Little Red" after my cape. The "Little" part had thankfully dropped over the years, and I didn't mind the "Red" part. I liked most things about Forrest, just not... not the part he perhaps wanted me to like.

Trying not to think on that, I unlatched the door and shuffled into the hut. The wolf limped in after me, stretching out beside the empty hearth, as if awaiting a fire. He panted, and I took a dish from the table and filled it with water from the lake, which he guzzled happily.

The hut was a small space packed with firewood, housing a rudimentary bed, a simple table and chair, a couple of chests of supplies and shelves and shelves of jars and bottles, all stuffed with herbs... and poisons.

The wolf glanced up at them as if he could read the faded labels. *Belladonna, nightshade, foxglove.*

"I know what you're thinking," I said, as if he could think at all, "but I'm not a witch. And I'm not trying to poison anyone. I'm a herbalist. I just like knowing how it all works." I took one of the jars from the bottom shelf. "This one might help your paw, if you'll let me?"

The wolf made no motion to move, sliding back down to the floor. Deciding he was no threat to me, I started a fire, boiled up some water, and carefully cleaned the bloodied limb. The wolf whimpered a couple of times, but never once tried to bite me in retaliation.

"You really are a very good boy," I said, scratching behind his ear. "I'd take you home with me, if I could. Although the villagers would *definitely* think I was a witch, if I managed to tame a wolf. Best not inflame those rumours, sweet as you are."

The wolf leaned into my touch, closing his eyes. I pressed a poultice against his paw, and bound up his wound. It was late by this point, far too late to think about going home. Darkness had folded around the lake, and the whole room was awash with the deep amber glow of the fire.

I got up from beside the hearth and pulled the shutters to, blocking out the night. The catch was broken and I couldn't fully close it. Too dark now to fix it; a job for tomorrow. It would keep some of the warmth in, at least, even if it wouldn't quite block out the dawn.

I took the flask of Grandma's broth from my basket and poured a little into the wolf's dish. "I don't have much, I hope you're not too hungry."

The wolf, of course, devoured every last drop, while I sipped the rest from the flask. It was a thin evening meal, but I was glad of it nonetheless, stroking the wolf's fur absent-mindedly as I slurped.

"I suppose we best stay here for the night," I told him. "I daresay it's better than your usual bed."

The wolf gave me a sleepy, wolfish grin, and settled down by the hearth. He was asleep within minutes.

I glanced over at the cot in the corner of the room, wondering why we'd set it so far away from the fireplace and then realising that neither of us, to my knowledge, had ever actually slept over here. It was just something we'd made to pass the time, to make the place seem more homey. I might have napped on it a couple of times before, but never during winter.

Forrest had added a fur to our collection of blankets and quilts, and I tugged all of them from the bed now to pile beside the hearth. It would be warmer to sleep next to the wolf, who seemed about as fearsome as a puppy.

And how many opportunities did one have to curl up beside such a beautiful creature? His fur was a mix of rough and satin, and he smelled of cold earth and pine as I huddled next to him and breathed deeply into his neck.

I didn't expect to sleep easily on the floor with the wind howling outside, but very quickly I felt myself drifting into darkness, lost to the pleasant aroma of soft and easy dreams.

I didn't stir an inch until faint whispers of dawn light came slithering through the broken shutters.

Half asleep still, my fingers reached out for the warmth of the wolf, only to be met with smooth, human skin.

I opened my eyes.

Next to me was an impressively sculptured man with dark, tousled hair.

And he was very, very naked.

I drew a sharp gasp. His eyes opened.

"Morning," he said sleepily.

I started to scream.

3
A WOLF WITHOUT

I scrambled to my feet, snatching up my dagger and punching open the shutters fully, as if hoping to dispel this vision with sunlight. It went nowhere. Lying across the floor was a very naked, perfectly chiselled figure of a man.

"You're a man!" I shrieked.

The man—perhaps more of a boy—leapt upright, light as a cat despite the well-muscled form of him. "Well, clearly," he said, gesturing to the vaguely hidden part of him that rather proved it.

"But you were a wolf! And now you're a man!"

"Oh good, we've established that. I was worried you were going to think I was a random stranger who'd crawled in here uninvited."

"I invited a wolf in, not a man! A very, very, naked man!"

"Which part is bothering you most? I'll happily cover up if you have anything I could—"

"Stay where you are!" I hissed, brandishing the dagger. "I will stab you!"

"I believe you, but I must say, I'm not entirely threatened."

I picked up a log from beside the fire and threw it at him. It smacked him on the foot. It had the rather unintended side effect of making him drop his hands to clutch his toes, displaying everything I was desperately trying to avoid. I squeaked and wheeled around.

"Oww!" the wolf-boy hissed.

"You shouldn't have come in here if you were actually a man!"

"I was hurt! You were helping me. I thought I'd just slink off in the night but then *you* decided you wanted to snuggle!"

"I wanted to snuggle the *wolf!*"

"Who wants to snuggle a *wolf?*"

"What…" My mind whirred, the thoughts turning gummy on my tongue. "What *are* you?"

"A lycanthrope," he returned.

"A what?"

"It's the name given to wolf-shifters. There's a few types —"

"You're… you're a werewolf?"

"Um, not quite. Traditional werewolves are bitten, and change into a wolf-monster every full moon. I can shift at will, more or less, although I sometimes shift unconsciously when I'm asleep… as you see."

He stared at me, as if waiting for the next question, but my mind had gone completely blank. *Werewolves are real. Or shape-changers are real.*

Magic was real. All the stories my grandma used to tell me

—how true were they really?

"There's quite a bit to get through, shall I make some tea?" he said eventually. "It's been a long time since I had some tea and I rather fancy some."

I stared at him, mind still bare, but somehow summoning just enough conscious thought to be amazed over the boldness of the suggestion. "This is *my* hut."

"Then you'll know which leaves make the best tea." He flashed a wolfish grin. The tips of his canines were slightly more pronounced, not quite fangs, but sharper than the average human.

I inched towards the shelves, trying to work out if I should run for it, or kick him out, and if it was completely ludicrous to be even thinking about sitting down to tea with a not-quite werewolf.

But it was awfully cold, and he was naked, and I was curious.

I took off my cloak—still fastened around my shoulders as an extra blanket, and hurled it at him.

"Cover up."

He took it gratefully, offering the fabric a sniff. His blue eyes darkened to the point of black.

"What is it?" I asked.

He sniffed the air again, pausing carefully. "Bakery?"

"What?"

"Do you work at a bakery?"

"I... yes."

"Your scent is delicious."

"Umm... thank you?"

He was still staring at me. Not in the way that men sometimes did, with an ugly kind of wanting. It was more like surprise, a little wonder. "You're welcome."

I crept towards the fire, adding in kindling, stoking the low embers. I was careful not to take my eyes off him, even as I unlatched the pot hanging over the fire and shuffled towards the door. My dagger never left my side.

I slipped outside, a freezing chill fastening on my skin. A thick frost gnawed at the ground, and I made my way carefully towards the stream that trickled into the lake, filling the pot halfway. I tried not to gasp at the cold, bitter and biting though it was. My body craved the warmth of my cape.

I marched back inside, re-hanging the pot over the low flames. The wolf-man had moved over to the cot, which made it easier to keep an eye on him as I picked leaves and herbs from the shelves, adding them to the slow, simmering waters.

"So... how much of last night do you remember?" I asked, my voice low. It seemed as good a place to start as any.

"You mean, how much am I conscious of in wolf form?"

"Yes."

"Pretty much everything, most of the time," he explained, "but it's... muted, perhaps is the best word, and sometimes overruled by instinct. Yesterday, for example, when I was stuck in the trap, I just tried to get out of it before trying to work out *how* to do that, exactly."

My eyes caught his hand, still wrapped up in a bandage, now looking uncomfortably tight. Should I offer to remove it?

But doctoring a person felt an awful lot more intimate than an animal, a lot more strange.

You slept next to him, I realised, my cheeks hot, *and he was conscious of it. How much more intimate do you want to be?*

My traitorous gaze fell to his impressively sculptured chest, to his toned arms and muscled legs, and I felt a hotness on the back of my neck.

A bit more, apparently.

"What's your name?" he asked.

"Andesine," I told him, my voice little more than a whisper. "You?"

"Finn," he replied.

Finn. White, or fair. It suited his wolf form, and even this one, despite the dark curl of his hair. His skin was pale as milk.

My mouth went dry, but I pulled out my words. "About eight years ago, I was saved by a white wolf. That *was* you, wasn't it?"

He nodded.

"And the other wolves that day—"

"Like me."

"Where are they now?"

"Not here. That's all I know."

"Are you alone here?"

"Yes."

"Why?"

He shrugged. "Complicated."

"How long have you been alone?"

"A year now, or coming up to it. I split from the pack last

winter." His eyes cast over me, as if he could see something else on my face, or was remembering something else. Whatever it was, he didn't share.

I chewed my lip. "How old are you? Do wolves age differently, or—"

"Our wolf forms reach maturity before we do, if that makes sense, but our human bodies age much as yours. Heal faster, though. Tend to be prettier." He flashed me another grin, but I did not return it. "I'm eighteen," he finished. "You?"

"The same."

I stirred the tea, inhaling the smell of brewing herbs. "Have you been in the woods all of this time? I haven't seen you for years."

"I've been here for the better part of a year," he said, "keeping my head down. Mostly sticking to wolf form. Going human for a while if any of your hunters got a bit overzealous."

"And before that?"

"Travelling with the pack."

"You've travelled?"

"Everywhere," he said, his pupils wide.

A thousand other questions burned inside me, but I tried to stick to the point. "The legends say that wolves can be killed with silver bullets," I said. "Is that true?"

"Well, yes, but it seems like a jolly good waste of silver. A regular bullet would work just fine, in the right place."

"So silver is fine, what about wolfsbane?"

"Should I be worried that you're so interested in killing

us?"

"I—" I dropped the ladle. "I've never met a lycanthrope before, and I'm curious."

He glanced up at my shelves. "You just like knowing how things work, right?"

I nodded, spooning out weak herbal tea into rough receptacles. Finn shuffled forward, cape hugged around his middle, and took one of the cups. He sat down beside me, not too close.

"Wolfsbane is deadly, even in very small doses, unless we receive an antidote."

"Mountain ash?"

"We can't cross a circle of it."

"What about grapes?"

He blinked. "Grapes?"

"Yes, or raisins. Daffodil bulbs?"

"What... what are you talking about?"

"They're deadly to dogs, so I thought maybe..."

Finn crinkled with laughter. "I've never munched on a daffodil bulb before. As for the others... I can confirm I can eat them in human form. Never tried as a wolf before. But I'll stay away from them now." He turned his eyes back to my herb collection. "You know a lot about this stuff for a bakery girl."

"Everyone needs a hobby," I declared, and looked awkwardly down at my cup. I took a long sip. "The villagers think I'm a witch. They caught me collecting herbs in the graveyard a few years ago and it spurned a rumour. No one wanted to buy my bread for a week. Mama was furious."

"So you moved your little laboratory out here?"

I nodded.

"Anyone else know about it?"

"I have a friend who helped me fix it up, but he's never told. He sometimes uses it for fishing."

"A friend?"

"Yes, a friend. Do you know what that is?"

Finn did not move.

"That wasn't supposed to be a hard question to answer."

"It's not supposed to be hard to have friends, and yet, here I am."

I wanted to ask why he'd separated from the rest of the pack, but despite all the rest of the information he was giving me, he hadn't volunteered that when we'd brushed past it earlier, and it seemed rude to pry. "So, you can shift any time you like? The full moon thing is a myth?"

"Ah, no. On the full moon, we *must* shift, and we become a little… wilder, then. More like a normal wolf."

"You don't have a choice?"

"It's very painful to resist. I don't recommend it."

I paused. "Does it hurt? When you do it now?"

He shook his head. "Not anymore. As natural as breathing. The first few times… those can be rough."

A strange shred of sympathy stirred unbidden inside me, for this stranger I hardly knew. Something inside tingled with the notion of reaching out and touching him, to expunge that memory of pain.

But I don't know you.

And I was rarely the most sympathetic of people at the

best of times. I wasn't usually cruel, but most of the time people told me sad things, I wondered why they were telling *me,* as if there was someone better they should speak to. I seldom felt truly sorry for anyone outside my immediate family, except Daisy. Maybe Forrest.

My family. What was the time? Mama would naturally assume I'd spent the night at Grandma's, but I seldom tarried long when I did. I ought to head back to help with the baking.

"I should go," I told Finn. "I'll be missed at home."

"Right," said Finn. "Need an escort?"

"You're naked."

"I don't have to be."

"Do you—"

"What?"

"You do have clothes somewhere, right?"

"Ha! Yes. I've got a cave a little upstream where I keep some supplies. It's not quite as cosy as your little hut, but it suffices."

"Right, well..." He still had my cape wrapped around his middle. "I need my cloak."

"Oh, of course," he said, biting back a grin. "Ah, er, do you want to close your eyes?"

Not really, and yes, definitely.

I shook my thoughts away, glad that mind-reading wasn't a werewolf power. I shut my eyes tightly and without complaint, saying nothing as I heard the slow rustle of fabric and felt the drop of it around my shoulders, warmed by his skin. I was aware of how close Finn was to me, his body radiating heat, his face only inches from my own.

Calloused fingers slid under mine, and raised my hand to his lips. They were just as soft as they looked.

"I thank you for your hospitality, Andesine," he said, his voice rough and gentle. "Perhaps we'll meet again."

The door banged open. I glanced towards it, but he was already gone, a fleck of white fur skittering along the frosty bank, away into the trees.

In the days that followed his first transformation, his mother told him the basics: he was a wolf, like his father. He would one day be able to shift his form at will, but during the full moon he'd had no choice. No, it wouldn't always hurt. Yes, he would always be out of control.

After that, she became something like a ghost, her touches transparent. And although she met his eyes, her gaze seemed filmy, like there was something between them. He was only a child and could not quite explain.

It happened once more before his father came again. It was bad, but not as bad as before, although the shredded bedclothes and ruined furniture told another story.

This time, though, it was limited to his room. His mother locked him in. He didn't hurt her.

And she didn't stay with him.

His father arrived late one night. Finn woke to them talking. He was used to listening to the two of them, sometimes spying them through the gap in the door when they thought no one was watching. His mother would sit in his father's lap and he would play with her hair, flaxen strands weaving through his calloused fingers. He would murmur soft things in her ear, too quiet for anyone to hear, and the image was warm and bright, smooth as velvet.

There was nothing soft or warm about this conversation.

"Fix him," his mother said. "Make it go away."

"I can't," his father replied. "You know I can't. You knew this would happen—"

"I didn't know," his mother wept. "I didn't know then what I know now. I didn't know what it would be like…"

Finn's stomach clenched. He knew what she meant, or thought he did. She didn't know how awful it would be, how he could hurt and destroy.

Make 'it' go away.

Make him go away.

"He should come with us," his father said.

"No." His mother's voice was dark. "No. Absolutely not. I forbid it."

Finn's mind flashed back to another conversation he had overheard, years beforehand.

When he comes of age, you'll never come for me again.

It was not him that she didn't want to lose, but his father.

He didn't want to hear the rest. He crept back to his bed and slammed his head under his pillow, praying for the release of sleep.

His father spoke to him in the morning, told him that it soon wouldn't hurt at all, but echoed everything else his mother had said. He spoke of the pack, of a group of men and boys just like them, "brothers" he called them.

Finn frowned. "No girls?"

His father shook his head. "The wolf gene is uncommon in females. Not unheard of, but rare."

"So what do you do if one of them *is* a girl?"

His father's jaw tightened. "Our alpha thinks that women shouldn't join our pack. That it would stir up trouble, that they wouldn't be suited to our way of life."

Finn didn't know what to say to that, but it didn't feel right or likely. "What's an alpha?" he asked instead.

"Our leader. The strongest. We follow his orders."

"Why?"

"It's good to have rules."

"Like not having girls?"

At this, his father said nothing. "You belong with the pack now, Finn. With me."

Finn looked over at his mother, but she would not meet his gaze. "I'm not going if Mama can't come."

His father sighed, but he patted his head. "I'll come back in a month. We'll see if you haven't changed your mind, then. Try not to hurt your mother again in the meantime."

After he left, his mother sobbed.

"I'm sorry, Mama," he said.

"It's not your fault," she said, dabbing her eyes. "We'll... we'll have to find another way to control your wolf. Don't worry. It'll be fine."

On the next full moon, she bought him chains and tied him to the beams. There was a muzzle, too. Finn could feel the wolf trying to escape all day, but she would not comfort him, other than uttering, "it's fine, it's fine," in a shapeless, ghostly fashion.

Finn did not feel fine, and he knew she didn't either.

But when his father came again, he still said no.

After the next full moon, when the neighbours complained of noise, when he noticed the hollows under his mother's eyes, how pale and grey she looked, he wondered if he shouldn't just go to spare her.

4
A STORM OF WOLVES

I swilled out the cups, put out the fire, and headed back to the village. My mind swirled with the impossible truths I'd just learned. I shouldn't have been surprised—there were enough local legends about werewolves and whispers of magic—but I was still shaken.

And yet, underneath all that shock and surprise was a stranger feeling, almost like grief, like I'd said goodbye too soon.

I wondered if we would meet again.

It must have been lonely out there in the woods, especially given how long he'd been there. Had he ever wandered into Thornwood for supplies? Had I served him once at the bakery? I didn't think I'd forget a face like his, and yet some days I was utterly oblivious to everything around me, dreaming up new concoctions and recipes and thinking eagerly of fleeing to the woods once we shut up for the day.

I was not always the most observant of people.

Yet my mind now had a narrow, pinpoint focus, and I could not scrub Finn from it.

Daisy and Mama were busy in the bakery when I arrived home, but I was permitted to change and grab a bite to eat before joining them. Mama twittered asking after Grandma and how she was grateful I'd stopped overnight rather than risked getting caught out after dark.

I flushed, hoping the hotness of the oven could disguise my roasting cheeks, wondering what Mama would say if she knew I'd spent the night in the arms of a man.

Boy.

Wolf-man.

"Are you all right?" Daisy asked when Mama had slipped into the back.

I wanted to tell her. I rarely kept secrets from Daisy. But I didn't know how to explain it, or if Daisy would understand. Maybe she'd tell someone else.

Forrest wouldn't be happy to learn that the wolf they were tracking was secretly a human, not when—

I stopped kneading the bread. His mother. Killed in a wolf attack.

But what if it wasn't a wolf at all?

It could hardly have been Finn, who would only have been a boy then, but maybe… maybe a member of his pack. Maybe the rest of the wolves were a bit more… wolfish.

Maybe that's why he hadn't wanted to talk about them.

I should have asked more questions.

"I didn't sleep too well at Grandma's," I said, guilt curdling inside me at the lie.

"Wild animals in the bedroom, again?"

"Something like that."

My palms felt hot against the dough, flushed with the memory of that split second when they had reached out for fur and found hard, taut muscle instead.

I should probably take a walk after I was done for the day.

Alas, by the time work was finished, Rowan was home too, and needed some help with his school work while Mama was readying dinner. By the time all was done, only the faintest trickle of light remained along the horizon, and I was sure any walk I took would tug me into a new kind of danger, one that could not be dispelled with a dagger.

"You're quiet this evening, darling," my mother remarked. "Late night at Grandma's?"

"We should try and patch up her roof." It was a nothing statement, neither a lie nor a truth, just something to keep her from pulling at that thread.

It worked, too. Mama gave a non-committal sound, knowing there was little money to even fix parts of that crumbling estate, let alone a roof, and returned to her mending.

Rowan climbed into my lap and demanded a story. Half the time he declared he was too old for such a thing, and he was getting to the age when he squirmed away from me whenever I reached for him, so I tried to savour the moments when he still wanted me. Daisy had little siblings too, and they were all now completely disinterested in getting her attention. Daisy never complained—she never complained about anything—but I knew she missed that time.

So I read until my voice was numb, and then took him up to bed, tucking him into the little bunk beside my own and drawing up the patchwork quilt. It was another creation of Grandma's, and the squares were printed with flowers and trees and the occasional whisper of a wolf. Despite his fears, Rowan was almost as drawn to them as I was.

"Song," he whispered, "Please."

I smiled. "Which one would you like?"

"The one about the lonely wolf."

At this, I paused. Mama hated that one. We'd learnt it instead from our grandma, and I'd always loved it, even when Mama twitched whenever we sang it.

"Please," Rowan repeated. "Mama won't hear if you sing it quietly."

"All right," I said, and brushed his soft curls.

"Midnight, moonlight, the dusk is swept away,
Sleep now, children, night is the wolves' day.
Under the moonlight, the lonely wolf cries,
Deep in the forest, the trees have turned to lies.
Sunlight to shadows, the woods are painted dark
The river turns to silver and the moon into a heart—"

Rowan was fast asleep before I could finish, bunched up under the covers. I disentangled myself from his limbs, tucked him in tight, and went to close the shutters.

A sharp shaft of wind bit against my skin, and the first flakes of snow drifted under the faint light of the lamps.

It would be very cold in the woods tonight.

The thing about being exposed to any kind of magic, is

that you were never quite the same afterwards. If something went missing around the house in the days that followed, I wondered if it was fairies. When someone spoke of memory loss, I wondered if they were under a curse. Once even the smallest bit of magic drops into your life, it is only natural to fixate on it.

Which was surely the only reason I was still thinking of Finn.

And how cold it was.

And if he spared a thought for me.

There were also the traps. I had no idea how many the hunters had laid, only that Forrest had come back grumbling that at least two had been dismantled, which suggested Finn was being smart and travelling about in human form where he was hopefully a little more observant.

On the fourth day, I got up early in the morning and set off into the woods in search of berries. The fresh snow meant the delivery from the city had been delayed, and Mama was moaning about plain buns and the lack of variety. I grabbed a long stick to set off any traps I came across, although most were now buried beneath the snow.

The search for berries brought me deep into the woods, further than I'd been in a while. I kept my eyes peeled for Finn, and sang loudly, possibly foolishly, in the hope that he might hear it and appear out of nowhere.

Snow started to fall as I trekked back, basket bursting. It got heavier just before I reached the lakes, whipping into a frenzy. It was a blinding, blistering, howling wind, a wadable frost, thick as mud that fastened on my clothes and features.

Cold snapped at my bones, burned at my skin. Several times I stopped, unable to move, the storm iron against me.

I'd have to stop at the hut. I couldn't go on like this.

But when I looked up, I realised that the snowfall had covered *everything.* I couldn't tell south from north, east from west. The trees, usually as familiar to me as the houses of the village, were all at once utterly unfamiliar, mere wisps in the bitter wind.

I crouched down beside an embankment, trying to steady my breathing. I could do this. I just needed to rest for a moment, gather my bearings. *Think, Andie, think.*

But the cold gnawed at my clothes, and my bones would have rattled if I wasn't frozen stiff. I knew I needed to move, but which way?

A pair of black boots appeared before me, sinking into the dense snow. A hand, large and calloused, stretched out.

And a voice, unfamiliar and known.

"Get up."

Finn.

I took his hand and hauled myself up, my legs nearly buckling under the heaviness of the rest of me. I crawled up his arm, clinging to him.

Arms circled round my back, under my legs, and lifted me against his chest. His breath brushed my forehead. "Hold on," he instructed, as my fingers coiled around the fur strapped to his shoulders.

His warmth radiated through his chest, dusting my own, and I clung to that as we jostled through the forests, the world blurring into white, his feet guided by something other than sight.

Eventually, a pleasant darkness flooded my vision, the cold peeled back, and I realised we'd reached the hut. Finn placed me down beside the hearth, closed the door, and swept the furs and blankets from the bed to pile around me. He wrenched off my gloves and rubbed my fingers and arms, willing warmth back into my chilled flesh.

"You're freezing," he commented.

"I thought wolves didn't feel the cold?"

"We feel all extremes."

I waited for the chastising, the telling off. How foolish I was to get caught in a snowstorm. It didn't come. Forrest wouldn't have let me live it down.

Instead, his fingers crept over to my basket. "Poisonous?" he asked at the contents.

"No."

"Hmm." He popped one into his mouth, and grinned. "Delicious. Definitely worth nearly freezing to death." He licked his lips, and I tried not to notice the way his tongue lingered on the berry juice. He took another handful.

"Those are mine."

"Consider it payment for saving you."

"I freed you from a trap!"

"Good point." He huddled closer, tucking himself in beside me. "For the warmth," he insisted. "I'd start a fire, but hopefully the storm will blow over soon."

I stared at him, the warmth of his body shirking through the layer between us. We were far too close, so close I could pick out the crystal flecks in those glassy eyes of his.

He's a wolf, I reminded myself *A genuine, magical creature. He probably has some kind of power. Concentrate.*

"What?" he said. "What is it?"

"I'm wondering what to ask you that isn't impolite."

"Ask anything," he shrugged. "I am not easily offended. I may not answer, but I shan't bite." He gave me the sort of smile that suggested *unless you ask me to,* and I tried desperately not to think of those teeth nipping at my neck. Tried, and failed.

I blamed the proximity.

"All right," I started. "Why did you leave your pack?"

"We had a... disagreement over how things were done. Other wolves... they're a bit more aggressive than me. I wasn't exactly a favoured member as it was."

"Is there only one pack?"

He shook his head. "There's a few others we've come into contact with over the years. There's an uneasy alliance between us, for the most part."

"Have you always been with them? You said you were born a wolf—"

Finn prickled, and I wondered if I'd touched a nerve. "No. There aren't very many female wolves, see. Most of the men mate with human women, and come for the boys after the first change. Usually around ten, or so."

I bristled, imagining someone coming for Rowan in a couple of years. "The mothers just hand them over?"

"Would *you* want to raise a monster?"

"A wolf is hardly a monster."

"Most of them are," he said darkly.

I went quiet for a moment, watching his eyes, the way they soaked up the thin light, lost in some old, painful memory. “Not you, though,” I added quietly.

“She didn’t know that.”

I wasn’t sure what I could say to that, but I had this strange, powerful urge to kick this woman, or the pack that had taken him. If someone ever came for Rowan, I’d fight them until my last breath, and he was only my brother. If it were my child…

I’d not given much of a thought to children growing up, initially accepting I’d probably be forced to have them at some point, and then deciding that maybe I was odd enough to be ignored by most eligible men. Then, of course, Forrest had started showing more of an interest, and somewhere in the back of my mind, I’d started to think maybe I could reconsider my options.

If he asked, I didn’t want to hurt him.

But I also didn’t think that was good enough of a reason to be with someone.

“You stare off into the distance a lot, are you aware?” Finn said, nudging my elbow. “Dreaming up new poisons?”

“Usually,” I said. “But not today.”

“What are you thinking of?”

“A boy from the village.”

“A sweetheart?”

“Maybe.”

Finn had nothing to say to this. I rubbed my hands together. “Do all the wolves have eyes like yours?”

“What? Beautiful ones?”

I glared at him.

"Ice blue? No. We have all sorts. Blue, gold, violet.. a few emerald green. They're all a little unusual. Brighter. Darker. Slightly inhuman."

"And... the teeth?"

Finn ran a tongue over his, and then promptly shut his mouth, as if he wasn't aware he was doing it. "Some can hide them," he said, tight-lipped.

"I don't mind them."

"What?"

"Your fangs. If you're self-conscious about them, don't be."

"I'm not self-conscious."

"You're pouting."

"I'm regretting saving you."

I smiled. "No," I said, surprised by my own boldness. "You're not."

"No," he said, returning the smile, "I suppose I'm not." His gaze turned back to my rows and rows of jars. "Tell me more of this habit of yours."

"Why?"

"I'm curious. I get the remedies, but the poisons?"

"I told you, I—"

"Just like knowing how they work, I remember. But how do you *know* that they work? Have you ever tried your poisons on anything living?

I blanched at this, because I didn't know quite how to answer, which response would make me seem less bad. But I disliked lying, so I aimed for the truth, shaking my head. "I thought about trying them on fish but everything kills them, so it would have been pointless. I once caught a rabbit but didn't want to hurt it… there's a difference between hurting for fun and killing for food, I think."

Finn nodded, understanding clear in his gaze. "I've killed a lot of creatures, and I always try to make it quick."

"Pain is worse than death, I think," I told him.

At this, he shrugged. "Depends on the pain. Some is worth enduring."

I didn't want to pick at that wound, but I wondered what pain embroidered his past, and why I wanted to hear it at the same time hating that it existed in the first place. Perhaps he was just thinking of the first change, which he'd already told me was unpleasant.

"I wouldn't know," I told him. "My life has been free from most pain."

He raised an eyebrow. "Most?"

"I make poisons for fun. I'm not exactly popular."

"No?" his face twitched curiously. "No friends at all? What about your family?"

"I have a mother, and a little brother. Ro. Rowan."

"Your father?"

"Abandoned us just before Ro was born, although sometimes I think mother killed him. She doesn't speak about him often but I don't think he was very nice."

Finn blinked.

"I'm joking, about the murder," I added. "I… I have a dark humour."

"I think I rather like it," said Finn, and half-smiled at me.

"What are your family like?"

"I love my mother, but she's a bit distant, and I don't think she gets me much."

"Your brother?"

A certain warmth rose in my chest at the thought of Rowan, the sort that only he could elicit, at least whenever I wasn't cross at him. I thought of his cheeky grin and brown curls, the way he still whispered to his toys when he thought no one was watching, the way his eyes lit up when I told him a story.

"He's all right, I suppose," I said, knowing my expression conveyed far more than my words.

Finn cocked his head. "Any friends? You mentioned a boy earlier..."

I didn't want to talk to Finn about Forrest, so I told him about Daisy instead, how she moved to the village three years ago and how I was determined to dislike her before she could dislike me. Everyone gravitated towards her, bees around the honeypot. Newcomers were rare and Daisy was lovely.

And yet, that first day of school, she came to sit by me at lunch.

"Why me?" I had asked.

"You looked lonely."

"I'm used to it."

"Don't be."

We still weren't friends immediately. I was sure as soon as she saw my weirdness, all that kindness would wither away. I told her she didn't want to be friends with me, that I was mean and cruel. She said if I was, she wouldn't be my friend anymore, and she stayed, and kept staying, and coming over to see me, and hissing at others who said cruel things.

For my birthday that year, she gifted me with a beautiful handmade jug, painted with flowers and jewels.

No one but my family had ever given me something made by hand before, no one had ever put so much thought into a present.

"Are you crying?" Forrest jeered.

"Oh, shut up," I said, and hugged the jug to my chest. "You're just jealous because no one's ever made you something so pretty, or ever will."

Forrest scowled at this, although he smiled when Daisy assured him she was more than happy to make one for his birthday, and then I got to tease him over that instead.

By the time I'd finished my story, the storm had let up.

"Come on," said Finn, "let's get you home to them."

Six months after his first transformation, before he was even eleven, someone who wasn't his father came to see them. He was tall and broad-shouldered, with brown, curling hair, a short beard, and eyes of gold, drained of warmth.

He knew Finn's name, and Finn knew *him,* even though he was quite certain he had never met the man before. He felt this strange pull towards him, but it was uneasy and unwelcome, in the way one sometimes hovered over a ledge, as if wanting to fall but not to land.

"My name is Vincent," he said, his voice like black silk, smooth and dark and impossible to ignore. "I'm your alpha. Your father sent me to claim you. You're *mine,* Finn. And I will have you."

"He's not *your* anything," Finn's mother snapped.

"Hush, woman," snarled the man, and she fell silent in an instant. "Come with me, boy, be with your father and brothers. We will teach you how to control the wolf, to become one with it. You will have power and freedom, riches, if you want them. We are kings of the forest."

Something in Vincent's voice stirred him in a way no words of his father's ever had, and he glanced over at his mother, and wondered if she wouldn't be happier without him.

Say something, Mama, he begged. *Tell me to stay.*

But once more, she did not meet his eyes.

"When I learn to control the wolf," Finn said, "can I come home again?"

Vincent's eyes narrowed, as if something in Finn's question had offended him. "No, lad. Because this isn't your home. *We're* your home, your family. Your mother has done her bit raising you till now, but you don't need her anymore."

Finn could not imagine a time ever not needing his mother, although he pretended in front of the other boys that he was fine by himself. "No," he said, as solidly as he could manage. "No, I'm not going with you."

The gold in Vincent's eyes changed to something more like black. "Go to your room," he said.

"You can't tell me what to—"

"Bed," Vincent hissed, "*now.*"

This time, Finn found it impossible to refuse. He went to his room, closed the door, and slid under his sheets. He thought it would be impossible to sleep, but a strange heaviness came upon him, and he closed his eyes almost immediately, even though it was not yet full dark.

It was black when he awoke, but the edges of the room were still sharp and crisp. He'd grown used to his strange new sight this past few months.

Vincent was shaking him awake.

"Come," he said. "There's no need to pack. You won't need anything where we're going."

"I'm not going with you!"

"You will," he said. "Your mother doesn't want you here anymore."

Finn flinched. He'd suspected as much himself, but she'd never said it. To finally hear it… "No," he whispered.

"It's nothing personal, boy. Women just don't understand us wolves. They don't know what to do with us. But we—we understand."

Finn's chest tightened. He felt hot and slightly sick. Tears pressed at his eyes.

"Come, now, no need for that. Man up, lad, and get up."

When Finn didn't, or couldn't, he seized the back of his shirt and hauled him to his feet. How he got out of the house was something of a blur. He wanted to say he struggled, but he was fairly sure he didn't. He remembered his mother sitting beside the fireplace, not looking at him, telling him to go, saying everything he'd always dreaded she would.

"I don't want you. You need to go. Do not come back here again."

He remembered screaming, but that might have just been his own.

5
CAVE OF THE WOLF

Cold as it was outside in the storm, it seemed colder at home, as if Finn had leached some of the warmth from the house. Even the glow of the ovens barely met me.

"Going out in a snowstorm for berries!" Mama twittered. "What were you thinking?"

"There wasn't a snowstorm when I went out!"

"You need to be more careful."

I mumbled something about how I was more likely to die of boredom than anything else, which sent her off on another rant, and it was a relief to be sent out to the front of the shop with Daisy.

For two more days, I ghosted through my old life, my thoughts in the woods. I'd always thought of the village as a cage, but now it felt as stifling as a snowglobe, like the air inside wasn't the same as the air in the rest of the world.

I was not keen to face my mother's wrath again, but by the third day I craved the outside so much I would have risked anything for it. I gave up being evasive, gave up being nervous and silly, packed a couple of buns and an old blanket into a basket, and set off into the woods.

The snow was crisp and fresh, and a fine, golden haze covered the woodlands, the sunlight sheathed in mist. I set off on the path towards the woods, still checking for traps with a stick. I only found one, and reasoned that the hunters wouldn't be foolish enough to set new traps with the snowfall.

"That seems a little strange, young lady," said a voice from behind me. "What are you trying to save?"

I turned. Behind me on the snowy path was a handsome, middle-aged man with dark brown curls and a voice like silver. He was rugged and dressed in furs, but was clean and well-kept. His boots crumped along the ground, polished and mud-free.

"Off to grandma's, little thing?" he asked.

I inched backwards, fingers sliding into my basket for the hilt of my dagger.

"Something like that," I said.

"Why are you disarming the traps?"

"I… I don't want a traveller to fall into one by accident. They were laid before the snow—"

"You're lying." His voice had a hard edge to it, despite the smile on his face.

My throat tightened. "I'm not supposed to speak to strangers."

"You're hardly a child."

"I'm also not an idiot."

I flashed my knife, but he caught my wrist in his vice-like

grip. His breath was against my face, hot and tasteless. His eyes flashed, and something like a snarl rose to his throat before his gaze fell against the jewelled hilt.

"Pretty knife you have there. Where did you get it?"

I tried not to shake, to steady my breathing, to look unafraid. "It was my father's."

"Was it now?" His mouth twisted into a smile. "Know how to use it?"

I wrenched free of his grasp and slashed his hand, stumbling backwards in the snow. Blood dripped to the ground, but although he seethed and clutched his hand, he made no move to follow. He looked up at me on the snowy bank with something like a grin.

"I bet your father didn't teach you that." He laughed, and then he turned his back and walked away, his boots making soft imprints in the snow.

I turned and fled, wanting to put as much space between myself and the stranger as possible, to forget the flame-gold of his eyes, the strength of his grip, and the toothy smirk...

Not a wolf. Surely. My mind was playing tricks.

I stumbled through the snowy ground, hardly looking where I was going, running like he was hot on my trail, not stopping until I collided with something hard and warm.

The scream stopped when I turned to face the person I'd smashed into.

Finn.

"You all right?" he asked, hands hovering at my elbows.

Stranger though he was, it took all of my self-restraint not to throw myself into his arms.

"There was a man," I muttered dumbly, and realised I was still holding the dagger in my hand, wet with his blood. "He, he..."

"Did he hurt you?" Finn's hands closed over my arms, his eyes examining my face.

"No, I hurt him. Not badly—"

A thin smile dusted Finn's cheeks.

"He's all right, he walked away, he just..."

"What?"

"He frightened me." I looked down at the floor, flushed with shame. "I suppose you think I'm silly."

"Not at all," he said, still standing so close that his iced breath brushed against my hair. "Let me walk you back to the village."

"No." I shook my head. "Not yet, please."

Finn's hands dropped away from me. "All right. What do you want to do?"

I held out my basket, not meeting his eyes. "These are for you," I said.

Finn stared at me for a long, pointed moment, as if I'd just spoken in a foreign language. "For... me?"

"Yes."

"What for?"

"Because... because it's cold, and I... oh, wait, wolves don't feel the cold, do they? You said—"

"Trust me, at this time of year, we do," he said, and his eyes misted over again, as if lost in another memory. "Not to the same degree, but sure, we do."

He wasn't wearing much today; a loose shirt, black trousers and boots. Nothing else to keep back the cold. His skin was prickled into tiny goosebumps, but he wasn't shivering.

"Can we... can we go somewhere out of the cold?" I asked, teeth chattering.

"Of course," he said, and he took my basket. I wiped my dagger in the snow. "My cave isn't far away. Follow me."

He led me through the snow, closer to the lake, on the other side of the shore from my hut and further upstream. The terrain turned rocky and difficult to traverse, but Finn seemed to know the perfect steps to reach the caves safely, even in the snow. He turned back frequently to ensure I was safe, helping me over the rougher bits until we reached a long alcove cut into the rock.

A heap of furs lay at the back alongside an ornate chest, behind a screen of woven branches. A bookshelf had been carved from pine, but it served as more of a kitchen, cluttered with wooden bowls of herbs and berries. There was a fire pit dug at the entrance, but no pot. There was little personal about the space except for a pile of wooden figurines: birds and bears and leaves cut from the bark.

I picked one up as Finn tore through my basket to get to the rolls. "You made these?" I asked.

He gave a gesture that was half a shrug, half a nod. "I have a lot of time on my hands."

I traced the carved lines of the feathers on one of the birds. "They're beautiful."

"So are these rolls," he said, devouring the final piece of the first one with something of a moan. "I haven't had proper bread in forever."

"You've been here for almost a year."

"What of it?"

"There's no pot… how do you cook anything?"

Finn cringed, scratching the back of his neck. "I usually just hunt in wolf form and eat raw."

"Delightful."

"It really isn't."

I sat down beside the empty fire pit and wordlessly added more kindling from the stack at the side. There were still embers from earlier, which I tried to goad back to life. "Why?"

"Why what?"

"Why live here? You've obviously a deft hand at carpentry. Why not go to the city and find employment there? Or any town, even. Why stay here in the dark and the cold?"

Finn sighed, sitting down opposite, picking apart the second roll. "I guess I'm more used to living like this. The pack travelled around a lot. We'd stay in towns some of the time, but we lived outdoors a lot, too. Simpler. Safer, even."

"But you're not with them now."

"No. But… I don't know. I think I kind of forgot how to act human after a while."

"You seem to be doing an all right job at the moment."

Finn smiled. "There's the change to consider, too. It's only once a month, but if you're going to live in a town, you need to have somewhere safe to go when you're wild and out of control, where you won't hurt others or be hurt. You put down roots somewhere, one day someone is going to notice you sneaking away every full moon and get mighty suspicious."

So the alternative is to not put down roots at all?

I wondered what that must be like, drifting by your lonesome, endlessly, listlessly. I quite liked silence and solitude, my favourite moments being when I was alone in my hut, but I also loved curling up in bed with Rowan and Mama on cold mornings, and listening to Grandma read, and chatting with Daisy as we kneaded the dough. I couldn't imagine being on my own forever.

"Aren't you ever lonely?"

"Not when I'm chatting to curious girls with poisonous habits."

"Oh, does that happen often?"

He snorted. "It gets a little lonely, sure, but you don't notice as much when you're a wolf."

I thought of the wolf I'd sometimes hear howling at night, and wondered if that was true.

"And when you're human?"

At this, Finn didn't answer.

I picked up one of his carvings. It was a woman, but the face was roughly cut, too messy to resemble human features. "This one could do with some work."

"I'm beginning to regret inviting you into my hovel."

"I gave you bread!"

"But it's gone now, and I'm forgetting how delicious it was."

"Well, I suppose I shall have to bring you some more, another day."

At this, he smiled.

"I... I can come back, right?"

"My cave is your cave."

My eyes drifted to the bed at the back, and I tried not to linger, tried not to think about sharing anything with him at all.

"Tell me about your travels," I asked him. "I've never been outside the village."

"What, never?"

I shook my head. "I once went to the outskirts of the forest and climbed a tree there. I could see for miles, but the nearest town was barely a dot on the horizon. It seemed impossible that I would ever reach it."

"Lyonne," he said. "That's the nearest town. Noisy, bustling place. You aren't missing much, there."

"So tell me what I *am* missing," I begged.

Finn smiled crookedly, and told me everything. He told me of white, sandy beaches and skies as blue as cornflowers, of hot, bustling cities with terracotta roofs. He told me of forests so dark that the sun never reached them, of open fields and meadows and flowers I'd never heard of. He explained the sound of a hundred carts moving at once, of festivals of light, of spices my mouth couldn't comprehend.

His voice spoke of colours I had no name for, of lands my mind couldn't fathom. I felt like my whole life until that point had been lived in shadow, in black and white, devoid of sound. I basked in every word he uttered, and time rolled meaningless beneath his tongue.

"Have you ever been to Loussant?" I asked, as he paused to draw breath.

"I have, why?"

"They have a university there with an excellent programme for keen herbalists. I've always dreamed of attending but..."

"But?"

"Money. Fear. It's a long way from my family, and what if the people there are as bad as the ones here?"

"What do you mean?"

"You know. 'It's not right for a woman to make poisons, soon she starts getting ideas and thinking...'"

Finn laughed. "You *need* to get away from here."

"Says the boy living in a *cave*."

"Ah, but no one questions my choices in a cave."

A narrow shaft of sunlight permeated the rock, and we both became at once aware of how long we'd been here. It must be almost lunch time. Mama would be worrying.

I climbed to my feet.

"May I escort you back?" asked Finn. "In case there are any more wolves in the woods?"

"They're not what I'm afraid of," I said. "But yes, you may walk me to the village."

We set off together, Finn telling me of Loussant, and I clung to every word until the village gates appeared ahead, dark demons cutting into my haven. They had never looked less inviting.

Finn squared up to me, and took my gloved hand. Somehow, the warmth of him rippled through the fabric. "Until you stumble into the woods again, Miss Andesine..."

"De Winter," I said, "but you can call me Andie."

"Andie," he said, the word flattened into felt. In all my life,

I'd never heard it sound so warm or rough or soft, all at the same time.

If kisses were words, they would sound like that, I thought, and tried to ignore the hotness tingling at the back of my neck, a hotness that spread down my spine when he bent over my hand, and kissed it.

His voice followed me home, like a thawed ghost.

Andie, Andie, Andie.

6 THE WOLVES IN THE NIGHT

For the next three days, I searched for excuses to go into the woods, whilst simultaneously trying to talk myself out of it. I ought not to have been thinking so frequently of Finn. I ought not to have been chasing after a boy. I ought to have some excuse to see him. At this point, I was probably bothering him. Maybe he was just being friendly. Of *course* he was just being friendly. He'd been isolated for so long he probably hungered for any kind of company. I wasn't special. I should just put him out of my mind and move on...

But I couldn't put him out of my mind, and as the nights grew colder, I thought more and more of him alone in the cave by himself, and found that a coldness had crept into my own bed, too, one that no little brother snuggling up against you could dispel.

"Something's going on with you," said Daisy one afternoon as we were closing the bakery, wrapping up the leftover buns and sweeping the floor. "You're quieter and more faraway than ever."

I didn't like keeping secrets, and I disliked keeping them

even more from Daisy. I chanced a quick look around to make sure Mama wasn't listening in.

"Don't tell anyone?"

Daisy lowered her voice. "Of course not."

"I met someone. A… a boy. A traveller. In the woods."

Daisy's dark eyes widened. "A boy? But what's he doing there?"

"It's complicated," I said. "I rather think he's hiding."

"Is he in danger?"

"I don't think so."

"Are *you* in danger?"

I blinked at her. "Why would you say that?"

"I've just… I've never known you lose your head over a boy before. I don't want you to get hurt."

"I haven't lost my head over him," I assured her. "I barely know him."

"But you *want* to."

"Yes."

Daisy smiled. "Poor Forrest."

I felt white with shame. "Please, Daisy, don't tell him. Don't tell anyone. It'll probably come to nothing, I—"

Daisy pressed a finger to her lips. "Quiet as a church mouse, promise."

"Thank you," I breathed. "I'll finish up here. You go home."

"If you're sure?"

"Of course."

She dusted off her apron and hung it on a peg by the back door, collected her cloak, and took a few of the leftover buns.

I finished cleaning, my chest feeling a little lighter, and went to empty the dust pan outside.

On the back step was a dead rabbit, neatly presented, and a small wolf token carved out of wood.

My heart skipped a beat, thrumming in my chest like a sparrow. I smiled, slipping the carving into my pocket, and took the rabbit back inside. My cheeks were flushed. *All* of me felt flushed.

He had thought of me after all.

Mama looked up from the kitchen where she was stacking bags of ingredients ready for tomorrow. She smiled at me, her dark hair dusted with white smears of flour.

"Nice rabbit. Did Forrest bring that?"

"Must have."

"Unusual for him not to give it to you in person."

"I should go and thank him," I said, gathering my nerves. "I'll take some of the buns. I won't be long."

Mama took the rabbit. "I guess I'll skin this beauty." She stopped for a moment, staring at a small wound on the rabbit's neck. I'd barely noticed it; it was otherwise a pretty clean kill.

"What is it?"

"Nothing," she returned, "it's nothing. Thank him from us both."

I readied myself quickly, heading off with unusual speed, hurrying into the woods before Mama could catch me going in completely the wrong direction. I ran, I told myself, so that I could get back before my absence was notably long. Not for any other reason.

I slowed down as I approached the hut, deciding to check there first before a possibly wasted excursion to the caves, and found Finn perched on a rock nearby, grinning.

"I take it you got my offering?"

"I did," I said, gathering my breath, "and thank you."

"Needed to thank you for the bread."

"I brought more."

"I am forever indebted." He bounded from the rock and strode across to pluck a roll from my basket, leaning against the wall of the hut. He tossed the roll deftly from hand to hand with a skill that rippled through me. It was a relief when he finally bit into it.

"How did you know where I lived?" I asked him.

Finn's cheeks reddened. "Aside from the fact that you told me you worked at the bakery, I have to admit you give off a rather fetching scent that is impossible to mask, although that cape of yours seems to do a rather good job."

"My cape?"

He nodded, biting into the roll. "Where did you get it?"

"My grandma made it."

"Is she a witch?"

"That's the rumour."

"The fabric is fey-made, I suspect, whether or not she knew it. Casts some kind of protective charm."

"I..." I startled. "What do you mean by *fey*?"

"You know, fairies?"

"Fairies are real?"

"As real as werewolves."

"Have you met any?"

He shrugged. "They rarely leave their realms, now, but we've had occasional dealings."

"What... what are they like?"

"Like us," he said. "Strange and ordinary, flawed and perfect, ugly and beautiful." He looked up at the final word, catching my gaze.

My collar heated, despite the cold. "What do I smell like?"

Finn swallowed, hard, as if this was an extremely personal question. "Like a bakery," he said eventually. "But also... not."

"Not?"

"It's difficult to explain."

I wasn't sure I would get more out of him than that, despite my burning curiosity. Perhaps it *did* defy explanation. I was left to wonder. I slipped my hand into my pocket and brought out the miniature wolf carving. "Is this a gift, or your calling card?"

"A gift, if you want it."

"I do," I said, and hesitated. "You didn't need to bring me a rabbit, though."

"I felt I needed an excuse to see you."

I swallowed my smile, thinking of all the wasted hours I'd spent, trying to find the exact same thing. "Oughtn't you act the part of the brooding hero, and tell me to stay away from you?"

He raised a black brow.

"I read a lot of gothic romance novels."

He snorted. "It's been a long time since I read anything," he said, "and I don't want to stay away from you. Well, apart from one day a month."

"One day a month, I'll bite your head off too."

Finn clapped his hand to his mouth, barely hiding a chuckle. "And it's *such* a pretty head."

My mouth ran dry, and I found myself lacking the words for a witty retort or even the ability to confirm. "Are all wolves as smooth as you?" I asked when I'd regained something like composure. "I would have thought your tongue rusty from underuse in the woods."

"There is nothing dull about my tongue, I assure you," he said, flashing me a grin that made my cheeks turn scarlet. "But it must be said that yes, most of us can be quite charming."

"Best beware of the big bad wolf."

"Indeed," he said, squaring up to me. "Or even the medium-sized ones."

"That *does* sound like you're telling me to stay away from you."

"It might be for the best," he said, "but I hope you won't."

His gaze lingered on mine, striking me dumb again. My heart thumped loudly against my ribcage, my stomach doing acrobatics. "Shall we continue this conversation inside?" I suggested, flinging out the first words I could find. "The more human amongst us are getting rather cold."

Finn gestured to the door, "After you," he said, with a flourished bow.

We slipped inside and sat down beside the empty hearth. "I can't stay long," I continued. "Mama believes I've only popped out. She'll be suspicious if I'm gone too long, and besides, I hear there's rabbit for dinner."

A grin flickered across his face. "Tell me more about your family."

So I did. I told him about the day Rowan was born. Forrest's mother had been the village midwife, so my grandma came to assist with the birth, and I was kicked outside. It was cold, and I had nowhere to go, so I was already predisposed to dislike this child before he'd even got here.

I skirted the fence surrounding the village and banged a stick along the bars. I dreamed up a magical potion that would hurry this whole process along, and then one for instant warmth. A drop of sunlight, a dash of pepper, a sliver of a rainbow...

Grandma found me just as I was working out the finer details.

"Andesine," she said, "you have a little brother."

I was still determined not to like him when she brought me to Mama's bed, any signs of the messy business already carefully hidden away. I was second to see him, after them. The second to hold him.

He was a scrawny, red-faced, wailing thing, dark hair plastered to his scalp. He ought to have disgusted me, and yet the minute he was first placed in my arms, I loved that little creature. There would be moments over the years when I'd hate him, moments of kicking and hair-pulling and unbridled toddler anger, but in that moment, when he'd stopped squawling, and looked up at me with those brown-gold eyes, I'd known I would do anything in the world to keep him safe.

Finn was staring at me when I finished the tale.

"Sorry," I said, "I got a bit carried away there."

"It was a lovely story."

A smile twitched in my cheeks. "You're an only child?"

"Yes," he said. "And no."

"The wolves—were they like your brothers?"

"Not all of them," he said sourly. "But one. One was."

The wind kicked against the door, jolting us out of the moment. A bluish hue was gathering over the lake.

"It's getting late," Finn announced. "We should get you back."

A few days later, the monthly market came to town. The village square was cleared, a dozen stalls set up, and I was thrust out of the warm bakery into the cold to peddle iced buns and loaves and hot cakes that were not hot for very long.

I disliked market day. There were always some travellers who tried to flirt with me and once or twice one of them had gotten a bit too handsy. I'd threatened one with my knife before, but that didn't deter the others who came after. Forrest had noticed my troubles and had taken to setting up his own stall—selling pelts, traps and rope—next to mine.

"You don't have to do that," I told him once.

"Don't want to be saved?"

"I want to be safe," I whispered. "I shouldn't need to be saved."

Forrest went quiet. "You know that I would never—"

"Of *course* I know that," I hissed back. "But it doesn't really matter what you wouldn't do, when so many others clearly would."

His presence stopped the grabbing, but men still made me feel uncomfortable with their comments and leers, and I hated how one sharp look from Forrest would silence them but somehow my own displeasure wasn't enough. Why was his 'stop' worth more than mine?

I wondered if things were better or worse in Loussant, and if I'd ever get the chance to find out. The villagers called Thornwood their 'cradle and their coffin' and acted like this was a good thing, while I felt like I was being boxed in.

It was no bad thing, to belong to a place, but sometimes I stared at the iron bars of the village gates like a prisoner stared at the walls of their cell.

My mind whirring with old thoughts and biting cold, it was a relief when Daisy came to relieve me from the stall. I took the earnings so far, leaving a few coins for change, and handed the rest back to Mama who was busy baking another batch. Rowan was helping her, rolling out the dough. I ruffled his hair but he jerked away from me, and flour fell from his little hands like fragments of time, like snow, quickly melting, reminding me that he was growing up and away from me more and more every day.

Mama counted the coins and gave me a few more than usual, a bonus for putting up with the weather "and anything else that bites."

Pleased, I took my payment and wandered about the rest

of the stalls. I purchased some new parchment and a faded book from a merchant, some new thread for Grandma, and was just about to retire to the warmth when my eyes fell upon a tiny set of carving tools being offered up by the local blacksmith. My thoughts fell immediately to the carvings in Finn's cave, to the little token stowed beside my bed. I hadn't seen what he was using to make them, but it was probably just a dagger. The beauties he could accomplish with something like this...

They were a little worn, but the price was fair. I haggled it down a few pennies and tucked it into my basket.

It was too late by that point to steal away into the woods, the darkness encroaching upon the skyline. A full moon tonight, I realised. Probably not the best time for visiting. What was it like for him, to surrender fully to the wolf?

I hoped it didn't hurt.

I'd go and see him tomorrow, just to see he was all right. I had the whittling kit as an excuse now. Although maybe... maybe I didn't need an excuse. Maybe he *was* the excuse, and I should just tell him that.

I wondered what he'd think if he knew the way I listened to him howl, how the sound seemed to echo against my bones.

"The wolves are crying again," said Rowan that night, as I tucked him into the bed next to me.

"There's only the one."

"No," said Rowan softly, "there isn't."

I listened, and sure enough, somewhere in the distance, something else was howling, too.

The first night away from his mother, Finn cried himself to sleep. His father gave him an awkward pat on the back and left him to it. The other wolves ignored him completely, and when he cried again after that, he was teased and ridiculed for it.

He learnt to hide his sadness, but that didn't make it go away.

"I miss Mama," he admitted to his father one day during a moment of weakness.

"She doesn't want either of us, boy. It's better this way."

But knowing she didn't want him didn't make him miss her any less.

As promised, the pack taught him how to shift at will. He'd learned to run, and hunt, and fight. He learned to fear nothing outside of the pack. They were the strongest and most fearsome wolves of all, unmatched and unparalleled.

He learned to love being a wolf, even if he sometimes felt the human part of him suffered for it.

Despite what Vincent said about the pack being family, they didn't feel like that to him. His father felt more distant than ever, Vincent was quick-tempered, Jean was cruel, and although some of the other members treated him with something resembling affection, it was much in the way one teased a stray dog.

The only person who really liked him was Cassel.

Cassel was two years younger than him and had yet to go through the change. Ordinarily, he would not have been allowed to join the pack until then, but his mother had died and he had nowhere else to go. Vincent had relented and let him join them, although he was frequently left behind when he couldn't keep up with the rest of them or fell from his father's back.

Some nights, the men would head off into town. During the harsher months, they might rent rooms in an inn, but when the weather was fair they camped in the woods beneath the stars and left the boys to themselves. Those were the best nights; the nights Finn didn't have to pretend. And if Cassel was a little irritating and clingy, he'd take that over the snide comments and cruelty of the others.

One night, he picked up a piece of wood and started to carve. It had been a while now since he'd wanted to, but he realised as more time passed that he was forgetting his mother's face.

He couldn't rush it. He wanted it perfect.

To begin with, it was little more than an incomprehensible lump of wood, but little by little, day after day and week after week, a detail would bubble up in a dream. A flash of her smile, the slope of her cheek, the short gap between her brows, constantly furrowed at him in frustration. Teasing, mocking. Nothing sad or stern or strict, no matter how often those things might have happened too.

Slowly, almost imperceptibly, the wood took on her shape, until the rest of the pack started to notice it, too. Cassel said nothing. There was something knowing in his gaze, as if he wanted to peel another face out of the wood, too. Jean jeered at him, but was cut down after a hard look from Reed.

It was all fine until Vincent noticed.

Vincent, who never let anything slide. Vincent who acted like every stray thought was his to twist.

"What's this?" he said one evening, snatching it from Finn's hand. "Truly, the detail is excellent. Quite the artist, your boy, Reed."

Reed's face twitched. "He has skill," he agreed. "Why don't you give it back, Vincent?"

Vincent held it up to the light, as if examining it, but Finn knew he could see it just fine. Saw it, and knew it.

It hovered dangerously close to the flames.

"Looks just like your mother…" he said, with the smile he frequently wore, the one with all the warmth of ice. "A happy coincidence, perhaps?"

Finn swallowed, trying to keep his voice steady. It never helped to show Vincent your weakness.

And yet, the words that tumbled out of him were not the safe ones, the ones of denial or indifference.

"I didn't want to forget her."

"How sweet," said Vincent with a snarl, and let the carving tumble into the flames.

Finn let out a howl, racing forward to grab her back, but Vincent's arms were faster, seizing the young wolf and pinning him against the ground. Finn struggled against him, kicking fruitlessly, screaming into the air.

"Don't let my mama burn!"

"Let it burn, boy," said Vincent, pressing him harder into the ground. "Let all of it burn."

Finn stared at the blackening totem, and felt like he was watching his mother die. His eyes leaked, his hand still stretching out towards her. Cassel raced forward, fingers snatching at the flames, but Pierre yanked him back, shaking his head.

"You don't need her," Vincent hissed. "You don't need anything but us."

7
THE WOLVES RETURNED

Bright and early the next morning, I gathered my belongings and headed off into the woods, bumping into Forrest just outside of the gates.

"Morning," he said. "Where are you off to?"

"Grandma's, where else?" I returned, glad I'd had the sense to stow the whittling kit at the bottom of my basket. The lie prickled in my cheeks, and I felt ashamed the moment I'd uttered it.

Forrest regarded me carefully for a moment. "You've been taking a lot of trips into the woods of late."

"I worry about her, out on her own, this time of year." *Lies, lies, lies.*

"Agatha has weathered a lot of storms, Andie. She'll probably outlive all of us."

"Maybe," I said. "But she'll still be alone."

Something about the sincerity of the final word registered with him, and he moved around me. It was the nearest thing to truth I'd uttered so far in the exchange, but I wasn't thinking about her. Grandma had forged something of her isolation, a sword or a crown. Finn hadn't. He wore his loneliness like a shackle.

"Try to stay on the path, for once," Forrest warned. "There's been a report of more wolves."

"I'll be careful."

"I don't believe you."

He walked back towards the village, and I waited until he was safely out of sight before slipping through the undergrowth, down towards the lake and then up towards the cave.

I sang as I approached, both to steady my nerves and also to let Finn know I was approaching, in case he wasn't decent yet.

There was a moment when I thought about not doing that, though.

There was little movement from inside the cave, little life at all. The inside was as quiet as the rock itself.

"Finn?" I whispered. "Are you there?"

There was a low, quiet moan from inside, and I dipped into the cave.

Finn was at the back, heaped under the furs, his dark hair plastered to his face. When he turned to face me, a long slash down his cheek rose to the light.

"Finn!" I bolted into the space, dropping down beside him and seizing his face. It was a shallow cut, but ragged, and far from the only one. Thin cuts and bruises dribbled down his arms and torso, and he was chilled to the bone. "What happened?"

"It appears I'm not the only wolf in these woods anymore. We may have gotten in something of a kerfuffle last night."

"A *kerfuffle?*" I squeaked incredulously. "Have you seen yourself?"

"No," he said. "I just shifted back at dawn. Wasn't even awake until I heard you."

I clutched his hands. "You're freezing."

He smirked. "Going to crawl in here and warm me up?"

"And get blood all over myself? No, thank you."

"Perhaps you could tenderly clean my wounds while calling me a fool in a fondly exasperated tone?"

I sighed, heading over to his shelf to examine his collection of herbs, finding some witch hazel which would do for cleaning wounds.

"I was jesting," he said from the pile of furs. "You don't have to help me. I assure you, I've had a great deal worse."

"I want to help, and I assure you I'm quite good at this."

I took a bowl outside to scoop up a handful of snow and found a few clean rags to doctor him. I tried to spark the fire back into life and left it to its own devices, returning to Finn's side.

I sponged away the dry blood on his eyebrow, not meeting his gaze.

"Just my luck to befriend the village herbalist."

"I don't help you out of morbid curiosity," I insisted.

"No?"

"I help you because I'm really rather starting to like you."

I waited for him to tease, to say, 'starting?' with a smirk as if it wasn't obvious already, but instead he kept his gaze down.

"My mother used to look after me," he said quietly, "and clearly it never meant anything to her."

My jaw tightened. "Well, it means something to me," I insisted, dabbing at the cuts further down, realising he was naked again. How far down was I willing to go? "Why come with me when I freed you from the trap, if you don't like being helped?"

Finn looked down again. "It was more the wolf in me that went with you. He trusted you, for some reason."

"He?"

"*I,*" Finn corrected. "I trust you."

I smiled. "More than just a pretty face and idle conversation, then?"

"Yes," he said. "A lot more."

I twitched under the weight of his gaze, swallowing carefully and hoping wolves didn't have enhanced hearing, that he couldn't feel the frantic hammer of my heartbeat.

Finn's rough fingers reached for mine, ice-cold. I dropped my rag and seized them, bringing them close to my mouth and blowing on them for warmth. "Let's get you beside the fire. I can fix you up just as easily from there."

"I'm naked."

"I won't peek."

"I mean, you can if you want… I'm just warning you." He lumbered over to the fireside, dragging the furs and blankets with him. His gait was stiffer than before, not as languid and smooth as it usually was.

When did I notice how he walked?

I gave him something to eat as I worked, and questioned him about the other wolves.

"Are they dangerous?"

"Not really. Not unless they want something from you. They're territorial and don't quite understand *no.*"

"Why did they hurt you?"

"The alpha was none-too-pleased when I left the pack, and we couldn't exactly have a friendly chat about it in wolf form."

"Can you… communicate at all, when you're like that?"

"It's not quite conversation, but we can understand each other."

"Do you have any other powers?"

"The alpha exercises some minor forms of mind-control over the rest of them. Nothing too severe."

"Them? Not you?"

Finn shook his head. "He lost that power over me when I became an omega, an outsider."

"Why would anyone join him, if that was the cost?"

"You're stronger in a pack. The more pack members, the stronger you are—individually and together. Me by myself? Practically an ordinary wolf."

"Are you?" I queried. "Ordinary, that is? When you're in human form—"

"I'm a little faster and stronger than the average man, sure. Faster healing." He held up the hand that he'd wounded in the trap, now no more than a whisper of a silver scar.

"And… your hearing? Sense of smell?"

"Minor heightened senses."

My heart thumped. He *could* hear it.

"You don't need to be nervous."

"I'm—those aren't nerves."

"No?"

"No, they're..." I shook my head. "No matter. Tell me something else. Where did you grow up?"

"The city of Voulaire, in the east. Busy, bustling sort of place. Glad to leave it."

I suspected that was not the full truth, but wasn't sure I'd get more out of him on that note.

"What's your surname?"

"Why do you want to know?"

"Perhaps I'm trying it on for size." I smirked, pleased by my own boldness. I'd been flirted with a great deal but never really flirted back. "Although, you should know, I'm very attached to my own. It's my mother's surname and it sits awfully nicely on a page."

Finn smiled, surveying me me carefully for a long, steady moment. "Whitethorn," he said. "My surname is, or was, Whitethorn."

"Was?"

"Names don't mean much to wolves," he explained, and then, barely a whisper, "Much like I didn't mean much to her." He paused. "I like De Winter."

"I like Whitethorn." I hesitated, cleaning out the rag. "Have you ever thought about..."

"What?"

"Going back. Showing her who you are. Finding out... whatever there is to find out."

"Yes," he said slowly, "more often than I'd like to."

"Why don't you?"

"Because I dream of her telling me it was all a terrible mistake, or a misunderstanding. I want her to tell me that she never meant it, or she did it for my own good, but..."

"But?"

He paused, swallowing a lump in his throat. "But what if it's not that? What if she meant everything, or said something worse? I couldn't... I couldn't go through that again."

I paused, words all slipping away from me. "I'm sorry," I managed eventually.

"What for?"

"For bringing it up. And... and for whatever she did." I crept closer to him, wondering if he'd believe me if I told him I'd never do that, wondering why I wanted to tell him that after knowing him so little.

But I couldn't find those words, so I slid under the blankets with him instead.

Finn's eyes went wide as I leaned against him.

"What... what are you doing?"

"Warming you up. You're still freezing."

"Right," he said, his throat bobbing, "is that the only reason?"

I smiled against his shoulder. "No," I told him, and brushed the back of my hand against his. His knuckles slowly pressed against mine, until our fingers slid together, entwined. My heart spasmed hotly against my ribcage, and I wondered if this was how wolves felt all the time, like there was something separate inside them waiting to break free.

He can hear your heartbeat, I reminded myself, *so get a hold of yourself.*

His hand squeezed mine, and there was a strange permeance to the action, like threading a tapestry. It would not be easy to untangle.

I wasn't sure I wanted it to be.

"Tell me of yourself," he whispered, a phrase longer than four words, an instruction that asked for other things.

Unravel yourself. Show me who you are. Let me see you.

It was a gentle kind of perverse, like I was stripping off my clothes, inch by inch and stitch by stitch. I felt him pressing against my skin, or my shell, tapping at my mortal form. *Andie, Andie, let me come in.*

So, word by word and story by story, I let him.

Satisfied his wounds were minor and he was warm and fed, I slipped away before lunch. I left behind the whittling knives, trying not to take too much satisfaction in the glassy-eyed look Finn gave me when I presented them to him.

Tired and sore, Finn did not accompany me down to the path, but his fingers took a long while to leave my own.

"You'll come again?"

"Wild wolves couldn't stop me."

I tried not to take too much satisfaction in the redness in his cheeks, either, but I failed.

I kept a sharp pace on my way to my grandma's, and was greeted with a warm hug and settled beside the fire within seconds. Grandma prattled on for a good hour about the scrapes the chickens were getting into, her battle with yet another hole in the roof, the latest adaptation she made to a recipe and some old story about her very short-lived marriage to my grandfather, which had ended abruptly with his death almost forty years ago.

When I was little, I made out Edwarde De Winter to be the great love of my grandmother's life, the reason she never looked at another man again. Grandma had laughed when I'd expressed the assumption out loud. "*Marriage* is the reason I never looked at another man again, dearie. Besides, widows live longer. I used to pray to the gods to just give me a few weeks without your grandfather, and they saw fit to give me decades."

"But surely... you must have loved him, at some point?"

Grandma shrugged, as if that was neither here nor there. "Things change, dear. Pass the salt."

Looking at her now, the picture of stubborn, wilful independence, I wondered what my own future held, what I'd be content with. What I wanted.

I thought of Finn, of the increase of breath whenever he entered my mind, and if I wanted those thoughts to change, if I wanted them to simmer away or spark up like flames. Which scared me more? Caring, or not caring at all? Enjoying his company or learning to despise it?

Even now, I couldn't ever imagine laughing off his death, and while I could imagine myself comfortable living alone... I imagined I'd be lonely.

"You're quiet today, Andie dear. Something on your

mind?"

Plenty.

I thought about asking Grandma about the origins of the cape, but I wasn't sure how to admit what I knew without explaining Finn. Grandma was always less uptight than Mama, but that didn't mean she'd approve of her granddaughter stepping out with a wolf.

Perhaps Grandma didn't know about the fabric's magic. She'd made it to replace the old one, after all. Perhaps she just bought the fabric because she liked it.

Or perhaps she did know, but just thought it cast a protection of sorts. What grandma wouldn't want that for her grandchild?

"You do enough talking for both of us," I said coyly.

Grandma laughed. "Cheeky! Come. Tell me of the village. That strapping young hunter boy proposed yet?"

"Grandma!"

"What? I'm old, but I've got eyes. He's fancied you for years."

"I, um, Forrest is lovely—"

"But?"

"He's not for me, Grandma."

"Good. Wouldn't want to see you settle. What will you do instead, then? The village is too small and narrow-minded for you. You ought to study."

"We don't have the money."

"We'd find it. I could sell this old crumbling place, if you really wanted it."

I stilled. "You... you'd do that?"

"Why not? I shan't be around forever, and your mother isn't interested in it."

"You *love* this place, Grandma."

"Aye, dear, but I love you more."

My chest warmed. "Thank you, grandma. But I don't want you to sell this place. I kind of like it, too."

Grandma raised an incredulous eyebrow.

"I mean, I'd like it more with a new roof..."

Grandma laughed, gave my shoulder a squeeze, and bent to stoke the fire.

∞∞∞

The next morning, I went to the library. It was a small place attached to the side of the schoolroom, and run by the same crotchety old school mistress who had taught both me and my mother. She was as old and ancient as the books she stacked, dusty and paper-thin.

She looked up at me as I entered, glaring through her half-moon spectacles. "Miss De Winter."

"Madame Clare."

"What brings you here?"

"I need to find the addresses of the parishes of Voulaire," I said, hoping she wouldn't ask more.

The old lady groaned, and went over to a book of maps, thudding it open at the index and turning to a page about Voulaire. She thrust it in my direction. "Find the names of the parishes, then I'll see if I can help with the addresses."

Voulaire was divided into seven parishes, or at least it had been when this map was made, which was clearly some time ago. If it was still accurate, I was grateful; cities could often have dozens. Voulaire was on the small side.

Madame Clare was grateful, too. It was less to look up.

"Why the sudden interest in Voulaire?" she asked.

"I'm thinking of travelling," I said quickly.

Madame Clare gave a huff that sounded suspiciously like, "good", which I assumed meant *good riddance.* Nevertheless, I made a note of the addresses and ran home to pen seven identical letters.

To whom it may concern,

I am seeking the address of a woman by the name of Whitethorn, who was living somewhere within the vicinity of Voulaire at least within the last decade. She would be perhaps around forty years of age and had, at one point, a son who would now be around eighteen.

I thought about mentioning that I was writing on behalf of Finn, but decided against it in case the parish manager was familiar with the situation and Finn was right about his mother's abandonment. I wondered if this was a gross violation, but at the same time... I had to find out.

If only to write the woman a very terse letter.

I decided to keep it impartial, signing off with a cordial wish for news, and folded all seven letters.

It was a few days until the next post was due out, and I had no way of knowing how long, if ever, a reply would take.

But soon.

Soon Finn would know I wasn't the only person who had cared for him.

8
THE BLACK WOLF

For days trickling into weeks afterwards, I seemed to exist for the narrow snatches of time that I could spend with Finn. With the night drawing ever darker, the evenings were usually surrendered to time, so I had taken to going out at the crack of dawn under the guise of gathering berries. I could usually only afford a few minutes before I had to rush back to open the bakery, but each moment seemed worth it. Finn had taken to meeting me in a glade beside the gates, to maximise our time together, and sometimes, if I had been unable to make our morning meeting, he ghosted the iron fence at the back of the churchyard, and we'd whisper words between the bars.

Finn told me stories of the places he'd been, the things he'd seen, countries he'd visited and experienced. His voice was animated in one moment, wistful the next. I could listen to him for hours.

"Why don't you travel again?" I asked him one evening. "What keeps you here?"

"Your pretty face and delightful company."

"Finn!" I hissed through my laughter. "I meant, before. Why stay here?"

He shrugged. "Travelling isn't so fun by yourself."

I knew, from his tales, that there had been times he enjoyed with the wolves, that whatever had caused them to part, he'd enjoyed the company of them in some ways. He spoke of hurtling through forests like the wind, unattached from the earth beneath, chasing the pack. There was a soft wistfulness that graced his words, but only for a moment before he managed to steel it, much like I managed to control the urge to say, *I'd travel with you.*

"Come into the village," I said instead.

Finn stared at me, eyes wide with disbelief. "And do what?" he said eventually. "Meet your family? I think your mother might have a few questions."

"Maybe we could explain it to her."

"And maybe she would call those fine hunters I've seen prowling about the place." He shook his head. "Do you want to risk it?"

"No," I said quietly, *no, I would not risk you.*

But how long could we do this? How long could we meet in tiny bursts, me hiding this growing part of my life? Until it fizzled out or I exploded? Until I gathered the courage to run away with him?

Stupid, ridiculous, foolish thoughts.

I could not live in the forest, and I could not leave my family.

Although occasionally a low howl would hurtle through

the forest, we saw neither hide nor hair from the rest of the wolves, and they did not seem to bother Finn, aside from once when I arrived at his cave and found him curiously quiet.

"What's wrong?" I prompted.

"I spoke to my father."

"Oh."

"He asked how I was."

"That's it?"

"That's it."

He would say no more about it.

I heard nothing of note from Voulaire. Two of the parish managers had written back to confirm that they knew of no-one matching the description I provided, and I imagined plenty of the others wouldn't bother with a reply if they had no news at all.

This secret, the one I was keeping from Finn, weighed more heavily than the gathering of ones I was keeping from my family. I knew I should tell him, but I was afraid he would hate me for it, and I liked him liking me.

I should have asked him before, but I hadn't. His pride would have prevented him, and I had to, *had to* discover what had happened.

And I would.

My days off from the bakery, I went to Grandma's, Finn beside me every step of the way. I'd spend a little time with her and then walk in the woods with him, gathering wood and berries and the occasional stray rabbit.

Sometimes, I'd chase him, or he'd chase me, and even

though he was as fast as an arrow he always let me catch him, and we'd roll about the snow and go home powdered with the stuff, breathless and giddy with our sides hurting from laughing so much.

The sound of Finn's laughter fragmented through the air every time I heard it. It reminded me of an old painting in my Grandma's house, of firelight burning in a rainbow of colours. It was bright and warm and colourful, and crackled deep against my bones.

I wondered if my laugh had that kind of effect on him, if anything about me conjured such a feeling, but although we talked of everything and nothing, I could not find the courage to ask him that.

Sometimes, we wouldn't talk at all. We'd sit in silence, Finn whittling while I stripped and boiled herbs and potions. He'd ask me questions, taking an interest in my tasks, and sometimes I'd stop and just watch him as he drew wonder out of a scrap of pine.

"How do you do that?" I asked once.

"Do what?"

"Just take a knife and make *that.*" I gestured to the face of a bear in his hands, the size of a large coin and just as detailed.

"I don't know," he admitted. "I just see it there already, and use my knife to tug it out."

"Who taught you?"

At this, he paused. "My father," he said eventually. "Every time he visited, he'd make me a little wooden toy, and I watched him doing it. One day I tried it for myself, and he said I had a gift for it. My mother looked so pleased. I think I did it for them originally, but I do it for myself, now." He paused, got up from his seat beside the fire, and collected a small figure from the mass of others. He pressed it into my hands. It was a faceless girl in a long cloak, arms wrapped around a wolf. "And you," he said. "I do it for you, too."

I took the carving and ran my hands over the smooth lines. "Where's her face?"

"I couldn't do it justice."

The all too-familiar heat prickled in my cheeks. I tucked the carving away in my basket. "I love it. It's beautiful."

"Yes," said Finn, in the low light of the fire, "she is."

"You're not talking about the carving now, are you?"

"I am not."

The worst thing about winter, I decided, was that one could not blame scarlet cheeks on the heat. And the worst thing about being with a wolf was he knew precisely how hard my heart thumped against my chest.

I was sure I'd blushed more in these days and weeks with him than in my entire life beforehand. And not an awkward, uncomfortable, 'please-stop-now' blush. The kind of blush that begged him to do it again, more, deeper, even if I lacked the confidence to say such a thing, pinned back by fading notions of propriety.

You cannot court a wolf from the woods.

I wondered, sometimes, if I could pretend to spend the night at Grandma's, and instead sneak away to the hut or the cave, and while away the night with him instead until his voice lost the magic that it held. I doubted *he'd* have any objections to the impropriety of it all.

The thought of curling up beside him in that pile of furs was a sinful, delicious temptation. I imagined the soft hardness of his body beside mine, the warmth of his skin blurring through the thin fabric dividing us...

The thought of nothing dividing us at all came too, and that was probably why it was an utterly terrible idea. The last thing I wanted was to be like my mother, raising a child by myself.

Although… maybe I wouldn't be. Maybe Finn would stay.

And there were ways to avoid conceiving, I knew from my study of potions.

Foolish, foolish, don't think about that.

And yet sometimes when Finn was speaking, I noticed the gentle curve of his lips, and imagined his mouth on mine. My gaze would travel down the slope of his chest, the parting of his shirt, and far, far too often my mind tried to recreate that first meeting, and every naked inch of him.

Yes, staying overnight would be a terrible idea.

One evening, I came back after visiting Grandma and dozed off in front of the fire, seduced by its warmth and Finn's soft, shimmering voice. I awoke to Finn shaking my shoulder carefully.

"Andie," he whispered, "it's getting late."

It *was* late; outside was nearly completely dark.

"Perhaps I should stay," I suggested, quite forgetting in the moment how terrible that would be.

Finn swallowed, and I watched the slow bob of his throat. "You'll be missed."

"Mama will assume I'm staying with Grandma."

Finn looked like he might be considering it, but a low howl sounded in the distance.

"No," he said. "Not tonight. Come, I'll walk you back."

Finn took my hand, an action I ought to have been used to by now but somehow still sent ripples through me, and we walked back together through the freshly-fallen snow. The thin light lit the woods with a kind of purple radiance. It was bitterly cold, but I refused to tug my hand from Finn's to pull my gloves back on; I wanted his skin on mine.

Shortly before the village, Finn tensed, stopping in his tracks. He sniffed the air.

"Finn?"

He flung out his arm as a black shape dropped onto the path ahead. A large wolf with dark fur and ice-blue eyes. Finn let out a low snarl, but the wolf stood up on his hind legs and shifted into a man. A tall, broad-shouldered man with black hair, eyes as piercing as the wolf's, and a blue coat trimmed with fur.

"He's fully dressed," I whispered. "Why is he fully dressed?"

The man smirked. "A little skill I've picked up over the years."

Finn's face was terse. "Father."

"Finn. Nice to see you've been keeping some company, at least, and one who doesn't seem surprised by what we are. Finally taken a mate? Vincent will be pleased."

"I really don't care what Vincent thinks."

"No," said the man carefully, "I suppose you don't." He

cast a look at me and dropped into a low bow. It was action almost identical to the ones Finn had given me. Inherited, or rehearsed? “Forgive me, where are my manners? I am Reed, fair lady, Finn’s father.”

“Oh, um, I’m—”

“Don’t answer him,” Finn snapped.

“I don’t mean her any harm,” said Reed, his face drawn up defensively.

“It appears the pack rarely means any harm, and yet harm happens wherever you go.”

To this, Reed had no reply. “Come back with us, Finn. I’ll convince Vincent to recant his words. We’re short on members. A wolf shouldn’t be alone.”

“I am not alone,” said Finn, clutching tightly onto my hand.

“You know what I mean.”

“I do, and yet I find I do not care. I’d rather waste away in these woods than return as one of you. Either way, I’d be dying alone. Good day, Father. I’m sure we’ll speak again, although frankly I’d rather not.”

He marched past him, tugging me behind him. Reed gave us both a curious look, and then shifted back into his wolf form and bounded away.

I waited until he was out of earshot. “You won’t really waste away in the woods, will you?”

Finn managed a slight smile. “Not the way you keep feeding me.”

“There’s not some wolf curse that the omegas sicken and die, then?”

"No, but it's as dangerous for us as any other wild wolf. I could still die of illness or injury, maybe even cold."

"You survived last winter."

"Barely," he shivered. "I barely survived last winter. There was a time I was sure..." He trailed off, his fingers brushing snowflakes from my cheek. His words were lost.

I thought about how cold he'd been the day after the last full moon, despite his assurances that wolves didn't feel the cold as keenly as we did. There were nights now when I woke too cold to sleep again, where the pillow felt frosty and my nose ached from ice. Rowan was nearly always in my bed now, or Mama's, and we had walls and shutters to lock in heat.

The cave would frost over if the wind changed direction.

"Finn?"

"Yes?"

"Could you please reconsider coming into the village and trying your hand at an apprenticeship?"

Finn sighed, and shook his head. "I am ill-suited to lies, and dislike telling them. I'd have to make up some story that wouldn't make sense, and someone *would* notice I was absent during the full moon in a place as small as Thornwood. I cannot be what I am not; I will not pretend to be."

"So you'll risk *death*?"

"I won't die," he said. "Someone offered me use of her hut."

It was warmer than the cave, to be sure, but it also wasn't fully mine. I couldn't imagine Forrest turfing out some vagrant into the cold, but if Finn wasn't careful, if Forrest discovered a wolf rather than a man…

"You look worried," said Finn, stroking a lock of hair behind my ear. "It's attractive, but I'd expunge your worries nonetheless."

"Stay in human form if you use the hut," I told him. "And avoid death. I'm growing rather fond of you, you see."

I kissed his cheek and darted through the village gate, trying not to glance behind me at Finn, touching his skin as if it had been graced with silver, and trying not to think about where else I could have kissed him.

A couple of years ago in high summer, Forrest, Daisy and I had gone bathing in the lake with some other village youths. Forrest and I had crawled up the stream, clambering through the rocks to a secluded glade. I had slipped, laughing, and as Forrest had pulled me up, his own laughter had melted away.

He swept his face to mine, and kissed me.

It was light and brief, over in an instant, so swift I could almost have imagined it. But when he moved away, I clutched his wrist, wanting to experience more of that touch.

Just the touch. Not him.

Even then I was somehow aware that I wanted the kiss more than I wanted him, and that even though I didn't fully understand Forrest's feelings then, I knew that wouldn't be right.

I think he must have had an inkling too, because he never spoke of it again, never once tried another kiss.

I wanted Finn's kiss, too, but I wanted more than that. More than a kiss, more than his touch, *him.*

If he kissed me, I wasn't going to let go.

My lips buzzing with the thought, I slipped in through the back door of my house.

And found the golden-eyed man from the woods standing in the kitchen.

9 THE BIG BAD WOLF

The door banged shut behind me, and my basket slid to the floor. Mama's eyes flew towards me. "Andie—"

The man grinned, cutting across her like a knife slides through butter. "Well, well," he said. "Andesine. I did think as much when we met a few weeks ago, but that didn't seem like the best moment for a reunion."

Reunion?

I frowned, and the man smiled back, as if reveling in my confusion.

"I'm glad you kept the knife I gave you."

I flinched. "No..."

Mama's eyes dropped, but her voice was hard as steel. "Andie, take Rowan and go to the forest house."

A strange phrase. An unnatural phrase. The forest house. Did she mean the hut? No, she didn't even know of it. She didn't mean 'go to the forest' at all. She meant 'go to *Forrest's* house'.

She meant fetch the hunters.

But why? What threat did this stranger hold?

No. Not a stranger. My father.

I had never spent enough time with him for his face to hold any kind of lasting memory. I'd known his hair was brown and slightly curled, and that his eyes were a brownish gold, like autumn leaves, but his features had blurred away behind the years.

He tilted his head, turning back to Mama. "Who's Rowan?" His voice was cold as rainwater.

"The dog," said Mama shortly, the lie rolling easily off her tongue. "She can't be alone in those woods."

It had not occurred to me until that moment that my father wouldn't know who Rowan was. I knew he'd left before he was born, but I had assumed he had looked in on us, or that Mama might have sent word, or...

I don't know what I thought, but I didn't expect this.

Why was Mama trying to conceal Rowan's existence? He must have known she was with child when he left. He must have known he had two children. It would be only logical to assume—

"Mama?" Rowan appeared at the top of steps, rubbing his eyes.

Something in the room shifted and tightened, like the wires on a violin, taut to the point of snapping. All eyes fixed on my brother.

"Well, well, well, Clarisse," said the man eventually. "You didn't tell me you'd remarried, and the midwife so sure you'd never carry again..."

Midwife? Forrest's mother?

Mama trembled, her face white. She balled her fingers into fists, stepping between him and Rowan. "Don't," she said. "*Please.*"

He paid her no need, sweeping across to the staircase. I crept beside Mama as he knelt in front of Rowan, not understanding, but knowing I didn't want to be alone, wanting to be close to her, even though I also didn't want him near my brother. He pulsated something, something I couldn't name but felt, as if everywhere he moved he splayed out cold, shadowy tendrils.

"What's your name, little man?" he asked, his voice was soft and gentle, the hard edges of it filed away.

"Rowan," he replied. "But sometimes they call me Ro. Who are you?"

"My name is Vincent," he replied. "How old are you, Ro?"

"I'm eight," he said.

Mama let out a tiny sob. The man's jaw tensed. "Are you, now?" He peered at Rowan closely, his eyes flickering as they beheld the specks of gold in Rowan's own. He sniffed the air, and wheeled around to face Mama.

"He's—"

"He isn't!" Mama insisted. "I swear he's—"

"Liar!" Vincent's hand flew out and struck Mama in the face so hard she crumpled into the ground. Without thinking, I leapt between them as he raised his hand again, but Rowan launched off the steps and wrapped his entire body around Vincent's arm.

"Don't you hurt my mama!" he screamed.

"Your mama is a lying whore, boy, and I am your father!"

There was no soft edge now, only fire and fury. "You will do as I tell you!"

Rowan trembled, as if he'd been struck. "You're not my father," he wobbled. "My father left."

"And I've come back. To claim you. You're to be my heir, boy, when you come of age. I will give you power beyond your dreams—"

"No!" Rowan yelled. "You're not my father! I say you're not!"

"Quiet!" Vincent turned towards him, his eyes dark and twisted. I scrambled for my basket, snatching out the dagger and plunging it into his thigh. Vincent snarled, spinning to strike me, but I yanked back my blade and darted away.

Blood pooled onto the floor. Vincent clutched the wound, face twisted. "That's twice now you've struck me, girl," he seethed. "Never again."

"Then leave," I hissed, with more courage than I felt. All my fear twisted into rage. "Leave and don't come back."

"I will have what is *mine*—"

"My brother isn't yours to take!"

A shot went off; Mama had grabbed the pistol she kept in one of the drawers and fired it into the wall. "Get out of my house!" she screamed, reloading. "The next goes through your head!"

Vincent smiled. It was not a kind smile, but cold and hard and full of teeth. "You wouldn't—"

Clarisse fired again, the shot blazing narrowly past his ear. "Missed," he said, and lunged for her.

The pistol went flying, skittering along the floor. Rowan

screamed. The air ripped from my lungs. And something else ripped too, shifting in the air.

Vincent was gone.

In his place was a huge grey wolf.

He was twice the size of Finn, his teeth like daggers. Claws dragged along the floor. His jaw rippled into a monstrous snarl, eyes gold and gleaming. Rowan was still screaming, but I stood utterly silent, even when he lurched towards Mama.

The back door banged open. Russell Carter, Forrest's father, stood on the threshold, crossbow drawn. He fired it into the wolf's shoulder, flying into the room as the beast reared. Another bolt shot through the dark; Forrest.

Mama scrambled towards Rowan, but I couldn't reach them. I dived behind the counter. The room strained with bolts and fur, snarling, screaming, ripping, thumping. Raw fear pulsed inside me. I was immobilised, numb.

This was not happening. This couldn't be happening.

Bowls smashed against the floor. The table flipped over. Blood splattered.

A terrific crash resounded through the air, and the wolf fled into the dark, howling.

Something howled back. The others. The others were there.

Russell glanced at Mama. "Are you hurt?"

"Go after him!" she yelled. "Don't let him get away, he'll —"

Russell streamed out into the night. Forrest waited, looking at me. "Are you all right?"

A tiny, quivering voice, not at all like my own, made its way to my mouth. "I'm fine," I said. "Go."

He disappeared, hurtling after his father.

Rowan was sobbing in Mama's arms, and she was weeping too. I had no energy for tears. I had no energy for anything. I sat on the ground, staring at the ruined room, my muddied thoughts whirring.

My father was a wolf, stronger and larger than my mind could possibly have conceived.

Did Finn know? No, no, he would have told me. He wouldn't have lied...

Finn. I wanted him here.

I was not a wolf, but it still seemed like I was howling.

But he didn't come. I couldn't call him. And for a moment, the other two people in the room didn't matter.

I was completely alone.

Get up, said a voice inside. *Stand up. You're not hurt. You're all right. Stand.*

Nobody's dinner, nobody's dinner.

Slowly, somehow, I rose to my feet, grabbed a broom, and started sweeping up the debris.

By the time Mama had finally managed to get Rowan back to sleep, I had dealt with most of the damage and scrubbed my father's blood from the floor. The task had kept my mind focused, had stopped me from shattering as easily as the jug Daisy had given me, smashed beyond repair.

But now the task was over, and there was nowhere for my thoughts to hide.

I turned to my mother, not quite meeting her gaze. "My father is a wolf."

Mama's chest heaved, half sigh, half sob. If she was surprised that I knew of such things, it didn't register. "Yes."

"And Rowan..."

"He'll be one too, when he's older."

I put my head in my hands. "Oh, Mama, how did you think you were going to keep this secret from us? From *Ro*?"

"I don't know," she rushed. "I couldn't... when he was born, I thought I'd have time. Time to explain it, or find some way of stopping it. But I haven't found anything. I didn't know what to do—"

"You could have told us! Told *me*! I'm hardly a child anymore—"

"I know," she wept, "I know, I'm sorry—" She trailed off into sobs, stuffing her face in her apron, trying not to wake Rowan again.

I sighed. I felt like crying too. Frustrations at my mother, yes, but also at the situation.

My father was a wolf, probably one of the ones that had hurt Finn.

"I'm not a wolf, right?" I whispered. "I would have changed by now, wouldn't I?"

Mama rose her head from her apron. "It rarely affects the women."

"So... I'm just an ordinary human, right?"

"More... more or less."

"*Mama,*" I pleaded. "Please."

"You give off a certain… scent. One that marks you as a desirable mate."

Everything in me sank. I recalled Finn's remarks about my scent, how my cloak masked it…

Did he only like me because of that? I rarely removed it in his presence, but…

Priorities.

"That's, that's…"

"Your grandma bought this red fabric of protection from a travelling fairy," Mama continued. "To mask you, in case any of the wolves ever returned, to stop…"

"To stop them mating with me, like my father did with you?"

Mama's jaw was tight. "They're wolves in and out of their forms. They have a strange magnetism, this sort of… pull. The minute I locked eyes on your father, there was no one else for me. No matter how much I wished it. The distance between us dampened it somewhat, and slowly I saw what kind of person he was. What he wanted more than anything was an heir. I tried to resist him, but I couldn't, and when I was pregnant again, I knew that if I gave him a son, I would lose him. I couldn't take that chance." She paused, dabbing at her eyes. "Perhaps I should have waited until I was sure, found another way…"

"Mama?" I tensed. "What did you do?"

"I had Beatrice—Forrest's mother—help me fake a miscarriage and convince him that I would be unlikely to conceive again. I couldn't have him come back. I had to make him leave—"

"What happened?"

"It worked. Your father believed it. He was… he was furious. With me, the world, it was impossible to tell. He stormed out and Beatrice went into the woods to bury the 'remains'—to keep up the ruse. Vincent… Vincent must have found her, hands wet with pig's blood, holding what he thought was his heir and… and snapped."

"He killed her." I sucked in a breath. "My father killed Forrest's mother."

Mama nodded.

"Does Russell know?"

"Yes."

"Does he know what he is?"

"Yes."

"Does he know… about Rowan?"

Mama's face went whiter than snow. "I told Russell that Rowan wasn't Vincent's, and that I had to convince him to leave me before the child was born, in case it was obvious. I begged him not to tell anyone."

"He believed you?"

"Women seldom lie about things like that."

That much was true, but I wondered if the lie would hold, if Russell wouldn't realise what Vincent was after, and why. If he saw the man's face, he might see the similarities between him and my little brother.

There was a brisk knock at the door. Mama startled.

"It's me," came Russell's voice.

"Come in."

Russell walked in, red-faced, dark, greying hair in disarray. "We lost him," he said, "and there are wolves *everywhere,* Clarisse. The woods were thick with them."

Mama looked up, tired and trembling.

"We'll catch him," Russell insisted. "You know we will. He won't get away this time."

Behind him, I spotted Forrest, hanging back. How much of the story did he know? Was this the first time he'd learned the truth of his mother's death?

Or had he always known that wolves could be men, too, and had laid his traps knowingly?

A sickness churned inside me, and I longed even more for Finn, hoping he was safe in the cave, that he wasn't foolish enough to go out with all this going on, that he'd got back to the cave before sensing anything amiss.

Suddenly I felt sick for a very different reason.

There was another noise in the garden, and Daisy's face peeled out of the gloom, a dark halo of curls loose around her fraught, lovely face. She cast a passing look at Forrest, briefly examining a cut on his cheek, and then rushed into the room.

"Are you all right?" She flung herself at me. "I just heard from the hunters... they say you were attacked by a wolf?"

It was too much, the final straw. On top of everything that had just happened, Daisy's kindness just toppled me over the edge. I burst into tears and sobbed on her shoulder.

"I'm going to take her upstairs," Daisy announced. Gently, carefully, she tugged me up the steps and into my room, helping me out of my clothes, into the bed and under the covers.

"The wolf broke the jug you gave me," I whispered in the

dark.

"I'll make you a new one."

"I liked that one."

"There are other pretty jugs." She squeezed my shoulder. "I'm so relieved you're all right."

But no relief came for me. I had no such assurances about Finn.

"Thanks for coming," I said.

"Of course I came." Daisy turned towards the closed window, facing the sound of wailing wind. "I hope Forrest's all right. He looked a bit scratched up."

"I'm sure he's fine."

I did not expect to fall asleep. My mind was still trembling under the weight of the past hour, under everything I'd learned. I knew I wasn't hurt, but the wolf—my *father*—had torn something away from me.

Or maybe my mother had, by not telling me the truth for eighteen years.

How had she hoped to keep them in the dark forever? Was she honestly so naive as to have hoped for a cure? You couldn't *cure* being a wolf; there wasn't anything wrong with them. You couldn't cure who they were, anymore than you could change the colour of your eyes.

Daisy stroked my hair until she thought I was asleep, dimmed the lamps, and shuffled away. I stayed awake under the blankets until exhaustion overpowered fear, and sank into a shallow, troubled slumber.

Around two years after he joined the wolves, Finn was playing with Cassel in a stream when the boy complained of a sudden headache. It was unusual for Cassel to complain about anything, unusual for anyone in the pack to complain about pain at all. Henri, one of the older wolves, ripped off a finger once during a fight with another pack. He hissed a bit and bound it up like it was nothing more than a minor inconvenience.

"Do you want to go back?" Finn asked him.

Cassel shrugged, his forehead scrunched with pain, and murmured something about wanting to lie down. It hardly mattered where he rested, when there was no home to go to.

His legs buckled underneath him, and he pitched into the stream.

Finn launched forward to catch him, flinging him over his shoulder, and ran back to the camp.

Reed and Pierre rushed forward when he re-entered the glade, but none of the others did much more than raise their heads. They lowered the boy to the ground, where he twitched and gasped.

"The change?" Pierre asked.

"Must be."

Vincent groaned. "He sure picked a moment. I was hoping to leave tomorrow morning. I suppose we better stay here until it's over."

Cassel groaned, oblivious to the world. "You're all right," Finn whispered. "It's just the change, Cass. You'll be fine."

At least Cassel had been warned. At least he knew he wasn't dying. Although Finn remembered how awful the first time had been, and wondered how much of a comfort that really was. He'd know he was going to live through it, but there would be moments when he wished he wouldn't.

Bizarrely, even though all the wolves had been through the change, even though they must have remembered how awful the first few times were, they seemed ill-equipped to deal with it, acting as if Cassel's moans were a terrible inconvenience to them all, so much so that after half a day, they decided to leave him to it and come back in a couple of days. Finn was assigned to stay behind and watch him, and only Pierre looked at all concerned about leaving them.

"You don't have to stay and watch," Reed suggested. "Keep within hearing distance in case anyone stumbles upon him, but you don't have to stay. You can't do anything."

Finn looked down at Cass, screwed to the floor, and wondered how it was possible that any of them could turn their backs.

"I'll stay with him," he said resolutely.

Reed shrugged, and walked off with the others. Only Pierre looked back, briefly and fleetingly, and cast Finn something like a grateful nod.

Had they honestly forgotten the agony of the first few times, now that it was little different to ripping off a bandage?

It was left to Finn to comfort him, trying not to think of his mother, of the way her hands had brushed his hair, how she had barely left his side.

He had hated her silence then, and he hated his own now. He could think of nothing, nothing to say to Cassel that would be on any help.

At one point, the young boy thrashed violently, and Finn caught his hands and gripped onto him tightly.

"It gets easier," he promised, with little else to say.

"I want it to stop," Cassel rasped, body trembling.

"I know, and it will, just a bit longer."

"I want my Mama."

Finn swallowed. "I know."

"I miss her."

"What... what was she like?" He wasn't sure he wanted to hear about Cassel's mother because he would definitely start thinking about his own, but he knew the boy needed a distraction and he couldn't think of anything to say himself.

Cassel's eyes brimmed with tears from a very different kind of pain. "I can't much remember her face," he whispered hoarsely. "But I remember her smile and the taste of her apple pie and the songs and stories she used to sing. I remember the way she used to hold me..." He paused, shuddering. "I don't quite remember the feeling of being held, though."

At this, Finn's chest tightened, because he was forgetting that feeling, too.

He slid his knees under Cassel's shaking body and tugged him into his lap, holding the smaller boy against his chest. He knew he made a poor substitute for the soft, warm arms of a mother, much like the trembling form of Cassel made a poor substitute for what he craved.

Cassel whimpered against him, fingers balling into his clothes. He whispered something that might have been thanks.

"Don't leave," he said at one point, although his vacant eyes could have been talking to another. "Don't leave me."

"I won't," Finn returned. "I swear I won't."

And this time, when he said thank you, Finn heard it.

10
COURTING THE WOLF

At first light, long before the rest of the village was stirring, I woke, the memories of the night before shuddering me into consciousness. It seemed strange to find my body unaltered, that my skin was as smooth and unblemished as ever. I searched my hands for scars, for bruises or bumps, evidence of the mess inside me made plain for all to see.

There was nothing, and even the pale-faced girl in the mirror betrayed little of the mudded swirl beneath.

I dressed quickly and raced downstairs. Mama was dozing in the chair beside the fire, angled towards the door, the loaded pistol lying on her lap. She woke as I hit the floor, wide-eyed and fearful.

I turned my gaze away, grabbing my basket and cloak.

"Where are you going?" she asked.

"To check on grandma."

"You should—"

"What? Take one of the hunters?"

"Yes." She hesitated. "It's not safe."

This was true, but I didn't care. I had to get out of the house, out of the village. Away from Mama and secrets and pain and confusion. To Finn, to the clarity and ease I felt only whenever he was around. Anything difficult about him, about us, had melted away in the mangle of the moment.

"I can't stay here," I told her. "But I'll try not to be too long."

"Andie—"

"What?"

"I... I really am sorry. I never meant... I never meant for any of this to happen."

I paused, my grip on the basket tight. "I know," I said. "But in the end, it doesn't really matter. It's awful all the same."

Mama said nothing as I left, the door banging shut behind me.

In a calmer, more rational moment, I might have felt sorry for her, might have found some faint sliver of sympathy for how *she* must have felt, all of these years, keeping my father's identity to herself. Raising us alone. But anger overpowered any softer emotion, the quiet fury of betrayal and bitterness.

She hadn't trusted me.

She hadn't prepared Rowan.

And now we were all in danger because of it.

Forrest and some of the other hunters were stirring for another expedition into the forest, readying a cart. His cheek was still slashed from yesterday. I felt almost jealous of his wound, of the proof of the chaos. I supposed I should ask how he was. Daisy would have.

"We're going to find some ash trees and burn them," Forrest explained, sensing my arrival. "Apparently there's an old superstition about it repelling wolves. Nonsense, right?"

So Russell hadn't told him. I wondered if I should, or if that put Finn in more danger. I didn't want Forrest to be in the dark, like I'd been. I wanted him to know what he was up against. But I also wanted Finn as safe as I could make him.

"I suppose if it makes people feel safer…" His voice trailed off, his gaze latching onto my basket. "Where are you going?"

"My grandmother's."

"I'll go with you. You shouldn't be alone—"

"Wolves are nocturnal," I snapped, knowing this meant nothing to werewolves. "So I should be just fine."

"Red—"

"Just leave me alone!"

I raced off, boots churning through the well-trodden snow, running as fast as I could. I refused to let him catch me, to stop me.

I am no one's dinner, no one's dinner.

I want to be safe, not saved. Safe, safe—

Finn.

I stopped halfway there to gather my breath, sides splitting, before continuing up on my journey towards the caves. Finn stood on the ledge outside.

"Andie—"

I raced forward into his arms, latching myself to him with such force that he almost stumbled backwards.

"What's wrong?" he asked. "Tell me."

I inched back, turning to the mouth of the cave. "My

father's a wolf," I said to the floor.

Finn tensed. "What?"

"My father. He's a wolf. Did you... did you know? Could you smell it on me—"

"No, no, I didn't know. I swear. I mean, it explains your scent, but I didn't know—"

"His name is Vincent."

Finn stilled. I thought about how large my father's wolf had been, unnaturally big, and the way his claws had scraped the floor.

"That's your alpha, isn't it?" I asked. "Or was."

"You're... Vincent's daughter?"

"Yes."

Finn's silence stretched on forever, as if he was calculating several things at once, trying to work out what to say first. "He came to your house, didn't he? Last night. What happened? Are you all right?"

"He..." I struggled to get the words out, stumbling on the events of last night, and eventually they all came out in a blubbering, intelligible mess. Finn grabbed me in his arms and held me as I bawled, fingers curled into his clothes. All the fear and anger gushed out against his chest. "He wants Rowan," I sobbed. "He wants to take him away from us."

Finn clutched me ever tightly. "I won't let that happen."

I pulled back, blowing my nose loudly on a handkerchief. "The hunters are placing mountain ash around the village."

"Smart."

"That means you can't get in either."

"But neither can Vincent."

"If it gets too cold out here—"

"I trust that a very pretty herbalist will come and warm me up with her own body heat—"

"Finn!"

"Too much?"

I threw myself back into his arms. "I wouldn't let you freeze to death."

"I won't let Vincent take your brother, either."

I clung to him like frost clings to the cold, and tried to pretend in his words, that we both had a power to keep the other safe by merely wishing it.

"I might not be able to come out and see you so much anymore," I whispered. "It isn't safe."

"I'll come by the cemetery just before sunset if you can't make it out."

"It… it might not be safe for you, either."

"I'll be fine."

"And if you're not?" I wiped my eyes. "Maybe… maybe you should go away for a bit, until the hunters have caught him." I didn't want him gone. I wanted him here more than ever before. But I also didn't want someone else I cared about at risk.

I also think that I wanted him to say he wouldn't leave, even if that was contrary to the safety I craved for him.

Don't go. Don't go anywhere I can't follow you.

Finn shook his head. "The hunters don't stand a chance against Vincent and his pack."

"Then what do we do?" Panic flared inside me. "What do we do, Finn? Just hope he gives up? Keep Rowan inside the village forever?"

"I don't know," he said. "We'll think of something."

I shivered, the warmth of the run finally trickling away. My body balked under the true weight of the cold.

"Come sit down," Finn suggested, tugging my elbow gently. "We'll get a fire going."

"I... I can't stay for long. I've got to see my grandma. And I promised my mother I wouldn't be gone long."

"All right. Just a little while, then." He brushed my hair over my shoulder, and pressed his lips to my forehead. I sat down beside the remains of the campfire, leaning against him, the thoughts of a fire abandoned.

"My mother said I smell different from regular females," I told him. "That I give off a scent that marks me as a prospective mate."

Finn tensed beside me.

"Why didn't you tell me?"

"Because it's vile, Andie."

"I smell... vile?"

"No! No, you smell delicious. What's vile is the entire notion of it, I didn't want you to think that I was..."

"You were...?"

"Well, your cape, as I said, disguises it completely, so I only really noticed it the first time when you gave it to me—"

"You seem to be dodging the subject."

"I didn't want you to think that I'd liked you because of your *scent,* all right? I didn't want you to think I was trying to mate with you—"

"Oh?" I said, with more confidence than I felt, "what are you trying to do, then?"

"I'm trying to—" He stilled. "I want to court you," he rushed in a blur of words. "I want to step out with you and go to dances with you and meet your family and do everything that comes afterwards, but I'm incredibly aware of what a terrible idea that is, that I have so little to offer, and that it's unfair of me to want anything other than your friendship—"

"What if I don't want friendship?" I told him, a heat rising inside me. *What if I just want you?* I swallowed, pushing the thoughts down, because he was right, it was stupid, it was foolish, it would end badly, and hurt, and we should just—

Stop. We should stop.

But I couldn't.

"My mother also says the wolves have a kind of magnetism, that makes them hard to resist. Makes them… makes people feel things for them. Is that true?"

Finn surveyed me carefully for a moment. "Alphas do," he said eventually. "Why are you asking?"

"No reason!" My voice came out oddly high, like the squeak of a mouse.

"Are you… feeling things for me?"

"I—"

He grinned. "You think I'm attractive."

"I think *you* think you're attractive."

"Your flushed cheeks suggest that is a view you share."

"It's warm in here."

"It's midwinter, and you are a liar." He paused, the smirk still high in his cheeks. "Luckily, you look good with red cheeks."

I punched his shoulder.

"You look good in *everything*."

I ignored him.

"And nothing, too. You look particularly good in that."

"You haven't seen me naked."

"I have a very vivid imagination." He paused, his face steeling itself. "I didn't tell you about the scent because I didn't want you to feel obliged to like me, or worse. I didn't want you to be frightened of the sway you hold over me, and leave."

I reached across and laced my fingers into his. "I'm not leaving."

His throat bobbed. "I see that."

"And you hold a power over me, too."

"I'm not sure I want to," he said. "No matter how much I..."

"Yes?"

Finn did not respond, but his hand grazed my cheek. My eyes flickered closed, and Finn's dipped too. Our faces moved together, guided by warmth. We were impossibly close and desperately far away.

"Andie!" called a voice from outside. "Andesine! Where are you?"

I scrambled upright, cheeks burning, hissing a curse. *Forrest.*

"Friend of yours?" asked Finn, a black eyebrow raised.

"Maybe he'll go away..."

"I know you're here! I tracked you—"

I swore again. If I didn't move now, he'd follow my tracks up to the cave, and find me with Finn, and I had no idea how to explain *that.*

"I've never heard you swear before," said Finn, twirling a curl around one of his long fingers. "I think I rather like your dirty mouth."

"Ssh! He'll hear you."

"Red!" Forrest hollered.

At this, Finn buckled. "Red?"

"I have to go," I rushed, pulling up my hood and reaching across to kiss his cheek. Finn turned at the same time, and for the briefest of moments, our lips brushed together.

We both inched back, startled.

Too much. Too much and too soon and not enough and—

"Red!"

"I'm coming!" I called, and tearing my eyes from Finn, flung myself out into the crisp, white cold. Forrest was down beside the lake, now thoroughly frozen over, red-faced from yelling.

"There you are!"

I inched forward, down the icy slopes. Forrest came forward to assist, but I waved him away. "What are you doing here?"

"I came to fetch you. It's not safe out here."

"I can take care of myself."

Forrest groaned. "You have a dagger, Andie. You're hardly going to stab a wolf."

"You'd have to be pretty lucky to hit one with a crossbow, too."

Forrest scowled. "Let's just go back."

"I'm going to my grandma's."

"Funny route to take."

"I just wanted some space!" I fought the urge to stamp my foot.

"I'll walk you there."

"There's no need—"

"For some foolish reason, I have a vested interest in keeping you alive, much as you might irk me."

"Fine!" I hissed, scrambling ahead of him. "But don't expect any thanks. Or conversation. I'm in no mood for company."

"Whatever you want," he said, holding up his hands defensively. He kept two spaces behind me as we trudged back to the road. I felt another pair of eyes on me, and glanced back in the direction of the caves. A shadow of a person behind one of the trees, staring out at us.

Finn.

I bit my lip, thinking of the ghost of the kiss that we'd almost shared, and my thoughts ached under the weight of wondering what else I would have done, if we'd not been interrupted.

Maybe I should apologise to Forrest. He didn't know what he'd done, and I couldn't fault his wanting to protect me. I'd have run out after Daisy.

But I didn't want his protection, or, at least, I didn't want to need to be protected.

"I'm mad at the situation, not you," I muttered in place of an apology.

"I know."

We said nothing else until we reached the rusted gates.

Forrest let out a low whistle. It occurred to me it had probably been a long time since he'd seen the place.

"Well, that's one place that could do with a bit of a spring clean once the snow melts…"

I did not laugh.

"I'll wait here for you."

"No." I shook my head.

"But—"

"You'll freeze out here in the cold, and I'm not coming back tonight. I'll stay over at Grandma's."

"But—"

"Forrest," I said, "I just need space."

He closed his mouth, and nodded. He had no idea about my father, but he must have sensed something else was amiss, an altercation between me and my mother, or something else.

"I'll let your mother know where you are."

"Thank you."

I watched him leave, but not for long. My thoughts had already turned back to Finn, and wondered if I would be able to sneak off again, to do what we hadn't managed to do earlier.

The kitchen door banged open.

"Well?" said Grandma, wrapped in a worn shawl, "Are you coming in?"

11 THE WOLVES ON THE ICE

I hurried up the drive, and into the warmth of the kitchen, stamping my snow-covered boots against the stone floor. Grandma ushered me into a seat beside the fire.

"How did you know I was there?"

"Grandmother's intuition," she barked. "What's wrong?"

"My father came home last night."

Grandma stilled. "I see."

"My father's a wolf."

"I knew that."

I prickled. "You too? And you didn't tell me?"

"Not my decision, dearie. Your mother didn't want you to know. I didn't want to go against her."

"Are you keeping anything else a secret?"

"Plenty. Tea?"

I shook my head. "Grandma, you aren't really a witch, are you?"

"There's no such thing as witches," she said stiffly. "Or at least, not how most folk imagine them. Humans can't *do* magic, see. Use enchanted objects or wield enchanted blades, sure. But only the Fey can do magic."

"The Fey?" I remembered to word from before, only dimly. Finn had used it too.

"Fair-folk. Fairies. Like the one that gave me the fabric for your cloak."

"You've met them?"

"We've had a few dealings over the years. They generally keep to themselves, see. Don't want the fuss. Can't say I blame them."

"What... what are witches, then?"

"Women that are too wise, most of the time. People can get a bit funny when women know too much. They'll stop doing all the hard work if they grow too wise. Maybe even uprise!" There was a distinct gleam in her eyes as she spoke. "Or stay in crumbling old chateaus in the middle of nowhere, whatever is easier."

"You are truly living the dream, Grandma."

"Ah, my dear, I am." She surveyed me carefully for a moment. "But that is not what you want, is it?"

"I'm sorry?"

"You, I think, would not be content to be alone, even with freedom."

I hesitated. "I think I would rather be alone and myself, than be somebody else with somebody else, but I would prefer not to have to pick. I should like to be myself *with* someone."

Grandma smiled, soft and worn, and for a moment I quite forgot that I was mad at her a moment ago. "You have someone in mind."

"I… I might."

"Not Forrest, I take it?"

I hung my head.

"Ah, young love. Never mind. He's sure to have other options. It's usually easy enough for affable young men."

"Grandma!"

"What?"

"Don't… don't…"

"Don't what? Make light of it all? When you live to be my age, dear, you learn what's worth making a fuss about."

"And what is?"

"True love," she said sagely. "But whatever he feels for you, it isn't that."

My Grandma spoke a lot about love for someone who famously detested her marriage. "Grandma…" I asked cautiously. "Have you ever been in love?"

Grandma paused, stirring the pot with her ladle. "There's different types of love, dear, and my life has not lacked for all of it. But nothing, nothing will ever compare with what I feel for your mother, and for you and your brother." She tapped my nose, dispelling the weight of her words with the action and a grin. "Care to tell me about this boy, then?"

"I don't know. Care to tell me one of your secrets?"

"Ha! That is fair." She pressed a warm bowl of something into my hands. "So, you know about your father," she said. "How are you feeling?"

"Scared, mostly," I told her. "Worried he'll come for Ro."

"We won't let that happen."

"Everyone keeps saying that, but I'm not sure how we're supposed to avoid it."

"We'll find a way. I have my means."

"You should come and live in the village with us, until this is over."

"I'm quite capable here."

"Grandma—"

She shook her head. "Don't worry about me, dear. I've survived this long."

I sighed, doubting anything I could do would change her mind. Still, I worried. Vincent might come after her and try and use her in an exchange for Ro. I doubted my mother would concede—Grandma wouldn't want that, either—but I hated to think what Vincent would do in retaliation. I was not ready to lose my Grandma.

"Are you mad at your mother?" she asked.

"A bit," I admitted. "I wish she'd told me sooner."

"Think, dear, if your mother had told you about who—what—your father was, what would have changed?"

I opened my mouth, but the ideas did not come easily. I wouldn't have been so surprised about Finn, and I might better have been able to defend myself when Vincent came back into our lives... but what else would have changed?

I might have been more wary of wolves, actually. Maybe I wouldn't have felt a kinship with them. Maybe I would have left Finn in that trap.

Maybe I wouldn't have strayed into the woods at all, too frightened of shadows. Maybe there'd be no hut in the woods, no hobby, no escape. Not much but a faint, simmering fear behind every action.

Afraid. The biggest change in my life is I could have grown up afraid.

"I'm still mad," I said, after a long pause.

Grandma shrugged. "You can be mad," she said. "Just try and be reasonable in it."

There was little I could say to that. I sipped my broth silently.

A short while later, Grandma stood up abruptly, as if alerted by a loud sound.

"Grandma?"

"Quiet."

I strained my ears. A shutter banged somewhere, a low howl of wind whistled through the rafters. Pigeons cooed. Nothing else I could discern, but Grandma's face pricked like a dog's.

She marched into the pantry, flung open a chest, and pulled out a crossbow.

"Grandma!"

"Get behind me. I'd tell you to stay indoors but we know that won't happen." She grabbed a quiver filled with bolts, the feathers tipped blue and red. She flung the crossbow at me as she strapped the quiver to her hip, moving towards the door, snatching back the weapon the second she finished buckling.

Once, several years before, Ro fell from a tree in her garden. I'd never seen her move so fast, like a grey blur across the overgrown lawn, desperate to reach him before he fell.

But now she seemed faster, more frantic than ever.

She wrenched open the door. At the gates, approaching

as if they had all the time in the world, was a pack of men, a dozen or more. Vincent stood at the head, Finn's father beside him. He frowned as he saw me, no doubt recognising me as the girl he'd seen with his son.

Vincent grinned as his gaze settled on us. "Agatha," he said. "It's been a long time."

"And here I was hoping it'd be longer." She lifted one of the blue-tipped bolts and took aim. "Get off my property."

"Come now, Agatha, there's no need for that."

"Stay away from my house," she hissed. "And away from my grandchildren."

Vincent's gaze darkened. "I will have the boy, Agatha."

Grandma fired her crossbow. It struck one of the younger men in the shoulder. He struck the ground, seething.

"That was a warning shot," Grandma yelled.

"A warning shot?" Reed hissed, crouching down by the young man's side and bracing him against the pain. "You hit him!"

Grandma tugged free another bolt, but this one was red. "This next one is laced with wolfsbane," she said.

At this, most of the pack shrank. Even Vincent seemed smaller than before.

"I've heard it's a terrible way to die," Grandma continued. "Do you keep the antidote on you? How much? I've got plenty of arrows. And I hear the hunters have plenty of bullets."

"You're bluffing," said Vincent, stepping forward.

Reed came up to his elbow and spoke into his ear. "Are you sure you want to risk this?"

Vincent shrugged him off, and snarled at Grandma.

"Shift," he commanded the pack.

The men dropped to the ground, backs and forms rippling. Some removed jackets and boots, others clothes seemed to merge with their bodies, fabric and flesh fusing together. Jaws elongated, hands shrunk and sharpened, until all traces of humanity were erased entirely.

A dozen wolves. Two women.

The number of bolts in Grandma's quiver didn't matter. She couldn't shoot fast enough. The wolves advanced, slowly, languidly. Was Vincent honestly going to kill us? Maybe not. Maybe he'd just wound us, use us as bargaining chips.

If my mother was made to choose between her children...

"Andie, go back inside," said Grandma coolly. "Shut yourself in the cellar and don't come out."

My knees trembled, my voice a breath. "No."

"*Andie.*"

If I left, I was fairly sure Grandma was going to die. She wouldn't let them take her alive.

I wasn't going to let that happen.

Do something, said a voice inside. *Do anything.*

If I ran, would they even follow? Surely they would just split up?

Unless I could make them follow me...

I thought of my scent, the one Finn described as *fetching.* What if it was something more than that, something they couldn't ignore in wolf form?

I could make them follow me, then put the cloak back on, and slip away.

I raised my hands to undo the strings.

"No," Grandma started. "Andie, *no!* Don't you dare!"

The cloak slipped from my shoulders.

The effect was instantaneous. One of the young, brown wolf's eyes went liquid, pupils black. He lunged straight for me.

I turned on my heels and hurtled down the hill towards the back gate, hearing a hard yelp as my grandma let loose a bolt, still screaming my name. I gathered the cloak into my arms and fled down the bank, sliding to the bottom. I leapt through the open gate and slammed it shut behind me, praying I could buy myself a few seconds.

I could not look back.

Tearing and skidding through the snow, I tore through the forest, keeping as far as I could to the path and praying for once for the hunters, for back-up, for any of the damn traps I hadn't managed to disable. The wolves were not far behind. I imagined hot breath on my neck, fangs at my ankles. Could they stop themselves now they'd caught my scent?

I pulled my cloak back on, but it didn't matter. They could still see me. They still had my trail. Frantic, I careened off the path, through the undergrowth, searching for shelter.

I was getting dangerously close to the lake. To the caves. To Finn.

Finn who would almost certainly run to my rescue and who didn't stand a chance against them.

No, no, no, not him!

I rolled down a snowbank and slid onto the ice. Something shifted beneath me.

I glanced back at the wolves. Many of them were unnaturally large, and together... together they were certainly heavier than I was.

I stood up, testing my weight on another patch. Nothing stirred beneath.

I sprinted over the ice.

The wolves followed. Something rumbled below, like ice turned to thunder. Lines of lightning cracked beneath their weight. I slid forward, rolling onto my stomach, spreading my weight evenly as one large wolf plummeted under the surface.

The others stilled, the power of my scent dispelled by the cloak, the fear of death taking over. The wolf scrambled in the water, limbs flailing, whimpering with cold and shock. He could not get out.

He was going to drown. It might take a while, but the cold would grip his limbs and lungs, he would stop struggling, and he would drown.

The black wolf—Reed—seemed to sense this too. He shifted back into human form and reached forward to grab him, but the wolf flailed again, clawing at the ice, making it crumble away from the side and making the hole bigger and bigger.

"Stop, Jean!" Reed hissed.

He did not.

My eyes scanned for something to help, unsure why I was trying to help the wolves who moments ago had been trying to attack me, but I didn't want them to die. I just didn't want to be used.

"The log." I pointed up the bank to a hollow log, long enough to slide over the hole, rough enough for the wolf to grip onto.

Reed said nothing, but followed my gaze.

I didn't wait to see what they did. I didn't wait to see if they regained their onslaught when the wolf was rescued. I turned on my heels and continued to flee across the frozen lake.

I was nearly to the other side when I heard another crack.

Don't stop, don't stop, don't stop.

Ahead of me, I saw a white shape drifting down the rocks, but I could not stop, could not fully register, even when my heart beat all the faster for it.

The ice was crumbling beneath me, splitting further with every footfall. If I stopped, if I paused, if I hesitated at all—

In the end, it didn't matter how fast I ran.

My eyes locked onto Finn's and I vanished under the ice.

As the years passed, Finn found more and more to enjoy in being a wolf, and learned to forget what he missed. There was a cold majesty in their lives, in their bodies, in being one with the wood. He was never the strongest or the boldest of his brethren, but he was as swift as the wind. His father praised him, and eventually he stopped wishing for another voice to praise him too.

He never went back to Voulaire. It was easy enough to avoid, not being on any of the main roads or routes. As time wore on, he forgot his friends' faces, even if he could never quite shake the sound of wooden hoops rattling down the cobblestones, the sound of laughter, and the chill ice water of the river they'd play in.

Cold didn't mean as much to wolves.

They did frequently pass through the Thornwood, though. It was on a major road and rarely avoided, even though Vincent liked to move quickly through it and stared at the wind in the trees like ghosts rattled through it. Every time they went, he kept his eyes peeled for the girl from before, and sometimes, *sometimes* he saw her. Older now, and more beautiful than he could ever have imagined her. A vision in red, utterly bewitching. He ought not to have been able to recognise her, the years blurred between them, but somehow he knew it was her, knew it from the pristine contours of her dewy skin, the redness of her lips and cheeks, the spill of her dark chocolate hair.

Bizarrely, the girl had no scent, but even so, he imagined one. She smelled like autumn and firelight, damp soil and cinnamon buns, and the first frost of winter.

He watched her as a wolf, but she tugged at the human part of him inside, a reverse full moon. The boy wanted to leap out and—

And what? Talk to her?

It had been a long time since he'd spoken to anyone outside the pack. He was wondering if he was forgetting how to.

Then, one day, just after he turned sixteen, Vincent came to him and presented him with new clothes, fresh, fine, crisp garments, dark blue and embroidered.

Finn eyed them with a wariness; Vincent never gave something unless it served a purpose.

"What are these for?" he asked carefully.

Vincent grinned. "Hunting," he said. "Dress up, lad. We're going into town."

Finn was used to the older wolves disappearing into the nearest town every month or so, stumbling home at dawn reeking of ale, great smiles spread across their faces.

Neither he nor Cassel had ever been invited before.

Finn was used to following orders by now, and obeyed without question. Nothing was explained to him until they reached the town and sauntered into the nearest tavern.

Finn liked the ale, and he liked the way the women seemed to gravitate towards them, even if the rest was a little loud and rowdy for his tastes. They had stayed in inns many a time on their travels, but he prefered camping beneath the stars.

Vincent had a woman on his lap, purring in his ear. He sent her to fetch more drink and explained to Finn what they were here for.

"We're here to bed women," he announced. "Maybe get a child or two out of them, if we're lucky. I don't know. None of these smell *ripe* to me."

Finn wasn't sure he wanted to ask what that meant.

"But still, there's fun to be had in it. Reckon I could fling that one your way, if you like. She seems up for anything." He jerked his thumb in the woman's direction. "Remember, we don't take women unwillingly, we're animals, not monsters. It's no fun when she isn't enjoying herself."

Finn had spent enough time among animals to know what was expected of him, enough time listening to the other wolves' stories of their past conquests. He ought to have been excited. Instead he was filled with a strange kind of dread.

He wanted to touch the women like the other wolves were touching them, but he was scared of what came next, and what could come after…

A child. A child that Vincent would take, whose mother

would grow to hate him.

But he did not want to risk Vincent's anger, so when the woman came back, and Vincent whispered something in her ear, and she came over and pressed her mouth to Finn's, he did not resist.

She tasted of cider. Her lips were soft, her body warm. He wanted more of her, and a heat deep inside of him quelled any gathering fears, at least for a little while.

The woman smiled. "Shall we take this upstairs?"

Finn swallowed his nerves, and followed her into the bedroom. She pushed him down on the bed and unlaced her corset, allowing him to touch her in warm, unfamiliar places.

"What's your name?" he asked.

The woman laughed. "What a little sweetheart. It's Margarete, but you can call me whatever you like."

"I'm Finn," he said.

"I didn't bring you up here for your conversation," she said, her fingers going for his shirt.

Finn liked being touched. He liked the feeling of his skin on another's. It had been a long time, far too long, since he'd experienced the sensation, and this... this was something else entirely.

But when the moment came, he couldn't bring himself to do it. Fear pulsed against desire. He didn't want to risk giving this woman a child, didn't want to bring another boy into the world to be hated by his mother, and he pulled away from her.

Margarete pouted, pulled her clothes back on, and sulked away downstairs.

When Vincent arrived, drunk out of his mind, it was easy enough to lie to him about how it went.

The second time was harder, and a third.

Eventually, Vincent figured out what he was doing. He scorned him for his lack of prowess in the bedroom, taunted him, and when that didn't work, he beat him.

"You will do as I tell you!" he hissed. "Bed the next woman I send to you."

But Finn spoke to the next woman thrown in his direction, learned that there were other ways of satisfying her, ways that they both felt counted as "bedding" so that he could sidestep Vincent's instructions.

He never once lay with a woman in a way that would have produced a child. He swore he never would.

12 WOLFSBANE

Ice gnawed at my chest, like a thousand tiny daggers stabbing at my lungs. Burning cold clawed at every inch of me. I knew I had to be alive, that no one dead could be in this much pain, but I felt like I was dying.

Somewhere, there was screaming. It couldn't be me, my throat fastened beneath the vice-like grip of the water, and it couldn't have been Finn; he was still a wolf. But the scream scraped against my ears, knives and foam, pounding in my head, against my chest, against everything.

Through the blur of water, I felt sopping fur, hard claws, and then something was lifting me out, but the air rolled against me with the weight of a rock. My eyes were frosted shut, and every breath I took was agony.

"Andie, Andie!"

His voice sounded faraway, faraway and lost, and afraid. I reached out to touch him, to guide him back to me, to comfort him, but I hadn't the strength to raise my eyes or speak.

I fell down, down, into the dark.

∞∞∞

A slow, heady warmth, thick and full, trickled back. A fire was crackling nearby, the room full of dark, amber light. Pine and woodsmoke filled my nostrils. In the background, something was dripping.

Outside, wind and wolves howled.

Someone was stroking my face. My damp hair was splayed out behind me, drying in the firelight, my cape thrown over the furs to dispel my scent, but I clung to the sensation of the person beside me, of a hot body beneath a pile of blankets.

Finn.

He was utterly naked, his body pressed against my own. I was cocooned in his chest, devoid of clothes, not a single scrap between us. I should have been alarmed or ashamed but I wasn't. There was nothing inside me except a delirious, delicious warmth.

"Finn," I murmured.

He inched back, just a fraction, whispering my name. "You're all right," he said, with a kind of breathless wonder. "You're all right."

"You came."

"Of course I came!"

"How did you know I was—"

"I heard you."

"I didn't scream."

He shook his head, taking one of my hands, and pressing

it against his chest. "I heard you *here.*"

It must have been a wolf thing, something I couldn't understand, even though I thought I might have heard him screaming when he shouldn't have had a voice.

Finn, Finn, my Finn.

I let my palm slide from his chest and drift round to his back, gathering him closer to me, our bare chests pressed together. This was wonderful, beautiful. I was overcome with the strange notion that clothes and jobs and everything else was just an utter waste of time, that lying together in bed beneath a canopy of warmth was what all any of us were born to do.

Finn let out a quiet, soft sound. "Ah, Andie, I feel I should point out… we are both quite naked. It was the only way I could get you warm. Your clothes are drying, I'll fetch mine later—"

He inched backwards, but I moved with him. "Don't go," I pleaded. "Please. Don't go anywhere. Stay. Stay with me."

Finn stilled, throat bobbing, looking somewhere between terrified and delighted. His body trembled.

"Are you uncomfortable?" I asked him.

"Uncomfortable is not the word I would use," he returned.

I slid my hand around his neck, and pulled his face to mine, covering his mouth with my own. Finn let out a sound half like a gasp, half like a moan, and then his hands sprang to my waist, drawing me into him. His lips were warm and bright, and he smelt like pine and woodsmoke, all the heat of summer with the cool, icy wonder of winter.

"Andie," he murmured into me. "*Andie, Andie.*"

I did not give him time or space to say anything else, my hands rising to his thick half-curls, clasping him against me, deepening the kiss. I felt transformed into soft, malleable dough as he rolled against me, hands, arms, lips, thighs—

Finn jerked back suddenly, taking half the blankets with him. "Wait, no, this isn't right, you're not—"

"Not what?"

"Lucid."

"Do I not seem lucid to you?"

"You can't be lucid."

"Why not?"

"Because you can't be lucid and still want..."

Oh, oh Finn...

I took his face in my hands, uncoiling my fingers gently around his cheeks. "I know what I want," I whispered. "I know *exactly* what I want. Who I want."

At that, his resolve broke, and his kiss burned against mine. He rolled me onto my back, covering my body with his, kissing every inch of my skin.

"Say that you're mine," Finn whispered into my ear, half a snarl and half a caress, "I don't care if you're lying, I just want to hear it. Let me hear it, I beg you. Let me pretend..."

"How about I pretend that *you're* mine?" I said, raking my fingers down his back. I wasn't quite sure why we had to pretend at all, other than it was too soon, and too much, and not enough, not enough at all. "Mine, Finn, mine forever."

He moaned into me, his hands hitching up my hips, hot palms sliding to my soft thighs, claiming my flesh as his lips claimed my mouth. "Tell me to stop."

I pulled his face back down to mine. "But I don't want you to stop."

His hot breath surged against me, his body arching over mine. I surrendered utterly to the feel of him, the taste of his touch, drinking in his warmth, drowning in the sensation of his flesh on mine.

All of a sudden, he pulled back again. "No, no, we can't," he said.

I sat up, crouching on my knees. His pupils widened at my nearness, and I wondered once more at the effect my scent had on him. "If you're worried about consequences," I told him, "there's a tonic I can take to avoid conception—"

"It's not that," he assured me, "Although, yes, I wouldn't want to lump you with that burden—"

It didn't feel like a burden, not anymore, not right now. Despite the fact it was too soon for any of that, I didn't mind the idea of bearing *his* children.

Albeit not in the middle of the woods.

"Then what?" I prompted.

Finn startled again, eyes widening, and threw a blanket over me. A second later the door banged open, and Reed appeared in wolf form, quickly shifting back into a man. He closed the door rapidly behind him, shutting out the cold. He glanced at us both, taking in our nakedness, but then his eyes settled on the clothes hanging over the fire.

"Survived your little dip then," he said to me. "Good."

Finn growled. "What are you doing here?"

"I need your help."

"I won't give it."

"I wasn't asking you." His gaze settled back on me. "You're Vincent's daughter?"

"Unfortunately."

"And Agatha De Winter's grandchild?"

"Is she all right—"

In the confusion, I hadn't spared a single thought for grandma. My insides twisted.

"Fine, last I saw," he said dismissively. "That was a very smart, or foolish thing, you did."

"My speciality," I said tersely.

Reed snorted. "His too. Which is why I'm hoping you'll help us again. One of the pack got hit with one of your grandmother's wolfsbane arrows. He's dying. I want you to fetch an antidote."

"What makes you think that I'll help you?"

"You helped us yesterday," he said. "And it's Cassel."

The name meant nothing to me, but Finn sucked in a breath. I turned to him.

"My... the youngest pack member," he told me. "A... friend."

I knew that warmth, that fear, that *my.* It was how I spoke about Rowan.

So I knew I had to help.

"How do I know this isn't some kind of trap?" I asked carefully. "That you're not just using me to get to my brother—"

"I'll take you to him," Reed insisted. "He isn't far."

"My father?"

"He's gone to see if he can secure more antidote from one

of our caches in a neighbouring town."

Finn frowned. "You didn't keep any on you?"

Reed's jaw tightened. "Cassel wasn't the only one injured last night. We used the rest on the stronger members."

Finn glared. "Of course you did."

"Not my call, Finn."

Full wolves seldom wasted time on weaker pack members. Only the strong survived in the wild. Why would Vincent run his pack any differently?

Although maybe the stronger members could have fought longer than the smaller ones. The neighbouring town was not close by. I wasn't sure how long wolfsbane took to kill you, but it was a risky game if Vincent was really playing it. It surprised me that he had gone himself rather than sending another. Maybe he hadn't gone at all, or had no intention of hurrying back. It seemed like the sort of thing he'd do.

Finn glanced at me, throat trembling. "Please," was all he said.

I nodded. "Let me get changed."

"Sensible. I'll go fetch my own clothes, too." He looked at his father. "You come with me."

"What, you can't trust your old man with your mate?"

"She isn't my—" Finn stopped. "I don't trust anyone. Come with me."

Reed held up his hands. "All right. If you insist."

They shifted into wolf form and left with a clatter, forcing me to slide out of the nest of furs to close the door. Thankfully, my clothes were mostly dry, and I crawled into them without much discomfort. I'd left my basket and my dagger at my grandma's, and I felt oddly naked without either. Forrest had left a couple of baskets for fish in one corner, and whilst not my usual design, they were perfectly serviceable. I added a few jars of various remedies to one of them. I knew they wouldn't be able to cure wolfsbane poisoning, of which I knew little, but they might be able to manage the symptoms.

I was packed and ready by the time Finn and his father returned.

Finn seized my hand, his jaw and body wound tight, and we marched almost silently through the muddied snow towards the glade where the rest of the pack was camped. They looked up as I approached, eyes wary, but a single look from Reed cut them down.

The injured pack member was lying to the side of a circle, piled under furs and blankets. Someone was keeping watch beside him, but no one was tending to him, even as he shivered and thrashed. He was young, only sixteen or so, with fair golden hair, clammy and plastered to his face.

Finn let go of my hand abruptly, and crouched beside him. I dropped down next to them both, extending a hand towards his forehead, beaded with sweat. He was hot enough to melt ice.

Finn squeezed his shoulder as I rummaged in my basket, firing orders for hot water to be brewed. The boy moaned under Finn's touch.

"Hey, Cass."

Cassel's eyes opened. They were a pale green, with little brilliance to them, only a faint remnant of the colour that must have once sparked there. "Finn..." Cassel grinned weakly. "Have you come to say goodbye?"

"No, we're here to help you," Finn insisted, gritting his jaw. "This is Andie."

He turned to me, blinking blearily. "Didn't her grandma shoot me?"

"You did attack her house, Cass."

"Fair... fair enough..." He looked up at me again. "Sorry I chased you."

"You're going to be all right, Cassel," I told him, even though I wasn't sure. I'd located the wound on his arm, a black, pulsating mess. Someone had tied a tourniquet above his elbow to slow the flow of poison, but it seemed to be having little effect. Even moving his head seemed to drain him. There was so little strength in his body. When the tea was ready and mixed with my herbs, I had to raise his head to help him to drink. "This should help with the fever, and the pain," I told him, directing Finn to help me. I packed snow into rags to use as compresses, anything to make him more comfortable. I could see how much his condition pained Finn, but I wanted to help *him,* too. Rarely had anyone wanted my services as a healer, too sure I was trying to poison them.

"Thank you..." Cassel rasped, murmuring under my touch. "You're nice."

"Yes," said Finn, glancing across at me, "she is."

Reed motioned to Finn to come over, and he pried himself from Cassel's side. There was little more I could do for him, but sometimes, I thought, it just helped to feel like someone *was* helping you. I cleaned his face and spoke to him in a low, soft voice.

"I won't last until Vincent gets back, will I?" Cassel asked.

"I'm afraid I don't know much about Wolfsbane poisoning, but try not to worry. I'm going to see if my grandmother has an antidote for you."

"And if she doesn't?"

I swallowed, not wanting to think about that. Not wanting to think about what that would do to Finn, and this boy. Another of the wolves hovered not far away, a wolf with the same green eyes. He looked like he was trying not to cry, his jaw clenched with silent agony.

Cassel's father. Why didn't he come over?

"I don't want to die," Cassel whimpered.

I stroked his matted hair. "Then I won't let you."

"Promise?"

"Promise."

He smiled, a weak, shadowy ghost of a gesture. "I can see why Finn likes you."

My attention drifted to Finn and his father, speaking at the side of the glade about the next course of action. I went to join them.

"We should leave," I announced. "There's nothing else I can do without the antidote. Keep him comfortable. I'll be back as soon as I can."

Finn's body was as tight as wire.

"Stay here," I told him. "Stay with your friend."

"I can't help him," he said.

"You can't help me, either. I'm only going to my grandmother's."

Finn bit his cheek, his throat wobbling. His father gave an awkward, flustered kind of look, and turned away. I pulled Finn out of the circle and into my arms.

"Talk," I said, "but quickly."

"I don't know what to do," he said, still holding in a sob. "I can't help him and I can't help you and I think I'll go crazy watching him—"

I took his face in my hands. Tears ghosted his eyes. "I won't judge you for whatever you feel you need to do," I told him. "You can come with me if you think you'd prefer the walk, but ask yourself maybe what Cassel would want. The rest of the pack don't seem to be particularly good at the whole comforting thing."

Finn swallowed audibly. "I'm no good at that either."

I raised up to kiss him, light, soft, slow. "Yes, you are," I told him.

"Andie..."

"What?"

"Thank you, for doing this. For helping him."

I shook my head, lacing his fingers into mine and squeezing them. "I won't let a boy die, and I will always, *always* help friends of yours. I will always help *you*."

He breathed deeply, as if his chest hurt. "And I, you."

He drew me in for another kiss, deeper than before, soft and desperate all at the same time.

"I'll be right back," I told him, and disappeared into the woods.

13 SAVING THE WOLF

The De Winter chateau looked shockingly undisturbed despite the events of the night before, or perhaps I was just used to the complete and total state of general disrepair. The only thing that was amiss were several spots in the ground where I suspected my grandma had buried traps. They'd be invisible after another snowfall.

Something of a trench lined the old iron fence, too, and I wondered if she'd ashed the boundary. The gate was undisturbed, although covering the entire estate was probably too much of a task. At least they couldn't surround her.

I wished she'd come back to the village.

I spied her down by the back fence, digging another hole. It occurred to me that this was the perfect opportunity to sneak in and search for the antidote, but before I could reach the back door, she looked up and saw me.

I raised a hand instinctively, and she bolted across the snow-covered lawn with surprising agility, yanking me into her arms.

"Andie, Andie my dear, I was about to set off for the village and send out a search party if you weren't there..."

"I'm sorry I worried you."

She held me away from her chest, examining my face for any signs of injury. "You're not hurt?"

I shook my head. "I lured them onto the ice and then hid in the hut until they were gone."

"You could have been killed."

"And yet I'm still alive."

She shook her head wearily. "No more brave or foolish gestures," she said. "Not for my sake. You wouldn't be doing me any favours, dear."

"Sorry for trying to save your life, Grandma."

"You better be. Hurry on inside. There's some porridge on the stove. I'll be in in a bit."

This was better than I could have hoped for. I did as she suggested, even scooping up a small bowl of porridge to swallow while I carefully raided the pantry. It seemed awful to eat while someone's life hung in the balance, but I'd not be helping anyone if I collapsed out of hunger on my way back. I held the bowl in one hand as I searched, carefully, through the meticulously well-stocked wares. Everything was labelled, but some of the vials were so old the ink had completely faded.

Too late, I realised I didn't even know what the antidote was called, that even if I *could* read the labels, I might not be able to identify it. What should I do? Take all the unknown vials and hope one of the wolves could work it out? There were so many. Grandma was sure to notice that many missing, or hear them clinking in my basket...

"Andie?" The kitchen door swung open. "Where are you, dear?"

I shoved the vials away. It would be easy enough to pretend I was searching for some dried fruit for the porridge, easy enough to lie, simple.

But in the meantime Cassel was dying and Finn was hurting with him and I was no closer to being able to help anyone.

Grandma opened the pantry door, frowning at me. Kindly, curiously, never for one moment suspecting that I was trying to steal from her. "Andie? What are you looking for?"

It was her smile that did it.

I burst into tears, and told her everything.

∞∞∞

"So," said my grandma carefully, as I dried my tears on my apron, "Despite your mother's story, you've fallen for a wolf, befriended the pack that attacked my home last night, and now are looking for an antidote to save the life of one of them?"

I sniffed noisily. "I haven't befriended the pack," I insisted. "And I haven't fallen for a wolf."

Grandma raised an eyebrow.

"Nothing's… nothing's happened between us."

She raised her eyebrow further.

"*Almost* nothing," I added. "We've been careful." *Though we nearly weren't.* "I'm not about to run off with him, or have any little wolf babies, I promise." *Though the idea is sometimes tempting…*

Grandma seemed satisfied with this answer.

"And I haven't befriended the pack," I repeated. "And Vincent's out of town. It's just one wolf, Grandma. He's only a boy, sixteen at most. I know you think they're all bad, but—"

"I don't think they're all bad," she said. "I think your father's bad, and that badness has a way of rippling into the rest, like a piece of rotten fruit in a barrel. But if you say this one's worth saving, then I believe you."

She disappeared back into the pantry, having dragged me beside the fire to tell my tale.

"Grandma?"

She rummaged behind the herbs, unstoppering vials, sniffing them carefully. "This boy of yours," she said, "what's he like?"

"Finn? He… he was the wolf that saved me the day I lost my first cloak." How many times had I told that tale over the years? "He hates the rest of the pack, or most of them. He's not like them. He's kind and thoughtful and I can tell him anything. He has the soul of an artist and the practicalities of a carpenter. He never makes me feel different. He makes me feel more myself than ever."

Grandma sighed. "Doomed," she said. "Oh well. He sounds decent enough." She handed me a thin blue vial. "That should save the little wolf."

"You're just giving it to me?"

She shrugged. "Never a big fan of killing, anyway."

I dried my eyes on the back of my sleeve. "I wondered why you didn't just shoot Vincent yesterday and be done with it."

"Ah," said Grandma, looking slightly embarrassed, "see, I do rather think maybe he *does* need to die, but between you and me, dear, I've never been the best shot. Complete luck that I hit the first wolf."

I half laughed, stowing the vial inside my basket, and preparing to leave. "What was he like? My father? Before. He must have had something about him for my mother to love him once."

"He had a silver tongue, that's what he had," Grandma said sharply. "A tongue that could spin lies into truth. He cut himself into the garment of the man he thought your mother wanted, and honestly I'm not sure he needed the power of an alpha to do that." She caught my hand. "When I was your age, I used to think I could solve the world with the right words. A fairy told me once as a girl that words are, and always have been, the greatest form of magic, that even a curse could be broken with the right ones. When I married, I searched in vain for them, the ones to fix the misunderstandings, to make him see my point of view... it was never enough."

"Why not?"

"It's not enough to have the right words, if there's no one really listening."

"Why... why are you telling me this?"

"Because you cannot reason with a wolf."

I frown. "Are you telling me that grandfather was a wolf?"

"Not one with claws," she said. "There is more than one type of wolf in the world, my girl. And Vincent is the worst type of all. Not all wolves are bad, but he's rotten to the core.

Don't make the mistake of thinking you can reason with him."

I think of the lengths Mama went to, to expunge him from our lives. A cost Forrest's mother paid for. I would not underestimate him. I would not give him a chance to hurt me or anyone else I loved.

And, I knew, my aim was better than my grandma's.

∞∞∞

I raced back through the woods, slowing only once I ran out of breath, just short of my destination. I paused against a tree, steadying myself. I could hear the pack speaking through the trees.

"How's he doing?" Reed's voice.

"Do you even care?"

"You know I do."

A pause. "Not good, Pa. But Andie won't be long. If it's there, she'll get it."

"You and she—"

"It's really none of your business."

"I can smell it on you both."

"Please," Finn scoffed, his voice unusually hard. "It's just carnal."

Something cracked underfoot at the same time I felt a sharp pain in my chest, jolted into being by the coldness in Finn's voice. *Just carnal.*

He was lying. He had to be. He was just trying to get his father to leave us alone. Otherwise he wouldn't have tried to pull away earlier, surely?

He's lying, he's lying, he's lying.

"Andie?" he called through the trees. "Is that you?"

"I'm here."

Two faces appeared behind the branches. "Your lack of a scent really is quite alarming," Reed said. "I didn't register your presence at all."

"I'm light of foot," I said briskly, climbing towards them.

Finn's eyes widened at the sight of me. "Did you get it?"

"I got it."

Relief flooded from every pore of him as I stumbled into the glade and hurried to Cassel's side. The boy was devoid of colour, and his body seemed to tremble with stillness. He was hard as iron when I approached, raising the vial to his lips. "Drink, Cass," I told him. "You just need to swallow. Everything will be all right, now."

Finn clutched his hand. "Come on, Cass. You can do it."

I trickled the liquid into his mouth and rubbed his throat, encouraging him to swallow. His pulse was thready beneath my fingers, weaker than a newborn kitten. What if it was already too late? What if he was too far gone to be saved?

He swallowed, almost imperceptibly. Reed bent down and pulled out his injured arm, ripping apart the tourniquet and massaging the limb, encouraging blood flow. He stared at the black mark, the inky spider-veins.

Slowly, the blackness began to recede. Cass took a deep, shuddering breath, his eyes open. They glittered in a way they hadn't done before. He grinned up at Finn.

"You're still here."

Finn's eyes glittered too, in an entirely different way. "Of course I am."

The older wolf I suspected was Cassel's father came and sat beside him, helping him sit up. He shivered as his chest hit the cold air, and I pulled the blankets up around him. His fever had broken.

"Keep him warm," I told the rest of the pack. "I should get going."

Cassel touched my arm. "Thank you."

"My pleasure, Cass."

Finn stood up. "Let me walk you back."

I shook my head. "Vincent is still abroad, I should be perfectly safe. You should stay here for a bit. You won't get much of a chance when he returns. Stay with Cassel."

"I'd rather..." He looked around, as if only just noticing we had an audience. His gaze flickered past his father.

Just carnal.

"All right," he said. "If you're sure."

I stepped away from the glade, murmurs of thanks whispering past the lips of the others, as if they were ashamed of the words. I wondered what story they planned to concoct to explain Cassel's miraculous recovery to Vincent; probably that they stole into Agatha De Winter's house. I did not begrudge them the lie, but it was strange how uneasy they were with their thanks, how even Cassel's own father could barely speak it.

All the way home, I thought of Finn, of the ice in his words, how he stiffened around the others, how he couldn't tell his father what I meant to him.

And I *did* mean something, I was sure of it.

Yet the words plagued me all the same, itching at the back of my mind. There had been such a sharpness to them, an indifference.

What if I didn't mean as much as I thought I did, and I was trying to convince myself otherwise? What if all his resistance to my advances was some kind of long game, some way to increase my affection for him?

There is more than one type of wolf.

I was so fixated on that thought, on everything that had happened, that I barely dwelled on how long I'd been gone. Mama fretted when I reappeared, then hissed that I should have been home earlier to help with the bakery. She set me to work the minute I arrived.

I kneaded dough beside Daisy, who said nothing, and thought of Cassel, and Grandma, and Vincent, and Finn. My mind whirred with pain and frustration.

I should have asked him to explain before leaving, but I didn't want to be wrong. I didn't want to risk knowing the hurtful truth, or hearing a pretty lie.

And yet that night as I tossed in bed, I trod the space between waking and sleep. I found myself caught somewhere between nightmares—bitter flashes of fur and fang, hot breath, full snarls—and hopes and dreams as soft as gossamer, fleeting as a sparrow in the snow, impossible to pin. Through it all was the memory of Finn's mouth on mine, the brush of his lips, the shaking of his body as it pressed against me. He was all nerves and quiet, tender desperation.

You wanted me, I told myself. *Not me as a body, as a shell.*

You wanted me—in a way that no one has ever wanted me before.

And I would have given it.

Mine, Finn, mine forever.

There was not one definitive moment when Finn knew he wanted to leave the wolves. It was a thousand grains of sand in a tiny hourglass, doomed to one day overfill. Day by day, little by little, something was added to it, like the day Jean almost took off Pierre's paw during sparring and the pack laughed like it was nothing… apart from Pierre, who had to hide his screams as Reed clumsily patched him back together.

Or the time that Vincent took Cassel "hunting" in the local tavern, and Finn caught Cassel weeping in the forest the next day, trying not to let anyone overhear him.

Or the evenings he spent with the women forced upon him, convincing them not to tell Vincent, wanting them and hating them at the same time.

Or the countless nights he lay awake, staring up at the stars, wanting to talk to someone about nothing and everything, and being too afraid to speak even if he knew who he would speak to.

I want to get out, I want to leave, I want to be free pulsed inside him like a heartbeat. He was an insect inside a cage, and just had to work out how to slip through the bars.

One day, he and Cassel were sparring under Vincent's watchful eye. Finn had the upper hand, as usual, but was letting Cassel get in a few good swipes. Vincent's order shimmered under a snarl. *Harder, faster.*

Finn wound up on top of the boy, claws pressed to his throat.

Wound him, Vincent commanded.

Finn felt the press of his command at his temples, inside his paw.

Wound him, teach him, learn yourself.

Finn did not want to hurt his friend, just like he hadn't wanted to follow a hundred, a thousand other of Vincent's instructions. He hesitated now like he had before, even though the urge grew, and the rest of the pack gathered round.

Cassel yelped beneath him.

I don't have to do this. I don't have to hurt him. I don't have to do anything.

He pushed back against Vincent's command. To begin with, it was like trying to stitch two bits of fabric together while a dozen other people tore them apart. Impossible, ridiculous.

But he kept going, struggling against the pressure, reeling his claws back in.

He shifted back to human form.

"No," he said to Vincent.

Vincent shifted back too, his expression livid. "No?" he

echoed, as if he'd never heard the word before.

"I won't hurt him," Finn said. "I refuse."

"You... refuse?" Vincent's eyes flickered. "I am your alpha, boy. Do as I command you."

"No," Finn said again, more steadily than the first time. "You are not my alpha. I renounce you. I am yours no longer."

A harsh whisper ghosted through the glade, a murmur of amazement.

Vincent looked ready to murder him.

"Have it your way, then," he said. "Leave us. Never return. Wander alone in the forests, see how long you last. Know you can never come back to us again, that you will be alone from this day forward. Packless. Omega."

Despite the harshness of his words, a lightness stirred in Finn's chest. Had he really done it? Was he really free?

The lightness vanished when Vincent reached out and slashed him across the chest. Finn hit the floor, gasping for breath.

"Outsider," Vincent snarled. "Enemy of the pack. Run."

Finn ran, swift as ever, hurling through the ferns and bracken. He bolted over hillocks and woodland, through streams and sludge, until his breath felt heavy and loose in his chest.

He wondered if Vincent intended to run him to exhaustion, or kill him, but he'd given them the slip so far. He was so, so tired though, fatigue pulling at his limbs.

He drew into a ditch, covered himself with mud, and let the pack overtake him.

He was too weary and wolfish to count, but he slipped

back into human form once they were gone, and went to guzzle water in the lake.

A shadow cut over him. Cassel, as naked as he was, his face as twisted and furious as Vincent's, but brimming with something else completely different.

"You said you wouldn't leave," he seethed, trembling. "You swore it."

Finn turned to face him. "Then come with me."

"I…" Cassel's throat bobbed. "I can't."

"I can't stay."

"Please… please don't go. They're our family, Finn. *You're* my family. 'The blood of the brotherhood is thicker than the water of the womb.' That's what Vincent always says. But I don't really feel that with the rest of them. Only you. You can't leave. You *can't.*"

"You know, I'm really sick of people telling me what I can and can't do."

He turned his back to leave, but Cassel lunged at him shifting mid-air and sinking his teeth into Finn's arm. Finn howled, punching him in the throat and flinging him from his back before shifting too, meeting Cassel's fangs with teeth of his own. They rolled in the mud, slashing and clawing, panting and snarling. Even severed from the pack, Finn was still bigger than Cassel, still had some remnant of borrowed strength. He could have finished it at any time, but he waited until the other wolf burnt out, until he rolled away from him and slid back to human form. Only then did he shift back, get up, and move away.

"Feel better?" he asked over his shoulder.

Cassel said nothing, his back a tight slab between them.

Finn took a step away from him. “No matter where I go, or how far away we are,” he said, each word painful, “you will always be my brother. Nothing changes that. But if *you* change… please find me. Farewell, Cass.”

And although the younger boy did not reply, Finn was fairly sure he heard him crying.

14 MARK OF THE WOLF

I did not go into the woods the next day, or the day after that. I had gone from searching for excuses to venture out to finding excuses to stay in. I was too tired, it was too soon, Finn was probably still with the wolves, Vincent had no doubt returned, it wasn't safe.

Forrest seemed pleased I wasn't challenging him, which actually made me more tempted than ever to go out, but I couldn't find the energy.

Perhaps a few days apart was good for us, anyway. I had been seeing too much of him. I didn't want to grow dependent.

Yet, on the third night, I could hear a wolf howling in the woods, and knew that it was him, knew because inside I was making that sound, too.

I was being stupid and foolish and I knew it, but now I felt like too much time had passed and I didn't know what to say.

Anything, said a voice inside. *Say anything. Just talk to him.*

My mind wandered towards the cemetery walls. I knew Finn had come by at least twice in the past couple of days. I wandered over there one morning when I was almost sure he wouldn't have been there, and found tracks, human and wolf, on the other side of the fence, evidence of pacing, of someone sitting there for a long time.

It was dangerous for him to be in wolf form so near the village. He must have shifted to beat back the cold.

Probably not the dedication of someone whose affections were limited to 'just carnal.'

"Something is bothering you," said Daisy. She'd been attached to my side for almost three days now, but her voice sounded foreign to me. I realised how long it had been since we had really, truly spoken. "That mysterious boy you mentioned?"

I tensed, a little of the truth trembling out of me. "We, er, kissed," I told her, not willing to admit how far the kisses had gone, how far they *could* have gone. "We kissed, and it was wonderful, but..."

"But?"

"I overheard him telling someone else that it was just... That he wasn't interested in me like that."

Daisy frowned. "Who else was he talking to?" she asked. "How many strangers are there in the woods?"

"Daisy..."

"Sorry, I mean, that's awful, obviously, and his loss."

I sighed.

"You really liked him, huh?"

"Yes," I said under my breath, "I do."

"Did you speak to him? About what you heard? Give him a chance to explain?"

"That would have been the sensible and logical thing to do, and therefore I did not do it."

Daisy snorted. "I mean, it was still an awful thing to say, and I don't think you should ever say something to someone that you don't mean, but maybe there was a reason. I don't know." She sighed. "Boys are silly and I wish I did not like them."

It occurred to me that in all our years together, I'd never really heard Daisy speak of any boy outside of a book.

"Dais?"

"Yes?"

"Is there someone *you* like?"

Daisy tensed, her hands stiffening on the broom. "You have your secrets, Andie, and I have mine."

"But—"

She shook her hand. "Nope," she said. "Quiet as a church mouse, me. Maybe one day when you tell me about your boy, I'll tell you about mine."

I snorted at this, and we went back to discussing work.

I resolved to find a way of speaking with Finn later that day, and ran out of the bakery during my break to place a note half beneath a rock, asking him to wait for me after dinner. I left a roll wrapped up, too.

At lunch time, a cart bearing the post and other supplies from the city rolled into town. Another letter for me from Voulaire, another person knowing nothing of Finn's mother.

I really needed to tell him what I was doing, there.

Maybe that night.

I was helping Mama start dinner when we heard a commotion from outside. Mama turned to me, frowning. "Keep stirring the stew."

"But—"

"Ro, go upstairs please."

"But—"

"Now, darling!"

She seized a lamp off a hook by the back door and hovered over the threshold while Rowan trudged awkwardly upstairs. Mama let out a sharp gasp, and a second later, Russell, Forrest, and two other hunters burst into our kitchen, supporting between them a fifth man, his chest slashed to ribbons.

"Heavens!" shrieked my mother, clearing the table to lie him down. "What—"

"Help him," Russell barked. "Wolf sliced right through his chest—"

"My mother, maybe, but me—"

"Please, Clarisse, you're a deft hand with a needle, we weren't sure he'd survive the journey."

The injured man let out a low moan, and I realised with a start that it was Laurence, my old childhood nemesis. His face was so pale and contorted that I hadn't recognised him.

Any resentment I had for him suspended itself, to come back down at a later date. I leapt towards the table and took his head, thinking of Cassel, of Finn, or maybe of no-one at all. Perhaps just seeing Laurence as a person in pain, a person who needed help, temporarily absolved of all his crimes.

"It's all right, Laurence," I told him. "You're going to be fine."

My mother, meanwhile, had stopped quibbling over who was best qualified to assist. She grabbed the kitchen scissors and snipped open his shirt.

Blood was everywhere, his skin torn like a pie crust.

Mama didn't flinch. She looked at the injuries as calmly as if she were examining ingredients for dinner.

"Forrest," she said swiftly, "would you kindly retrieve Rowan from upstairs and take him to your aunt's for dinner? We may be here some time."

Forrest said nothing, but followed her instructions. The rest of the hunters hung around, forming something of a barrier around the table and Rowan was escorted safely outside.

"Fetch my sewing kit, Andie," Mama instructed, firing off instructions to the rest. Clean rags, hot water, blankets. Then she whipped out a small locked box from the pantry, one I'd seen before but never opened, and handed it to me with the key while she went to stem the bleeding.

It was full of herbs and potions, all of the labels written in her hand.

Not Grandma's. She'd brewed these herself.

"Do you know what to do?" she asked me.

"I… I think so."

"Quickly, then," she said.

I added feverfew and a handful of other herbs into a pot of water for the pain, and handed her a vial of wormroot for clotting. Tea brewing, I hastened back to her side. She'd barked the rest of the men away apart from Russell, who was holding Laurence's hands as she scrubbed away at the wounds. Laurence was making an awful, ragged, whimpering sound, and I found my forgiveness stemmed even further.

"Nothing important damaged," my mother deduced. "It's just messy."

"You can fix him?"

"If you can hold him still."

Wordlessly, I took several of the clean rags and started at the other end of the slashes from Mama, sponging away the blood. The bitter tang of witch hazel protruded through the air, along with coppery stench of blood.

Laurence cried throughout, tears sliding onto the table.

The feverfew took forever to brew, and even as I pressed it to his lips, I wasn't sure what good it would do. He still twitched when the stitching began, knuckles white in Russell's hands.

"You're doing fine, lad," Russell told him.

I wrung out a cloth and placed it on his forehead. "Not much longer now, Laurence," I whispered. "The tea will start working soon."

He lapsed into silence a few minutes later, my mother's needle still working through his flesh. I cleaned as she sewed, sponging blood from his body, the table beneath, the sopping rags.

I'd never seen so much in one place before.

What would a serious injury look like?

Mama sent me to mix more herbs, and finally Laurence sunk into sleep. She scrubbed her hands in the sink, face flecked with red, while I emptied bloodied water into the garden and set rags out to soak.

Forrest and the other hunters paced nervously on the back step.

"Is he—" Forrest started.

"He's fine," I assured him.

The hunters breathed a collective sigh, the rest setting off to deliver the news to his family. Forrest leant against the side of the barn.

"Thank you," he said. "I know he hasn't always been nice to you—"

"It was all Mama," I returned tartly. "And he was never anything but beastly to me, but I wouldn't let someone suffer like that."

"He's better now. He'd never—"

"I've never locked anyone in a cupboard before. Have you?"

"I—"

"Don't make excuses for him."

"I'm sorry," he said. "I didn't mean… I don't know what I meant."

"Ever a problem with men, I find."

At this, he managed a snort. "You're so much better than most of us, Andie."

"Daisy's nicer."

"I'm not interested in nice."

I swallowed at this, because I was painfully aware of what he *was* interested in, and while I'd never led him on in any way, never given a reason to suspect there was more than friendship between us, I hadn't let him know that nothing else was on offer, either.

"Forrest, I—"

He grabbed me in his arms, shaking as he lowered himself to my shoulder. I felt the same kind of powerlessness as I had looking at Laurence, the same desire to help. It could not have been easy for Forrest to watch his friend go through that.

Then I thought of Finn, watching Cassel, of me not speaking to him since.

I wondered if he was waiting for me. I'd lost track of the time.

Two of the hunters trundled back with a cart to take Laurence home to rest. Forrest dropped away abruptly, and no more words between us were uttered. He offered me a tired smile.

I hoped he could talk to his father about what had happened, that his frazzled nerves would have some company. Laurence was like a second son to Russell, he was certain to be just as frayed.

But men, I'd observed, sometimes wound up their twisted nerves and shoved them away, as if they'd fix themselves if ignored for long enough. I sometimes understood this, but not always. Not in times like this.

I thought Forrest's best remedy might be company, a kind smile and a sympathetic shoulder.

But not mine.

Quickly, I bustled across town and rapped on Daisy's door. Her mother answered it, giving me the awkward smile that most of the kind neighbours bestowed, and called for her daughter. Daisy appeared, wrapped in a shawl.

"Andie? Is everything all right?"

"One of the hunters was injured," I started.

Daisy's face drained of colour, her dark eyes saucer-wide.

"It's not Forrest!" I added hurriedly. "Laurence, who, frankly, probably almost deserved as good as he got... but he'll be fine, too. No. Forrest isn't hurt. But he did seem a bit shaken. I thought, maybe, someone should go and check on him?"

Daisy's face softened, but the clutch on her shawl didn't waver. She gave a sort of nervous nod, whispered something to her mother, and stepped out into the cold.

Halfway across the cobblestone square, she stopped.

"Andie?"

"Yes?"

"Are *you* all right?"

I shrugged, missing the words to explain everything inside me, but not wanting to lie. I was still fairly sure Laurence's blood was underneath my fingernails, and now that he wasn't bleeding out in my kitchen, I felt a bit strange about aiding my former bully. Emotions to be unpacked later, tomorrow. I still had to speak to my mother.

And Finn.

As Daisy hurried off in the direction of Forrest's house, I craned my neck in the direction of the cemetery. I felt him before I saw him, felt a tug in my chest, pulling me towards him. He stood on the other side of the bars, wrapped in furs, stamping his feet against the cold.

I rushed across the yard, almost skidding in the frozen

snow. "I'm sorry I'm late," I breathed, icy spurts misting the air between us. "There was an injury I had to attend to—"

"It's all right," said Finn stiffly.

"No, no, it's not all right," I panted, rubbing my hands together. "I'm sorry. I'm sorry I've been avoiding you."

"Did I do something wrong? Was it... was it the kissing, and the... the other stuff? We can take a step back, I don't want you to feel pressured, I'm not even sure I—"

"It wasn't that," I told him. I took a deep breath. "I heard you speaking to your father. I heard you say it was just... just carnal between us."

"Oh," said Finn, after a pause. His eyes widened. "*Oh.* Oh Andie, I'm so sorry. I didn't mean that, I swear I didn't. The wolves, they're just so repressed when it comes to emotions. I couldn't have them know. I couldn't have my weakness exposed."

"Weakness?"

"You're my weakness," he said, and tried to move his fingers through the bars. He got within a few inches and then stopped, wincing as though in pain. I looked down and saw the disturbed snow, and remembered the ring of ash planted beneath.

I moved forward, closing the gap as far as I could, and his fingers found my cheek. "My weakness," he whispered again. "And my strength."

I grabbed his hand and kissed his fingers. "I'm sorry I avoided you. I knew—I *hoped*—that was the reason, but I couldn't ask. I was afraid."

"Of me?"

"Of my feelings, mostly," I admitted. I frowned, remembering something else. "Your father said he could smell 'it' on you. What did he mean?"

"It's complicated," he said.

"I wasn't planning on going anywhere."

Finn sighed. He tugged his hand away and sat down in the snow, back to the bars as if he couldn't quite bear to face me. "The reason I was so hesitant the other night, the thing I didn't quite get the chance to tell you, is that when a female mates with a wolf, it creates a sort of bond between them. Well, a one-sided bond."

I slid down next to him. "Go on."

"I told you before that only alphas have this natural magnetism to them. That's usually true, but after a woman mates with a wolf… she'll feel a strange loyalty to him. Attracted to only him. Something to do with ensuring she only bears his children, or other nonsense."

I swallow, suddenly understanding his hesitance. "How long does it last?"

"I've heard reports of it wearing off after a long time without contact, but for some, it's forever. One night and you're committed to someone against your will to the end of your days. It's awful and unfair and I hate it." He breathed rapidly, like he'd just wrestled out of a fight.

I took a moment to process this. "Have you… have you ever…"

He shook his head. "No," he said, almost bitterly. "I couldn't bring myself to do that to another person. But… I've come close. A lot. The other day with you in the hut… you've no idea how close I came."

"Thank you."

"For what?"

"For explaining. For not going through with it—"

"That's messed up, Andie. I shouldn't get praise for stopping myself. That's the bare minimum of what someone should do."

I couldn't think of much to say to that. I supposed I had low expectations of what I expected. "Finn?"

"Yes?"

"What do I smell like?"

This, at least, brought on a ghost of a smile. His cheek twitched. "Like vanilla and firelight and apple spice and damp earth and rainwater. Like the first frost and the crisp snow. Like warm dust and sunlight through fog. Like heat and fire and flesh and sweat. Like everything I've ever loved and desired and ever want to and will."

The intensity of his words kicked something into life, deep in the pit of my stomach. "Do you think I smell like that to all the wolves?"

"I think everyone smells what they want most. I *hope* you don't smell like that to all the others."

I reached through the bars and turned his face towards mine, gently tugging us as close together as I could, and kissed him through the bars. He let out a soft groan.

"You *taste* amazing too," he said. "Like baked goods and promises of joy."

I smiled. "One of those things makes sense."

"No, both of them do, I assure you."

He kissed me again, hands sliding through the bars to reach for me. I wished we could melt away the barrier between us. "You still haven't explained about your father's words," I reminded him, drawing back before his touch made me too giddy. "What could he smell on you?"

Finn's eyes widened. "Oh," he said, "I missed that part, didn't I?"

"You did."

"For... for some wolves, they also experience the bond. It's very uncommon and while the bond is respected in some ways, some of the wolves—and certainly Vincent—look down on it as it means the wolves are less likely to want to spread their wild oats elsewhere." He paused for a moment, not meeting my gaze. "I didn't think it was a thing that could be smelled," he said hesitantly. "And certainly not before, er, consummation."

I stared at him, unsure how to unpack my words, unsure if I had words at all.

Bond. He was bonded to me.

Perhaps I should have wanted to resist the pull. Perhaps I should have wanted more choice. But I *did* have a choice. We both did.

And I chose him.

"I have to tell you something, too."

"What?"

He looked up hopefully, which crushed my heart a little; what I had to tell him was not so sweet. A confession, one he needed to hear.

"When... when you told me your last name, I used it to

try and find out more about you. About your mother."

"Why would you—"

"Because the more I knew you, the more I liked you, and the more impossible it seemed that anyone would ever have given you up." I told him. "That if she did so willingly, she must have thought she was doing the right thing. That she must have regretted it every day. I wanted you to know that… that she loved you. Because she must have. Anything else seems ludicrous to me."

Finn was silent on the other side of the fence.

"I know it was a breach of privacy, I understand if you're mad—"

"I wouldn't have let you, if you'd asked. But I'm not mad." He went quiet again. "Have you heard anything?"

I shook my head. "Nothing yet, but, but… I wanted you to know. I didn't want to keep anything else from you."

"Thank you," he breathed, then frowned. "Anything else? You have other secrets?"

"Not from you," I whispered. "I think you know almost everything."

"Almost?"

"I… I'm not great with talking about my feelings. Never have been. It doesn't mean I don't feel them. And I do. Feel. A great deal. For you, that is."

"I'm not great either," Finn replied softly. "I was raised by literal wolves. They actively avoided talking about anything. For seven years, I was told that there were certain things I shouldn't feel for anyone, and I think I feel all of them for you."

I sucked in a breath, not sure of what to say to that, a nervous warmth hopping about my chest like the first sparrow of spring. Finn shivered against the bars, the little skin I could feel iron and ice.

"It's late, and cold," I said. "You should shift and go back to the cave. Or the hut. It'll be warmer there."

"If it's all the same to you, I'd like to sit here just a little while longer, saying very little, and holding your hand through these bars."

I smiled, leaning further against them, our heads resting together, uncomfortable though they were. "I suppose I can spare you a few more minutes."

15 THE NEXT WOLF MOON

"You were gone a while, dear," Mama said, when I finally stepped back inside, my lips raw and numb from kissing Finn so much through the fence.

"Needed the fresh air," I told her. *Needed Finn.* I flopped down onto the sofa, my gaze drifting unconsciously to the table, scrubbed clean. The smell of herbs still hung in the air. "Why didn't you tell me? That you were a herbalist too?"

Mama busied herself rubbing the rags in the sink, avoiding my eyes. "The village doesn't like women like us, darling. They don't like anything too new... or too old."

"Then why stay here? Why not go somewhere else?"

"Because there's more than one type of wolf in the woods."

She's afraid. I realised. *She's afraid outside is no better. She's afraid of failing. She's afraid of always being different.*

I don't think I ever understood my mother as well as I did in that moment, or even myself. Because I was afraid of all those things too.

But I was afraid of not going more. Of never finding out.

"I think I'd like to go and study in Loussant," I said abruptly.

Mama bristled, but she did not look as I thought she would. Trepidation, perhaps, but no fear, no disappointment.

"Alone?"

No, not alone. With Finn. Everything, always, with Finn. "If needs be. I... I don't know where we'd get the money from but maybe I could work while I studied. I want to be a herbalist, Mama. A real one. A healer."

She smiled. Not the sort of smile she usually wore when she looked at me—weary or amused or fond—but something more like proud.

"You showed an aptitude for it today. I didn't even think you liked Laurence."

"I don't," I said, too shocked at her softness to be annoyed by the assumption about Laurence, "but that didn't matter in the moment."

She stopped scrubbing then, and wiped her hands on her apron. She came forward and took my face. "You would be excellent, my dear daughter," she said.

"I thought... I thought you wouldn't want me to go."

"If you have the courage, you should go wherever that takes you. We'll find the money somewhere. It might take a while, but we'll manage. After..."

"After the hunters have caught my father, right?"

"Yes. After that merry occasion."

That seemed as much as a dismissal as any. I was exhausted, too tired to even think about the meal we'd abandoned. I turned to leave.

"Mama?" I asked, halfway up the stairs.

"Yes?"

"Did you ever love him? Vincent?"

"I love that he gave me you, and Rowan."

"That's not an answer."

She sighed. "I loved who he pretended to be," she told me wearily. "Take a bowl of stew with you to bed, I won't have you go hungry. Good night, darling."

∞∞∞

Although I knew it to be dangerous, I chanced a trip into the woods at first light the next day, hopeful that if the wolves had been out the night before, they would be sleeping it off this morning. Finn was delighted to see me, although he admonished my recklessness. He walked me back to a glade not far from the village gates so I could run back if any wolves approached us.

"How's Cassel?" I asked.

"Fine, fully recovered, thanks to you. I was able to see him the other day. He asked how you were. I think he's rather taken with you."

"Can you blame him?" I asked, twirling a lock of hair around my finger.

"No," said Finn shyly, "I cannot."

He kissed me throughly, back against a tree, and we kept kissing for a rather long time.

"How is your patient?" he asked during a moment of reprieve. "I forgot to ask."

"Laurence? Probably still an ass."

He frowned at this, and I explained our history. I explained what I hadn't been able to explain to Mama or Daisy, about how I didn't care but then I did, how strange and awkward it felt... and yet how it made me realise what I wanted to be.

"You... want to go to Loussant?"

"Yes," I said. "But..."

I want you to go with me.

"But?"

"I mean... not right away. We need to sort out this business with my father first. And there's the money issue. But yes, eventually."

Finn stroked a lock of hair behind my ear. "This village always was too small for you."

I kissed his lips, glad to have avoided asking whilst at the same time thoroughly annoyed with myself for not managing it and slightly annoyed he hadn't offered.

Ask me to run away with you, I begged.

But he did not, and eventually I had to slip back into Thornwood lest I worry my mother too much.

"Meet me again in the churchyard tonight," Finn whispered.

"You've already seen me today."

"Once is not enough."

I smiled at this, and promised that I would.

For days, we heard nothing from Vincent. We knew he was biding his time, waiting for his next chance. Finn reported that the wolves were posted along all the roads, preventing us from leaving if we were foolish enough to try it, but there were no attacks. They did not incense the hunters again.

It was not a relief. It was standing on the edge of a crumbling cliff.

"I heard from Cass that my father is trying to convince him to give up on your brother," said Finn one evening, trying to raise my spirits.

"I'm sure that's going splendidly for him."

Finn grinned weakly. "Well, the last time he raised it, I heard he didn't get slashed, so perhaps that's progress."

He kissed my freezing fingers, and for a moment, I tried to believe that Reed had the power to stand up to him, to sway him, to make him leave us alone.

But I could not imagine it. Peace with men like that was a passing thing.

This pattern of fear peppered with joy continued for several days, the rest of my hours seeming to span years before nightfall came, and I could slip away to Finn's side, to talk and kiss and hold his hand until I went numb with cold.

"This isn't natural," I told him one night.

He cocked his head. "What isn't?"

"There being something between us. Only seeing you at night. Sneaking away like there's something wrong with us being… us."

Finn thumbed my fingers through the bars. "The word 'us' is delicious when you say it."

"Could you stop flirting for one moment and be serious?"

"Of course," he said, stiffening. "What do you need?"

"I need you to promise me that this won't be forever."

He smiled, sliding his hand to my cheek. "Not forever, Andie. This won't be forever. Nothing's forever but..."

I waited for him to finish, but his words had gone numb. Perhaps he did not wish to speak a lie.

We kissed instead, and said goodnight.

Back in my kitchen, I was greeted by the sight of Laurence having his bandages changed by my mother.

"Ah, Andie, good timing," Mama chimed. "Why don't you try removing Laurence's stitches? It's good practise. I just need to see if I can find some fresh ragwort. There's a bit of swelling here which I'd like to treat."

I wasn't precisely keen to be left alone with Laurence now that he was decidedly conscious, but I gave a grunt of agreement and she scurried off outside. I picked up the scissors and tweezers and started to snip, my patient tense underneath me.

Minutes ticked painfully by.

"I'm sorry I teased you about being a witch," Laurence rushed, as if the words could choke him and he needed to spit them out as soon as possible.

"Oh my, if I'd known all I needed to do to get people to treat me decently was heal them, I would have poisoned the entire village years ago and produced a miracle cure."

Laurence blinked at me.

"I'm joking."

"Your humour isn't exactly... funny."

"Neither is locking people in a cupboard."

He looked down at his feet. "I'm sorry I did that."

"Are you?"

"Yes. Yes, of course I am."

"Then why did you do it?"

"I don't know. Everyone else was laughing. It seemed funny at the time."

I groaned, pulling out one of his stitches a little too roughly. Pack mentality wasn't just unique to actual wolves, it appeared. "Why do you do what everyone else is doing?" I asked him.

"Most people do that. Only you and your family do your own thing."

"You should try it some time."

"Should I? Because you don't look happy most of the time, you know."

I resisted the urge to jab him with the scissors. "I'm only miserable because of other people," I insisted. "If everyone could just accept that not everyone is the same, that we're allowed to be different, the world would be a happier place for everyone."

"Do you really think so?"

"Heavens, Laurence, do you even think *at all*?"

He rubbed the back of his neck. "Not much, actually, no."

I sighed. Thankfully, Mama came back in after that, and I was finally dismissed.

The next time I had a full day off, I announced my intention of going to Grandma's, thoroughly intending to spend most of it with Finn. It was, unfortunately, the night of the full moon, so I knew we wouldn't be able to see each other after dark. I'd make my way to her estate and spend the night, quietly terrified but at least not worrying about what could befall her in my absence.

Forrest, of course, insisted on walking me, and I didn't complain. I was courting enough danger as it was. Daisy came too, unusually quiet, and I wondered if she was worried about me sneaking off to see this boy of mine. I'd remained silent on the matter of his identity, and she'd stopped trying to probe.

"Are you all right, Daisy?" Forrest asked. "You seem a bit out of sorts."

Daisy blinked, as if she was surprised to be spoken to at all. That seemed odd to me; the two of them had always been good friends.

"Thank you for asking," she replied sweetly, "I am quite fine."

Forrest did not look entirely satisfied, and I wondered if he planned to interrogate her on the way back, and what he might ask.

I hoped she wouldn't tell him about my mysterious gentleman.

Finn, a gentleman!

"What are you grinning about?" Forrest asked, turning his attention back to me.

"Why, this fine day, of course!"

Forrest snorted. It was bright but bitter, the sunlight

sheathed behind a veil of cloud, turning the snow almost gold. We did not have many days like this in midwinter.

“Winter solstice, soon,” Forrest remarked. “It’ll start getting warmer and lighter after that. Can’t wait.”

I think he hoped that the wolves might move on when the seasons shifted, or that they’d be easier to hunt. I stopped suddenly in my tracks, smile evaporating, hating more than ever that he still didn’t know.

The wolves are men.

My father killed your mother.

I want you to kill him.

I don’t want you hurt.

“Andie?” Forrest stilled. “What’s wrong?”

“Nothing,” I insisted, because I had no idea how to tell him that, or even if it was right to. Would Forrest hate me for something my father had done? Would he hate Finn?

And the truth would surely hurt.

“Why do people keep secrets?” I asked my grandma once as a girl. “Our teacher says that lies almost always come out in the end.”

“Your teacher’s a fool,” she twittered. “Lies don’t always come out in the end, only the ones we hear about. And there’s a difference between secrets and lies. Secret is not telling something, lies are deception, telling a falsehood.”

“Surely *both* are deceptions?”

“Depends what they are.”

“I don’t think it’s good to lie.”

“Some secrets are there to keep us safe, dear.”

I understood that now, although I’d always hated it.

Everyone was always trying to keep me safe by shielding me from things. I rather felt like the things that could hurt me shouldn't have existed in the first place.

And yet now I was doing the same thing to Forrest.

He sighed loudly. "Now you're *both* being odd."

"I'm almost always odd," I said pointedly.

"Aye, but I usually get a bit more sense out of Daisy."

She did not smile at this, and walked on ahead.

They left me at the gate and trudged back along the frozen path. I walked up the winding drive towards the back door, mindful of traps. Fresh snow had indeed concealed them, but I was confident if I kept to where the gravel should be, I'd be fine. Grandma wouldn't want to wound her only granddaughter, and any regular visitors would know the way to the door.

She was happy to see me until I announced my intention of seeing Finn and coming back to spend the night with her.

"It's a full moon," she said.

"Which means nothing during the *day.*"

"I don't want you in the woods after nightfall."

"You're here!"

"I'm tough, I told you."

"You're not *an entire pack of wolves, tough,* Grandma! No one is."

Grandma muttered something stubborn under her breath and went to start cooking. For all that she said she didn't approve of Finn, she packed me a sizable portion of thick, creamy porridge 'for the road', packed with dates and berries.

I raced to Finn's cave, dropping the basket to the floor and throwing myself into his arms with such force that he toppled over. He laughed with a breathless kind of giddiness and laced my fingers into his, pinning him to the floor, cutting him off with a kiss that slid silently, slowly, into another.

It had been too long since I had held him properly, too long since I'd been this close to him. I coiled myself tightly against his body, wondering if it was possible to sink into a person, wondering how I could feel so utterly inseparate from him whilst feeling a strange kind of agony at the fraction of space between us. A hot pain sunk under my skin, into my bones, and I slid my hands under his shirt at the thought and kissed his neck.

Finn groaned, and a hotness stirred inside me. He gently tugged at the ties of my cloak and then swore, pulling his fingers back.

"What?"

"If I take off your cloak, all the other wolves will smell you too. We can't risk it."

"We can keep the cloak on. I'm sure I can get my clothes off around it..."

"Clothes... off..." Finn's eyes went wide, but he shook his head rapidly. "No, no, no, we can't."

I traced my fingers down his chest. "Because it would be forever, you mean? Because there'd be no going back?"

He swallowed. "Yes."

"Maybe I don't want to go back. Maybe all I want to do with the rest of my life is move forward with you beside me."

Finn lay his hand over mine and squeezed it, and then he

grabbed my face and plunged us into a kiss so deep it melted winter. I was swimming in the lake at high summer, the river molten gold and liquid light. Something burned beneath my skin as his fingers pooled into my clothes, his lips bruising mine. I wondered if maybe I was a wolf too, I was so desperate to break free.

I inched back, staring at him, half deliriously. I examined every inch of his face. It could not have been more perfect if he carved it himself.

"What is it?" he asked.

"Nothing, I'm just thinking of how glad I am you got stuck in that trap."

He laughed again, louder and softer than before. How would I ever grow tired of that sound? "I assure you," he said, brushing the tips of my fingers, "I am much more glad of it than you are."

We kissed until our bodies burned, brought to the brink of something neither of us fully understood. We touched too, hard and soft and everything between.

We broke at some point for a decidedly late breakfast, and talked.

And then kissed some more, our lips chapped and raw. The air turned thick with our breath.

Finn grew quieter as the day wore on, conscious, no doubt, of the darkening skies. He carved a little in the back of the cave. I re-organised his herbs. Mid-afternoon he gave up carving and just lay his head in my lap. I ran my hands through his soft curls and read to him.

Eventually, it was time for me to leave.

We linked our fingers together and set off through the woods.

"You're nervous," Finn remarked.

"It's not fair that you can hear my heartbeat."

"I was looking at your face."

I stopped shortly, staring up the drive towards the chateau. The turrets stood stark against the grey sky, like gravestones. "I'm worried that the pack will find you like they did the last time and hurt you again."

"Maybe," he shrugged. "Although I seem to be on friendly terms with most of them after the incident with Cass. I'm sure it'll be fine."

I was not so sure, certain only that he was coddling me, that even Cassel would find it hard to resist the pull of the alpha if it came to it.

Finn tilted my chin towards his. "I'll stay as safe as I can," he promised me. "And it won't be anything you can't fix."

"I'll come and find you tomorrow."

"I can't wait."

He lowered his lips towards mine, drawing me into him, his body tense and trembling. I couldn't let go. I wouldn't. I pulled him to his knees, palms digging into his hair, pushing him back against the snow and kissing him so fiercely my chest hurt.

His face contorted, almost as if in pain, but he did not stop, rolling me over through the snow.

Something cracked beneath us. He stopped. "We haven't accidentally rolled onto the lake, have we?"

"It's about a mile away, so no."

"Ah, good, just checking."

"It's just a stick," I said, gripping the back of his hair. "Please resume kissing me."

"Happily," he said, as his lips slid to my neck.

Something shuddered beneath us, and we both paused again. "What—" said Finn, shifting upright.

The ground opened beneath us, and we shot downwards in shower of snow, dirt and bracken.

16 DREAMS OF WOLVES AND WONDERS

For a long moment, I lay at the bottom of the pit, staring up at the sky, wondering how a fall of a few feet could make the growing moon look so much further away. The air was wrenched clear from my lungs.

"Andie," Finn groaned, moving beside me. "Are you hurt?"

I wiggled my toes and fingers, and pulled myself into a sitting position. I rolled my neck. The powdery snow and bracken had cushioned the fall, even though it was a good ten feet.

"I'm all right," I told him. "You?"

"I think so."

I crawled to my feet. The incline was natural, too imperfect and too deep to have been fashioned by human hands, but the branches we'd fallen through were woven.

It had not occurred to me when the hunters said that they were setting traps that they would have laid any like this. Why didn't Forrest say anything?

Perhaps he didn't know. Perhaps one of the others had spied the hole and thought they were being really clever. It was the type of thing that Laurence would probably do, forgetting about travellers and the snowfall making everything invisible.

I examined the drop for any handholds, any roots to grab onto. Nothing.

"Here," said Finn, appearing by my side. "Let me try and boost you up."

I didn't waste time arguing about how I'd get him out afterwards; the full moon was likely only a few minutes away. We'd dallied too long. I stood on his outstretched hands and tried to clasp the top of the hole, to no avail. My hands sank into the snow. Nothing to hold onto.

I tumbled back down, Finn panting.

We both searched for another way out, examining every side, every broken branch for an idea. We tried to slam the branches into the earth to use as footfalls, but the earth was frozen solid. Finn splintered one trying to force it in, slicing his palm.

"Finn!"

"I'm fine," he hissed, tearing off a piece of his shirt to try and bind it. "I'm..."

The air grew darker, and he slumped against the side of the pit. A sickly sheen spread across his skin. His face was a ghostly shade of white.

"Finn!"

"It's all right..." he murmured.

I caught him before he could fall, sinking to the ground

beside him. Even with all the layers between us, I could feel the heat radiating from his body. I wrenched off a glove and pressed my hand to his forehead. "You're burning up."

"I'll be fine."

"The moon's only just out—how long have you been feeling this way?"

"A while."

"You should have told me to go!"

He managed a weak smile, his jaw tight. "Didn't want you to go."

"You're an idiot."

"But you like me anyway, right?"

I kept my hands on his face. "You know I like you."

He tried to smile, but there was a flash of something else, and he hit the floor, convulsing. He curled inwards like a dying spider, a twisted cacophony of painful limbs.

My voice lodged in my throat.

"It's... not as bad... as it... looks..." he rasped.

"Liar."

"Talk," he said, "please."

My throat throbbed, hard and raw. "I don't know what to say." *Be all right, please be all right, shift, don't shift, be safe, don't hurt me.*

"Scream, then," he suggested. "Someone might hear."

"If the hunters find you, they'll kill you."

"But not you."

He let out a long, low moan, one that scraped against my heart. I called out his name again and pulled him into my lap. He tried to shirk away from me, as if he could hurt me in this state, but he had no strength. I gripped onto him fiercely.

"Tell me what to do," I begged. "Tell me how to help you."

A low, harsh word. "Can't."

"Finn, *please.*"

"You're... pretty... when you... cry."

I swallowed, my throat sore and tight. "I'm pretty always."

"No... arguments... there."

If I called out and the hunters heard me, they might hurt him. If I called out and the wolves came, they'd hurt me. Which was more likely? I already knew who I wasn't willing to risk.

"It's just... pain..." he seethed. "It can't kill me. I just... I just need a bit longer..."

I thought I might crack before he did. I couldn't watch this. I couldn't.

Pain is worse than death, we'd agreed once. And it was, only I didn't know it until now. I'd die to spare him this.

But I also knew if he hurt me, he'd be killing himself, and...

And I didn't want to die.

"Gods..." Finn's breath crackled. "This is rather unpleasant..." He curled inwards again, harder, his body pulsing with pain.

How long could he hold on for? Not until morning. At some point, he was going to lose it. We were just delaying the inevitable. Prolonging his suffering. *Our* suffering.

Claws would hurt less than this.

"Finn," I whispered, "you need to shift."

He shook his head, biting his lips. “No.”

“I can’t get out… you can’t stay this way all night.”

“Can try. Won’t hurt you.”

“*This* hurts me,” I insisted. “This hurts me a lot.”

I peeled his shirt off over his head, already plastered to his body with sweat, and pressed a hand against his chest. “Shift.”

“No.” His teeth were gritted, his flesh taut underneath me.

“You can’t stay like this!”

“I could hurt you.”

“You won’t,” I said, gripping his face, “I promise, you won’t. You don’t want to hurt me. You’ve never hurt me before. You won’t now.” I drew my dagger out of the basket which had mercifully rolled in with us. “And if you try, I’ll stop you.”

Finn stared at the dagger, kept his eyes steadily on me as I helped remove his other clothes. “Promise?”

“I promise.”

He shook his head. “I’m not sure—”

Before he could finish, I closed the fragile gap between us and pressed my lips against his. Finn trembled faintly beneath me, his body still spasming, but he somehow found the strength to raise a hand to cup the back of my neck, murmuring something incomprehensible into me.

And then, as I was sure it would, all strength to resist crumbled out of him entirely, and he shifted away into fur, letting out a long, mournful howl.

He cowered against the wall, ears flat, not snarling, not

quite. I clutched my dagger but didn't raise it.

Don't make me hurt you, don't make me hurt you.

Because despite my words, I wasn't sure I could. I certainly wouldn't be able to bring myself to do any more than wound him. I'd die too.

I wondered what happened to wolves when they were killed in wolf form. Did they shift back at the final moment, like Finn had a tendency to do in sleep?

What if death came so suddenly that they couldn't?

I could hear someone moving in the forest above. A hunter? It sounded human. If they discovered us in the pit, they were certain to shoot fast, ask questions later.

What if I never saw his beautiful face again?

"Finn," I whispered, holding out my hand, "Finn, you need to be quiet."

He turned towards the wall, growling low and harsh, shrinking away from me. His claws tore at the earth like he was trying to escape.

He was still trying to protect me, to control the wolf within.

A light appeared above, followed by a startled gasp.

"Andie! What on earth... is that a wolf?"

I stared up at the light, and found Daisy's face. "Yes, it's a wolf," I told her.

Daisy put down her lamp and grappled with something in her other hand. I realised almost too late that it was a crossbow.

"Wait—" I said, leaping between her and her target. "You can't!"

"It's a *wolf,* Andesine! Are you mad?"

"No, I'm not," I said, the secret falling out of me, "And he's not."

"Not mad?"

"Not… not a wolf," I explained. "Or, he is, but, he's a man, too. Most of the time."

"He's…" Daisy's eyes widened. "No," she said. "No, no, *no…*"

"This is Finn," I gestured to him, still not willing to step away. Daisy's crossbow was still fixed in his direction. In *our* direction. "The boy I—"

"A *wolf?*" she shrieked. "You've been stepping out with a *wolf?*"

"He's lovely," I whispered. "I promise you. He's kind and sweet and… look, could you please chastise me some other time? Go fetch some rope from my grandmother's shed—stick to the path, she's placed traps over her lawn."

Daisy groaned. "That's because your grandmother's a sensible woman." She glared down at me, sounding as furious as I had ever heard her. "Try not to get eaten by your wolf-sweetheart until I get back."

She marched off into the dark, leaving me alone with Finn once more. He stalked the edges of the pit, keeping as far away from me as possible, his snarls growing louder and more vicious.

Still holding back, still struggling.

"Finn," I whispered desperately, "it's all right, you won't hurt me."

He did not seem to hear. This was different from the wolf

I'd known before, the tender pup. This was wild and frantic and as un-Finn-like a thing as I had known. Daisy couldn't return fast enough.

But as she looped the rope around a nearby tree and levered me out, I found myself not wanting to leave. I couldn't possibly bring him with me. He had to stay.

If the rest of the pack found him… if the hunters did…

Daisy hung at my elbow incredulously. "Come on! What are you waiting for?"

There was too much to explain, and it would be foolish to do so here. "Coming," I said, but stopped her from unlooping the rope. "Leave it for him."

Daisy groaned and trudged up the road, a bobble of light in the gloom. I followed her, fighting her waves of silent fury.

"What are you doing here, Daisy?"

"Following you! I knew, I *knew* there was something else going on. I knew you weren't spending the night at your grandma's. So I told my parents I was staying at yours and came to check on you. Your grandma is all locked up for the night and you were nowhere to be found. Then I heard the howling…" She shook her head. "A *wolf,* Andie?"

"He's not always a wolf, like I said. When he's just Finn he's… he's charming and kind and funny—"

"Forrest is charming and kind and funny," she spat. "Why choose a wolf over him?"

"What does it matter to—" I stopped, noticing a tightness in Daisy's face, a stiffness in her, a reason for her anger, one that should have been clear to me a long, long time ago. "Oh, oh Daisy, I had no idea—"

"Of course you don't! You're too busy wrapped up in your own little Andie-world to notice anything about anyone!"

We stopped abruptly, halfway up the drive, the air between us stinging like a slap. Daisy's hard gaze dropped to the floor, and she turned on her heels and raced up the drive.

I followed after her, swinging into the kitchen. It was still early, but grandma was nowhere to be seen. Not that it mattered if I woke her. She knew everything.

"I'm sorry," Daisy wept, crouching beside the remnants of the fire. "That was unfair. You couldn't have known."

"It wasn't unfair," I told her, adding a log to the grate, "and I should have known."

Daisy dabbed her eyes on her handkerchief, sniffling and saying nothing as the embers pulled at the log, and dark light spilled into the room.

"Why didn't you tell me?"

"What would have been the point? It wouldn't have changed anything."

"I would have turned Forrest down sooner. Maybe by now he'd have realised you're worth ten of me."

"No one is worth ten of anyone," she said, although she managed a weak smile. "You can't weigh up people like that, especially not in relationships. You either fit together or you don't."

"I don't fit with Forrest," I told her. "I never have. Not like that. I've never understood what he saw in me. I think maybe I'm just comfortable for him, he's known me so long. But I'm not right for him. You'd make a much better fit."

"Try telling him that."

I laughed, hollow though it was. "You encouraged me to be nice to him."

"When you love someone, you want them to be happy. It doesn't matter how much pain it causes you."

I thought of Finn, howling outside, and how much pain I'd bear for his sake. "I know that," I said softly.

"This Finn then," she returned, "he's your match?"

I nodded slowly, and then I told her everything. *Everything.* Even the details I'd skipped with Grandma. I told her about how we met and the nakedness and the teasing. I told her about my father, and Rowan, and what Vincent had done to Forrest's mother.

"And he doesn't know?"

I shook my head. "I want to tell him. It's not right that he doesn't know. But I don't want him to hurt Finn by mistake, and... and he's smarter than his father. He might work out that Mama lied about Rowan."

"Forrest would never hurt your brother."

"No, but he might tell his father, and who knows what he might do."

I think Daisy wanted to object to that too, to object that anyone who was part Forrest could do anything like that at all, but she didn't. She knew how narrow-minded our little village could be.

In the distance, the wolves howled again, and I jerked involuntarily towards the window, in the direction of Finn.

"You're worried about him."

"If he's hurt—"

Daisy grabbed my hand. "There is nothing you can do for

him right now," she said gently. "Come, let's fix us something to eat."

I was in no mood for food, but the act of cooking gave me something to do, at least. I had always disliked this time of year when the days were enveloped in darkness, with only a few hours of faint sunlight a reprieve from the pressing night, but now I had a new reason to hate it; it was so many hours until sunrise. So much time to pass. So much time for something to go wrong.

"How long have you loved Forrest?" I asked Daisy, desperate for something—anything—to fill the silence.

Daisy smiled. "I cannot give you a precise moment. It was a collection of them, over the years. A hundred thousand tiny things. He'd compliment my flowers, carry my books for me, regale me with tales of the woods, talk to me when he saw I was alone, make me feel like there were no others even when I knew that wasn't true. He has a way of laughing that shimmers against my soul. It makes me realise that we have them, because he makes me feel mine. One day I just looked at him coming towards me and knew I'd race to stop an arrow if it was flying in his direction... a bit like you did today for your Finn."

I swallowed. "I didn't even know you knew how to use a crossbow."

She looked down at it, stacked against the brickwork. "I asked Forrest to teach me about a year ago. Any excuse for a little time with him."

I thought about the early days, trying to find a reason to speak to Finn, whereas now we just fell into one another.

I wondered if Daisy would ever have that, because I could think of few who deserved it more.

"Are you happy in the village?" I asked her.

"What?"

"The village. Are you happy there? You've actually lived outside it. What's it like?"

"I like it," she said. "It's quiet, peaceful. I know people have been poor to you, on occasion, but they've been kind to us. Our neighbours are our family. Yes, I like it." She looked up. "It's not for you, though, is it?"

I shook my head. "It's too small."

At this, she smiled. "I'll miss you, when you go."

"*If* I go."

"No, it's when. It's always been when. I'm just glad you see it, too."

'When' seemed a long time from now, and if something happened to Finn, I wasn't sure I'd have the strength to go alone, but I made myself a silent promise that I would, that I would leave regardless, and see the world he'd shown me through his stories. The village was my cradle; it would not be my coffin.

"Tell me of your plans," Daisy insisted. "And I shall tell you mine."

We whiled away the hours doing just that. I told Daisy of my dreams of studying in Loussant, of the tiny apartment I'd share with Finn, of working as a healer, of finding new and better ways to help people. I dreamed of somewhere I couldn't quite picture where we might one day raise a family, although I couldn't fully imagine that part so far ahead.

Daisy could. She wanted a spring wedding. She'd planned out the entire menu and what her dress would look like. She spoke of this old house on the outskirts of the village where Widow Marie had lived until her death last year, and had stood abandoned since. It had plenty of room for the family she wanted to raise there. She'd even picked out names for the first boy and girl; Hunter and Emerald, "in homage to her Aunt Andesine."

I knew then, that wherever I went, something of the village would always be a little like home. I could never say goodbye to Daisy even if I could scoop up Mama and Ro and take them everywhere with me.

They couldn't stay in the village forever, not after Ro started to change.

I wondered how Finn's mother had coped. Perhaps I would ask her that, if I ever found her. After my stern words, of course.

Eventually, we retired to the spare room. Grandma had made up a fire for us already, and I wondered once more at her absence and whether I should check on her. I decided against it, certain she would hate the fuss.

Daisy and I stripped down to our petticoats and slid under the blankets, talking ourselves into exhaustion. Daisy dozed off long before I did, the dark and silence stiffening in the room her consciousness had quit. The howling grew louder, and I could no longer pinpoint Finn's from the others. Were they close by? The wind whipped them everywhere, grating against the bones of the house, the stones screaming with them.

Be safe, be safe, be safe.

I was sure that I would never sleep, that I could never be tired enough for the sickness inside me to abate, that my fears and dread would pin me to this plane till daybreak, but the hours rolled, and the darkness slowly tugged me into bitter, broken sleep.

After leaving the pack, he left the forest, stole clothes from a line outside a farm and a pair of boots from a back step, and walked for a few more miles before collapsing for the night in a haystack. The next morning, he shed his clothes, shifted, killed a pheasant, redressed and continued onwards. He wished he'd learnt how to shift with his clothes intact, like some of the older wolves could, but he'd never been taught. Vincent had always said "the time would come." Only now did he realise that had been another way of controlling him, keeping him weaker.

Finn wasn't particularly hungry, which he knew was probably a bad sign, so he left most of the pheasant on the back step of some other farm, reasoning that someone else might want it, that he should give a little more back to someone to repay the universe for taking the clothes.

He continued onwards, sore and stiff. He hadn't bothered to do anything with his wounds, he was so used to them healing.

Before the second day was out, he spied the forests of

Thornwood. They'd passed through it so many times it almost felt like home. And home was what he wanted. A place to rest even if he couldn't belong.

He stumbled into the woods, aware his feet were dragging. He and Cass had found some caves here before. It was growing cold, frost nipping at the air. Even wolves weren't completely immune to the cold.

Cassel. He hoped he was all right, that he'd grow to forgive him. That maybe he'd find the strength to leave one day himself. They'd make a poor pack by themselves, but a decent family.

He dragged himself into one of the caves and collapsed on the floor, too tired and too weak at first to realise how hot he was. He put the pounding in his head down to lack of water, too much exercise.

It wasn't until he woke the next morning, clammy and cold and barely able to open his eyes that he realised something was seriously wrong. He could barely move. Worse still, his wounds weren't closing like they used to. The one Cassel had given him on his shoulder was better, but the slashes across his chest where Vincent had lunged for him still rung with pain, the edges turning black and ragged. It was almost certainly an infection, and he didn't know anything about medicinal herbs that might have helped him even if he had the strength to move.

He wasn't even sure that it was a wound that could be healed through normal means. It was inflicted by his alpha, and Finn wondered if it was cursed, if Vincent's words were true. He could never leave them, not for long.

He huddled in the back of the cave and waited it out. There was nothing more he could do.

For three days he stayed there, shifting when he could to keep warm, fizzling out of it when he was too weak to do otherwise. He dreamed of the first change, and of his Mama, her face as shapeless as ever.

He dreamt he remembered her voice.

Finn, Finn, hold on, my darling.

In the worst of it, he wondered if he shouldn't just let himself die. No one would miss him. He was adding nothing to the world. What was really the point of being alive?

And then he heard a voice, high and clear, like a sharp spring morning at the end of winter. It was a girl, singing down by the lake, a song about deserted lovers and death and poison. Despite the topic, it was a sweet voice, and he found himself stung by it, pried out of the dark.

One more note, he prayed. *One more line, one more song...*

He thought it would be nice not to die alone, and wished he could call out to her, but suddenly he didn't feel like he was dying anymore. A feeble strength trickled back into him, and he rose to see if he could catch a glimpse of her.

She was gone by the time he stumbled out, but shortly afterwards, his fever broke, and he knew he was going to live.

The next day, he stole a knife from the village, hunted a deer, and made his first pelt. He hacked down branches and built himself a fire. He cooked the remains of the deer, and the next day traded the rest for supplies. He kept an eye out for that girl, and an ear too, but he did not see her.

He knew that it was the same girl from before, the girl

with the red cape, and longed for her name, knowing even then that her name would never be enough. Her name, then her words, then her touch...

Sometimes, from the back of his cave, he could hear her singing down by the lake, her high, clear voice penetrating even his wolf form. One day he managed to find her before she faded back into the forests like a creature of mist.

She was every bit as beautiful as he remembered.

He told himself he was struck with her for empty reasons; that it was simply the colour against the grey of the rock, the crispness of her song, or the closest thing to company he'd had in months.

But the truth was that there was something else, even then, something in the soft slope of her smile that rumbled deep within, something in her quiet, dreamy gaze that seemed to whisper to him.

The living ghost of the woods.

He thought about leaving, of course, finding work as a carpenter, the only thing he was good at. But he didn't want to go to the city. He belonged in the woods. The loneliness suited him, because it meant he didn't have to pretend.

Yet sometimes, he knew that when he howled, he howled for her.

17
THE KILLER WOLF

It had taken me so long to fall asleep that the morning had lost its bluish quality by the time my eyes opened. Daisy was still asleep beside me, her dark hair unbound and splayed across the pillow like a halo. She looked like a princess from a fairy tale.

Forrest was a fool if he never grew to love her back.

I scrambled out of bed as carefully as I could, pulling on my clothes and trying not to wake her. The cold bit at my naked skin; the shutters had long since fallen off and there was little to hold back the cold but the flimsy curtains.

I peered through them, hoping to see something, but a mist had swallowed up most of the woods.

Be all right, I begged. *Please, please, be all right.*

I didn't want to think of the alternative. I didn't want to think at all. I laced my boots poorly, flung on my cape, and disappeared into the gardens.

Finn was not in the pit when I arrived. Neither were his clothes.

"Finn." My breath rasped against the cold. "Finn!"

"You look worried, and I'm trying not to enjoy that too much," said a voice, layered with warmth and humour. I wheeled around.

Finn stood behind me, hair tousled, clothes crumpled, but unhurt.

I flew into his arms. "You're all right," I breathed into his neck. "You're all right."

"I'm fine," he assured me, hands curling into my back.

I cupped his face, thumbing his cheeks. "I was terrified."

"I'm sorry."

"Not *of* you, *for* you. You know that, right? You know that I—"

But what words I had yet to utter were lost once more under the press of his lips. We cut apart the air with our kisses, raw and tender.

"I woke up a little while ago," he told me when we parted. "Freezing. Decided to risk your grandmother's ire and kipped beside the fire. You ran straight past me."

I blushed a little, embarrassed by my haste, my single-mindedness. Finn kissed the scarlet spots, his lips trailing to my neck.

There was a cough from behind us.

Grandma stood on the snowy drive, hands on her hips, hair in disarray. "Well, well, young wolf," she said, smiling daggers. "Why don't you come in for breakfast?"

Finn was silent as Grandma stoked the fires, silent as she

added oats to the cauldron, silent as she stirred. He managed a 'thank you, madam,' when a steaming bowl was placed in front of him, and a 'good morning,' when Daisy arrived.

"Are you nervous, boy?" Grandma barked.

"Um, yes madam. I've never met anyone's family before. I'm incredibly nervous."

"Good," she said stiffly.

"Grandma!"

"I meant good that he's honest."

"No, you didn't."

"No, I didn't," she said, holding up another ladle. "More?"

After eating so little last night, I was famished. Even Finn, nervous as he was, managed two bowlfuls, all the while steering around my grandma's questions.

"You grew up in Voulaire, I hear?"

"Yes."

"Happy there?"

"Largely, yes."

"Opinion on Vincent?"

"Not a fan."

"He's your alpha?"

"He was."

Grandma narrowed her eyes. "How'd you break free?"

Finn looked down. "I'm not entirely sure," he said. "I just knew I couldn't stay with them."

"*Why* did you break free?"

I paused now, too, waiting for his answer. It was something, despite all our conversation, he'd never spoken about. I'd been curious, of course, but I hadn't wanted to pry. He'd kept that part locked up.

"There wasn't one great defining moment," he said quietly. "It was a dozen, a hundred things adding up. A hundred things I never wanted to do."

Like chase terrified girls in the woods.

I waited for Grandma to probe him more, but she didn't. I was glad; I didn't want to think of the things that Vincent had forced the pack to do, didn't want to bear witness to that pain and humiliation again.

I squeezed his hand under the table.

"What was your mother like?" Grandma asked instead.

"Grandma!"

"What? You can tell a lot about a man by how he speaks about his mother."

"It's, um..." I started.

"It's all right," Finn answered. "Her name was Celine Whitethorn. She had hair the colour of wheat. It shone golden in the sun. She was, I think, always very sad, but she usually hid it behind a smile. She used to chase me around the kitchen and we'd play knights together with wooden spoons and pots for swords and shields. She sang lonely songs as she kneaded the dough. She rarely laughed, but I still remember the sound."

I stared at him. He had never spoken about her so much before.

"And I swear to you, I have no intention of making Andie as unhappy as she was."

Grandma's gaze was unwavering. "She's dead?" she asked.

"She might as well be," Finn replied, eyeing the bottom of

his bowl.

Grandma handed him a biscuit, and went to tidy something up. I kissed his cheek while her back was turned, but he remained a little numb under me.

Suddenly, his ears perked up.

"Ah," said Grandma, staring out of the window, "your escort is here, ladies."

The sound of footsteps over snow and pebbles sounded out over the ground, accompanied by Forrest's sharp whistle. I grabbed Finn's hand and yanked him into the hall.

"What—" he started.

I pressed him against the wall, which groaned under the pressure. Snowflakes fell from the hole in the roof, dancing around us in a flurry of white. I kissed him as deeply as I dared, his fingers against my face, my back, my hair. When we parted, he brushed snow from my skin.

"Someone ought to fix that roof," he said.

I half laughed. "That's all you have to say?"

He bit his lip, his eyes shifting uncomfortably.

"What is it?"

"That man coming up the drive... I remember you mentioning someone before. Is he your sweetheart?"

I carded my fingers through his hair, shaking my head and sighing. "Don't you know already? *You're* my sweetheart. That is... if you want to be?"

He kissed my fingers. "Till I'm dust, and even after."

We drew in for another kiss, but a sharp rap on the door cut us off.

"Tonight," I uttered. "At the cemetery."

His lips dusted my forehead, my hand still clutched in his. "It feels like twenty years away."

I broke from his side, scuttling back into the kitchen before I became too irreparably entangled in him. Forrest stood in the kitchen, barely looking my way as I entered. His eyes were rooted on Daisy, but he did not look pleased.

"What are you doing here?"

Daisy innocently sipped her tea. "Good morning to you, too, Forrest."

"Did you walk here by yourself?"

"I have two excellent legs."

Forrest's temple twitched. "It's dangerous."

"I brought my crossbow. I'm as well armed as you."

Forrest opened his mouth, and promptly shut it again. He muttered something about it being bad enough that he had to worry about me.

"Tea, Forrest?" Grandma held out a cup.

"I thank you, no. We ought to be off. I'm needed back at the village, and I daresay Clarisse has need of her staff."

"Indeed," Grandma returned, taking back the cup. "Well, take care, children. Keep an eye out for wolves and miscreants."

"Wolves are nocturnal," Forrest pointed out, as if he hadn't just walked here to collect us and chastised Daisy for coming alone.

"That's the rumour, isn't it?" said Grandma with a smile. "I'll see you later, dears."

She handed me my basket, patted us both, and sent us on our merry way. I was sure I could feel Finn's eyes on me and we walked down the drive, but I could not see him. It felt like the gaze of a ghost.

∞∞∞

Mama put us both to work, and for the first time in a long while, we chatted and sang while we kneaded the dough, swept the floors, counted out the coppers, oiled the scales, dusted the shelves and glazed the buns. We delighted in childhood clapping games and practised moves for the winter dance in a few day's time whenever the shop was cleared of customers.

"Forrest was certainly concerned over your safety," I said at one point.

She shrugged, as if it meant nothing. "Forrest worries. He's a worrier. It's one of the things I like about him."

I'd never liked Forrest's protectiveness, but if it suited Daisy, I was not going to judge.

"Finn's handsome," she added.

"But not as handsome as Forrest, right?"

We both started to giggle.

Mama appeared at the door to the rest of the house. "Are you girls giggling?"

"No, Mama."

She narrowed her eyes. "I know those giggles. Are those *boy* giggles?"

At this, we laughed louder.

"Andie, you haven't some sweetheart you've neglected to tell me about, have you?"

"Books are safer than boys," I said. It wasn't a lie, but it wasn't precisely the truth, either.

"Good girl. That being said, I wouldn't object to you settling down with the right fellow..."

I groaned, and returned to sweeping the floors, brushing out the constant trail of leaves the customers kept bringing in.

It was almost closing time when the cart arrived, carrying the post from the town. I'd stopped waiting for news from Voulaire at this point, so it was a surprise when one of the village children came in with a letter for me. I opened it without thinking, expecting nothing.

And promptly gripped the counter.

Dear Miss De Winter,

Firstly, please accept my apologies for the delay in responding to your enquiry. I am relatively new to the position and currently sorting through a backlog of paperwork. I have looked through our records and can confirm that we did indeed have a woman by the name of Whitethorn living within our district some eight years ago, and that she had a son that would now be around eighteen.

Unfortunately, Celine Whitethorn died eight years ago, and her son went missing at the same time. It is thought that the woman, who had a history of melancholia, took her own life and that her son ran off in fright.

I am sorry to be the bearer of such sad news, and do hope she wasn't a relative or friend of yours.

If I can be of any further assistance, please do not hesitate to contact me.

Yours sincerely,

P. T. Vandimere

She was dead. Finn's mother was dead, and had been for eight years. Had been since he disappeared.

The parish manager said she'd killed herself. Killed herself the night Finn went. Out of shame for letting him go? Or because… or because she never wanted to give him up in the first place?

"Andie?" Daisy hovered beside me. "What is it?"

"I need to go to Finn. Can you cover for me?"

"Of course," she said, the anxiousness in her face unwavering, "but—"

I stuffed the letter in my apron pocket, grabbed my cloak, and hurtled off into the forest. This couldn't wait until tonight, when I wouldn't be able to hold him. This couldn't wait one moment more. Finn was not to go another minute thinking his mother hadn't wanted him.

I hurtled over snow and woodland, stopping only once my chest hurt too much to move. I steadied myself against a tree, gathering my breath. I would need it for what was to follow.

How would I find the words to tell him what had happened? Maybe I could just give him the letter. Maybe the right words didn't matter, maybe it would just be enough that I had come...

Tears leaked from my eyes, remembering how Finn had spoken about her, just this morning. How he'd loved her in one breath, and said she might as well be dead in the next.

And she *was* dead. She'd been dead all this time.

Finn, oh Finn...

Something moved behind me, like a tangible shadow, silent and slick. I wheeled around, and Vincent stepped out from behind a tree.

"Well, well, if it isn't my dear daughter."

I swallowed, balling my fingers into fists. "Vincent."

His gold eyes flickered, and I realised my address angered him. He wanted me to call him father. Not for any love of me, I was sure, but for the power it held, for the notion that I, female though I was, belonged to him in the same way my brother did.

"So, my beta informs me you and the little omega have formed something of an attachment..."

I sucked back my trembling, remembering a lesson Forrest had given me once in how to handle a dagger, the right stance to take to hold my ground. Inwardly, I cursed myself; in my haste, I'd forgotten my basket.

"If you want to call it that."

"Ha! Where do you get that quick tongue from, girl? Not your mother, certainly. And I wasn't around enough to teach you. Agatha, maybe. Always liked the old bat."

"I assure you, the feeling is not mutual."

Vincent squared up to me, and for a second, I thought I

might have felt that *pull* that my mother spoke of, only it was more like a snare. “Come with us,” he said, his voice like rough velvet.

“What?”

“I need an heir, but maybe I don’t need a son. Maybe a grandson will suffice. Why don’t you come with us? Bring the omega, if you like, I’d prefer you pick someone a little stronger, but I’m willing to make sacrifices. Take him as your mate. You need not be separated from your babes, if that’s what you’re afraid of, and I’m sure you have other uses. You’ve proven quite resourceful.”

Every word that left his mouth sickened me. “I’m not a broodmare!”

“No shame in wanting to breed, sweetling. What’s awful about motherhood? Isn’t that what all women dream of?”

“Not *this* woman,” I said tersely. “Not just that.”

“What *do* you dream of, then?”

“Of my own path.” I steeled myself, sharpening the words inside me, summoning the courage for the question I had to ask. “What do you do if the women refuse to hand over their sons?”

“They rarely do. Well, some might resist at first, but hardly ever after the first change. They don’t know what to do with them then.”

“And Finn’s mother?”

“What about her?”

“She refused you, didn’t she? She died eight years ago. Round about the time he joined you.”

Vincent’s face tightened, and I knew even before he spoke

what his answer was going to be. "I didn't mean to kill her," he explained, as if this was excuse enough. "I just needed to make her see sense. To understand she couldn't keep a wolf in the city. That the boy belonged with us."

My stomach dropped, curdling with horror and pity and sheer disbelief at his indifference. "He belonged with *her*."

"That's what she said, right before she tried to stab me."

"So you killed her."

"Self-defense."

"And Finn?"

"As the child of my beta, he was already part of my pack. I compelled him, fiddled with his memories of that night. Convinced him that she'd kicked him out."

A strange, dark dizziness gripped me, his words like insects, alive and biting in the air around us. "You're a monster."

"That's what she said," Vincent sneered, "before I snapped her neck."

Something ripped through the air. An awful, penetrating sound, between a human scream and an animal howl.

I snapped towards the noise; Finn stood on the embankment, his fangs bared, his fingers extended into claws. He lunged at Vincent, shifting mid-air, sinking his teeth into his neck.

Vincent half-laughed, half yelped as the fangs sunk into his flesh. He shifted in a second, kicking Finn from his body into the crumbling snow.

I screamed. I didn't know what else to do.

They circled each other, snarling, testing the air. But

something else shimmered behind Vincent's hot breath. Like laughter, cruel and fine, like he enjoyed Finn's anger. Like he craved it.

Finn went for him again, but Vincent's claws sliced across his chest. He was twice the size of Finn, had twice the strength. He could kill him, if he wanted, and at the moment, Finn didn't care. The only person who cared about whether or not he lived was me.

"Stop!" I begged, whatever good it would do.

A bang went off, a bullet cracking against Vincent's shoulder. He let out a low yelp, and both wolves shot off into the trees, a trail of fur and blood.

Forrest stood on the path ahead, a smoking pistol in his hand. He stared ahead, not meeting my gaze.

"Did you... did you see the size of that *thing?*" he gaped. "I've never... it was almost as large as a..."

It took me a moment to recover my words. "What were you *thinking*?"

Forrest blinked. "That there were two dangerous wolves in front of you?"

"You could have shot—" *Finn. You could have shot Finn.*

"You were out of range, I never would have—"

"Don't ever do that again!"

I marched off in the direction Finn had fled.

"It's not safe—" Forrest called.

"I am not yours to protect!" I barked back, with more venom than I meant. I didn't care. Finn was hurt. He was hurt, and bleeding, and he'd just heard...

Oh gods, what he'd just heard.

Forrest did not run after me. Perhaps he thought I was shaken and needed time to cool off, or perhaps I'd finally hurt him so much that he didn't care.

I cared if he was hurt, but not enough to turn back.

I picked up Finn's boots and the remnants of the clothes he'd been wearing when he shifted. They were mostly intact. I wonder if Forrest had seen them or if they were too far up the embankment for him to notice. Vincent's clothes had shifted with him, of course.

Finn had bolted towards the lakes, but his trail in the snow led not to the cave, but down to the hut. It was a closer place to hide.

I found him there beside the empty hearth, naked, his eyes red-rimmed. I put down his clothes and fetched a blanket from the cot. He did not get up when I entered, didn't move a single muscle, didn't say or do anything until my arms were around him, and he shook violently between sobs.

"He killed her," he wept. "He killed my mother."

My throat went tight. "Yes."

"She didn't send me away."

"No."

"She loved me."

I took his face in my hands, thumbing away tears. "Of course she did. Of course she did, Finn. How could she not?"

His fingers coiled into bitter fists, and he looked away from me. "I'll kill him. I'll kill him, I swear."

"I'll help you."

"No. No, you can't. I won't let you become like me."

"But what if I'm already like you? What if I'm already dark

and twisted and you're just the only person I've ever shown that to? You're not the only one with a good reason to want him dead. Maybe you're the one helping *me.*"

"You want to help people. You aren't a killer—"

"I want to help people that deserve it—"

"You helped your childhood bully!"

"Because he didn't deserve to *die.* Vincent does. He killed your mother. And Forrest's. And who knows who else? And he will keep killing unless someone stops him. Let's stop him."

Somehow, I was going to find a way to do it. I didn't know how yet, but I was going to do it. He didn't get to hurt anyone else. No more dead mothers, stolen boys, or childhoods lost. I would take the dagger he had given me and plunge it into his heart.

Finn buried his face against my shoulder, swallowing noisily. "I spent all this time hating her—"

"But not anymore," I said, threading my fingers through his. "And if there's a world after this one, she understands."

He sobbed more at that, and I let him, holding him tightly against my chest. He was bleeding through my shirt, but I didn't think he could feel it. It didn't matter to me.

When his sobs subsided, I propped him up against the side of the hut, started a fire, and went to fetch snow to clean his wounds. They weren't deep, three long slashes down his perfect torso, but I bandaged them nonetheless, my fingers running over the smooth contours of his sculpted chest.

Finn caught my hand as it skimmed over his heart, and held it there. I could feel it thumping wildly beneath my touch, my flesh trembling with the sound of it.

Mine, mine, mine.

I looked up, and found his face inches from mine, and suddenly our mouths crushed together and we were kissing with wild, desperate, frantic energy, as if we could blot out pain with touch.

I slid my arms around his neck as his own went to my waist, lying me back against the floor. His palms gathered at the stays of my dress and hovered there, unwilling to go further. His heat burned through my clothes.

"Do it," I urged. "Unlace me."

There was plenty of time to stop, but neither of us did. I wriggled out of my dress, Finn tugging off my boots, his deft fingers sliding to the tops of my thick, woolen stockings. He paused, staring at me with huge, blue eyes. I wondered how anything could be so perfect, how anyone could be so still and radiant, and yet tremble with hopeful, nervous energy.

I nodded, my throat closed, and he peeled those off as well, flinging them behind him.

He took one ankle in his hand and kissed my calf, his lips travelling up my leg towards my thighs, kissing, teasing, caressing, resting his head in my lap with only my undergarments between us. I wasn't sure how to remove my petticoats without taking off my cloak, but everything below the waist was shucked off in an instant, a flurry of mutual haste. Cotton and lace scattered the wooden floor like piles of dense white snow.

Finn stared at me again. "Are you sure? Are you absolutely sure? It'll be forever, after this."

"Oh, Finn," I breathed, fingers tracing his face, "it's already forever."

With that, he moaned, and I claimed his mouth with mine, running my tongue over the pointed tips of his fangs and kissing him until my lips felt numb, over and over and over, his hands and fingers everywhere at once. When I finally released him, his mouth moved to other, softer places, places I didn't truly know existed. My mind went white with a hot, liquid shock, and after that I surrendered utterly and entirely to sensation.

"Finn," I whispered hoarsely, "Finn, I want you."

"Have me, then," he said, his smile breathing against my thighs, "for I am always and irrevocably yours."

I tugged his face back towards mine and raked my hands down his back, sliding my legs around him, making him groan and murmur.

"You seem to know what you're doing," he panted.

"It's easy, with you," I told him. "Everything's easy with you."

"Do you have a tonic prepared?"

I shot him a coy smile. "I have the ingredients ready."

"Good," he said, and with his next actions, I lost all words and thought entirely.

When he woke up that first day in her hut after she rescued him from the trap, in her arms, he was certain at first that he was dreaming. That was the sort of thing that happened after a year of talking to almost no one. You fixated on people, you made up ridiculous fantasies. You took a girl you'd never spoken to before and imagined her as everything you wanted.

And yet, when they spoke for the first time, the spell she'd cast on him didn't waver. Indeed, it increased in her absence, settled in her presence, and he found himself longing for her in ways he didn't know one could long.

She ghosted his dreams at night, and when they were together, he could barely take his eyes off her. It was just as well she always wore her cloak in his presence; her smell was intoxicating, suffocating, debilitating. A scent that almost made him feel sick.

There was something in the weight of her breath as it mingled in the cold ice air that stirred against his soul, as well as other, baser parts of him. He wanted to twin that breath with his, to claim it with his own, to unravel the layers dividing them and press the frayed edges of his core with hers, until the tattered parts of whatever he was had threaded to her irreparably.

It was like a bone coming back together. Pain in the joining, in not quite being one, but an inevitable merging, a release as bone knitted into one, a disbelief that they had ever been separate to begin with. He was conscious of a thousand different things whenever they were together; the softness of her sigh, the way she bit her tongue when she was thinking, the smooth, dark spill of her hair over her shoulder, the weight of her breath, the slow, steady heave of her chest.

He was conscious of her absence, too, of the way time flickered when she was away from him, of the weight of the air where she'd stood a moment before. How could you be haunted by someone living? He felt like she'd poisoned him, that he was dying some slow death without the antidote of her presence, and yet it was worse when she was around, and near, a pain cleaved into his centre. He wanted her more than he had ever wanted anything and he wasn't sure what to do about that, where to put his feelings where they couldn't hurt either of them.

Because he didn't want to turn her into his mother, wouldn't ever let her know the hurt that she had, and yet… maybe he could try at being human, for her. Maybe he could try living in a town again.

If not for her, then who? For what?

Finn watched her lying in his arms, nothing in the world

as warm and real as she, and suddenly everything was so perfectly and utterly clear.

18
DANCING WITH WOLVES

Afterwards, I lay in the crook of Finn's arm beneath a pile of furs and blankets, stroking the curves of his face as if hoping to memorise it through touch. "Do you feel different?" I asked him.

"Yes and no," he said, fingers tracing softly along my spine. "I expected to feel altered towards you in some way, but nothing has changed there. I love you just as much now as I did before. Perhaps I've already reached my limit, there. No mating bond could extend it."

A smile radiated through me, like a polished piece of burning gold. *I* felt a little different, like the threads between us had grown more tangible, like his heart had placed a ghost over mine. He was even more beautiful than before.

"I love you," I told him. "I'm not sure I said it, before. Or said it so plainly. But I love you, Finn Whitethorn."

He smiled, pressing his mouth against my temple. "How about Winterthorn?"

"What?"

"Finn Winterthorn. Do you like the sound of it?"

"I do, but—"

He took a bit of spare thread from the hem of my cloak, and tugged it free with his teeth. He wound it around my finger and kissed my palm. "I love you," he whispered. "Marry me?"

I blinked at him, certain I'd misheard. "But... how?"

"I believe one asks a priest..."

"I mean, where will we live? Where will we *go?*"

"Loussant," he explained. "Where you'll study, and I'll apprentice myself to a carpenter."

"How will we pay—"

"We'll figure it out. I haven't worked out the finer details yet."

"You haven't worked out *any* details yet..."

"I've worked out the most important ones," he insisted, "which are that I love you and don't ever want to be apart from you."

I swallowed at this, looking away, because we *had* to part, at least for a while. I had to go back to the village and he couldn't follow, and I couldn't stay there cowering under a cloak forever.

And even if we had the money, I couldn't go to Loussant until my brother was safe.

"Andie?"

"I will marry you," I told him, "when my father is dead."

Finn blinked at me, his eyes two gleaming chinks of deepest sapphire. "That is the most unromantic acceptance of any proposal ever. I'm half tempted to reject your acceptance."

I rolled on top of him. "Stop it," I said.

"You are naked and on top of me, I will do whatever you ask of me."

"Not *quite* naked," I said, gesturing to the cloak and the few undergarments we hadn't managed to remove.

Finn placed his hands on my hips, a wicked grin sliding across his face. "Naked enough..."

I laughed, and drew my hand to the top of my head to remove a single strand of long, brown hair. I wound it around his finger, too. "Marry me, Finn. Be mine forever in a way other people can see, other than the way you already are."

"Well, when you put it like that..."

He grabbed my waist and jerked me down to the floor, kissing me expertly, like he knew every crevice of my mouth.

"Would you like to know *why* I love you?" I asked him. I was certain, despite his bravado, that he did not quite have the ego to match. He had not had a life of much affection, not for a long while.

"I would, actually," he said, and then his smile melted away. He paused, sniffing the air.

"What is it?"

Finn scrambled into a sitting position, raking at the furs until it reached a spot on the floor where we'd been lying, before. Seeped into the floor were a few drops of blood, the size of large coins.

"Your blood," he rushed.

"What about it? It's perfectly normal—"

"You bled on the floor."

"Good grief, you're not bothered by a bit of blood, are you?

You bled on my shirt, you know."

"I can smell you." He rubbed at the stain, as if hoping to dislodge it, but it remained etched to the floor. "Get dressed," he hissed.

"But—"

"Andie, please!"

His voice frantic, I grappled at my discarded garments, tugging them on as quickly as I could. Finn shucked on his own, torn though they were, and seized my hand.

"You need to get back to the village."

I need to stay with you.

Of course, I didn't say that. I knew what he meant, what might happen if he didn't. I let him drag me through the forest, certain the trees had eyes.

Finn barely breathed until we were within sight of the village gates, and spun me round to face him.

"Don't come out again," he said, "please. Let me come to you. We'll find a way, Andie. We'll find a way to be together."

"Finn," I whispered, a tremble in my voice, "I don't understand, what's changed?"

"They'll know what you are to me, now. You were valuable enough before as Rowan's sister, but… if they know I'm your mate, if they threaten you… they'll use me to get to your brother. They'll find a way."

"You would never hurt Rowan. You would never hurt anyone."

Finn's jaw clenched, and tears sprung at his eyes. "There are no limits when it comes to you. Not anymore."

He kissed me, deep, but rushed and hurried, and tried to

move away.

I grabbed his hand. "Finn," I breathed. "I don't regret it. I still don't regret it."

Finn came back, kissing my forehead and lingering there. He played with the ties of my cape. "The next time I have you, when you have *me,* I don't want there to be anything between us at all."

"I love you," I whispered against his chest, still testing the shape of the words.

"I love you," he ushered back. "Stay safe."

"You stay safe."

"I'll do my best."

He kissed me again, sweet and swift, and bounded off into the forest.

For the first time in a long while, I felt alone. And for the first time in forever, I hated it.

∞∞∞

When Finn did not meet me at our allotted time that evening, I knew, in a way I hadn't before, that he was all right, but I hated his absence nonetheless. I hoped that my mother had never experienced this with my father, or that it had broken over the years and distance. It was uncomfortable to the point of sickening. I was almost feverish. When I slept that night, I linked my fingers together, tracing the band of thread, wondering, half knowing, if he was doing the same to his.

In some cultures, the exchange of vows and tokens would

make us already married, never mind that there was another name to call us.

I didn't see him the next day, either.

I knew something important kept him from me, I knew that he was all right, but I also knew that he had just found out about the death of his mother, and whilst physically he was unhurt, there were other pains.

I was surprised I couldn't feel them too.

There are no limits when it comes to you.

What if the other wolves caught him and used *him* to get to *me?* Would I really exchange my brother's life for his? If there was a path where Finn died, and on the other both he and my brother got to live...

I didn't want to think of that, didn't want to think of Rowan growing up like Finn. It would hardly be saving him.

On the third day, I found a note tucked under a stone on the other side of the gate.

Safe. Trying to keep them away from you. Don't come looking. I love you.

I tucked it into my pocket, treasuring the words. It occurred to me that for all I'd seen his carvings, I'd never seen his handwriting before. It was a bit childish, well-formed but underused, and I wondered how much, if any, schooling he'd had after being taken from his mother.

Taken from her.

I wanted to say that I couldn't believe that my father had done such a thing, but I believed well enough. The shock still rippled through me, the callousness of the way he'd said, *'right before I snapped her neck'.*

I imagined the sound. I imagined Finn sleeping in the next room, unaware.

I imagined being her, looking into the eyes of the man who was going to kill you, and who was going to put your son through hell.

Finn had told me only snippets of his time with the wolves, focusing more on where he was than who he was with or what they were doing, but it hadn't been pleasant. Vincent had almost broken him.

I wondered if this last revelation had.

One afternoon, the hunters rolled into town carrying the body of a white stag on a cart. I didn't see the antlers at first, only the flash of white hide, mistaking it in the moment for something else entirely.

A wave of dizziness washed over me, a faintness gripping my limbs. My mouth tasted like bile.

"Red?" Forrest frowned, appearing at my side, "Are you all —"

He didn't finish his sentence, because my knees gave way. I trickled towards the ground, but Daisy's arm reached me before Forrest's, and steered me safely into the bakery.

"Are you ill?" Forrest fretted. "Let me fetch your mother —"

"No," I whispered, "please don't."

"She's been working so hard making bread for the solstice tomorrow," Daisy said quickly. "She quite forgot to eat! A little rest and food and she'll be right as rain."

"If you're sure—"

"Don't worry, Forrest," she assured him. "I've got it from here."

As soon as he left, it all came crashing out, everything that had happened in the last few days, all my fears and hopes. Daisy tugged me into her arms, devoid of words for once.

I wanted Finn. I wanted him safe and happy and here beside me. I didn't want to hide, I didn't want to tremble every time the hunters rolled back in with a fresh carcass, worried one day it would be his.

And there was nothing, nothing I could do.

I wished I was a wolf. I wished I had fangs and claws and could take on the pack myself, take on my father. I would kill him and save us all.

But I was no wolf, no hero, and as trapped in this town as Finn was outside it.

I could save no one. Not Rowan, not Finn, and certainly not myself.

The best thing about the winter solstice celebration was that it afforded some distraction, a dozen tasks for me to set my mind to. I made myself as useful as possible, shovelling snow, setting up stalls, stringing lanterns and arranging tables. We'd done most of the baking yesterday, but I aided other villagers in roasting venison and spicing cider.

"You're unusually helpful today," Mama commented, "is

something the matter?"

I shrugged in lieu of lying, not being able to find the words.

"Come with me," she said.

She tugged me back inside and into her room, flinging open a chest at the foot of her bed. Once, my father shared that space with her. She'd borne me in it, and Ro.

Mama rooted around in the chest and pulled out something heavy, wrapped in brown paper. It was a dress, white as snow, with crocheted sleeves so delicate it almost looked beaded. It was the finest thing I'd ever seen grace the walls of our worn, shabby home.

"I've not had time to make you something else for tonight," Mama explained, "and your other good gown is getting a bit worn."

For a moment, tracing the fine cotton pleats, everything dissipated. "It's beautiful, Mama."

"Let's put it on, then."

She helped me into it, lacing me in. It fit as snugly as a tailored glove, perfect and pristine. And yet, when I beheld my appearance in the looking glass, I felt a twinge of dread. For a second, dressing, I had felt like a bride, but the pale-faced girl in the mirror looked more like a ghost.

I felt like I was dressing for a funeral.

"Beautiful," said Mama, draping the cape around my shoulders again, and adding a necklace of red beads as an embellishment. "If you did want a husband, you'd have no problem finding one."

It was a silly sentiment, albeit one born out of love. There was far more to making a match than looks, and yet... "What if I've already found one?"

Mama frowned, no doubt remembering our last conversation, about Loussant and studying. "Andie—"

A cheer went up from outside, and a band struck up. Music filled the air, cutting off whatever my mother was going to ask and giving me enough time to regret saying anything in the first place.

You have to tell her at some point.

Maybe after my father's funeral, if anyone bothered to give him one.

"We should join the party," I said quickly. "I wouldn't want to miss the dancing."

I had little stomach for food despite barely eating the rest of the day, but I forced down a bowl of soup before starting on the cider, spiced and piping hot. Village dances were one of the few occasions I tended not to feel left out, at least for a blissful period in the middle when everyone was at that pleasant stage of tipsiness, their sharpness was dulled. I never wanted to stay as long as Daisy, who would dance until her feet bled if we let her.

I remember one year, for the spring festival, she convinced me to stay out later than I liked. We'd both had too much blackberry wine and were giddy with the heat. I'd collapsed in a heap by the side of the square, but Daisy kept dancing until the pipers stopped playing, swaying to the ghost of their tune, like some kind of fairy. She eventually slumped down beside me, slippers in tatters, and we sat and talked for so long that the words turned gummy in our mouths.

Then Forrest, who had been lurking somewhere nearby, came over to ask if we were all right.

"Daisy, your feet!" he exclaimed.

Daisy looked down at her bleeding toes. "Oh, these are *fine*."

"Those are not fine!" he insisted. "Come. Let me take you home and I'll help you with them."

Daisy shrugged, taking the hand he was offering, only to be surprised a few seconds later when he lifted her into his arms. She let out a short gasp, but clung to him as he carried her away.

No wonder she fell in love with him.

I sought Daisy out, already among the throng of dancers, but it was Laurence who welcomed me into the group, pulling me in for a rowdy, fast-paced dance. The cider and music congealed within me, and although I didn't forget my worries, I felt them a little less. I danced until I couldn't breathe, and then I rested before dancing some more.

The night wore on. Rowan flung himself into my arms. Mama took to the floor with Russell. Everyone from the butcher to the carpenter to my crabby old school mistress joined in at some point. The music turned and twisted from rowdy to slow, the fiddlers pulling softly on their strings.

Forrest's hand slipped around my waist. "Can I have this dance?"

I nodded, even though I knew what this meant, what this was an invitation for. Perhaps it was just the excuse I needed. We started to sway. This was wrong, all wrong. "Forrest—" I began.

He shook his head. "Can I go first?"

"But—"

"I don't know where your mind's been these past few weeks. I know there's been something bothering you. But I want to know. I want to know everything about you, Andesine. There was a time I thought I was closer to you than anyone. I miss that. I want it back. I miss *you.* Whatever it is that's going on, you can tell me. I just want to make my own feelings perfectly clear. I like you, far more than as a friend. I want to be more to you. Please, Red. Give me the opportunity to show you how I feel."

I inched back, casting my eyes downwards. "I'm sorry, Forrest. I care about you a great deal, but not like that."

I couldn't bring myself to look at him, but his body was tightly set. "Perhaps if you just gave me a chance—"

"Forrest! I've known you my entire life! It's not about 'giving you a chance', it's about me knowing that we aren't right for each other—"

"But how are we not right? We're both smart and sort of funny and we get on—"

"There's more to it than that," I said, thinking of Finn, thinking of how I melted into his presence, how we didn't just 'get on', how we seemed chiselled from the same bark, trees knotted together. "There's so much more, Forrest. I'd just make you miserable. I could never like you the way you wanted to be liked."

"But... why not?"

"It's not so simple."

"Is there someone else?"

At this, I looked up sharply. "Would you respect my 'no' more, if there was?"

"I—"

"I don't want to hurt you," I told him shortly. "But I've made myself clear. I can't, Forrest. I just can't."

I turned my back and walked away from the dancefloor, guilt and anger and frustration all mudded up inside of me. I didn't owe him anymore than that. Why couldn't he accept it? Why did I have to prove my refusal was genuine? Why was I still trying to work out if there was a nicer way I could have said 'no'?

I should have told him sooner. Now we both hurt more because of it.

I'm sorry, Forrest.

Outside the village gates, I saw a white figure. A man, broad-shouldered in a white shirt, with dark hair, standing a little outside the lamplight.

My heart flipped. *Finn.*

He'd come.

I crept forward, but he darted backwards. Had he not seen me?

"Finn!" I called out softly, stepping over the gate. "Finn, where did you—"

A large hand closed over my mouth, smelling of earth and salt. Arms fastened around my wrists. I kicked and screamed, fear pounding in my chest, but everything was muffled. They dragged me into the bushes, out of sight, flashes of luminous eyes in the dark.

"Don't struggle, girl," came Vincent's liquid voice. "I've no *real* intention of harming you. Unless your mother doesn't cooperate, of course."

The person I'd thought was Finn stepped out of the gloom. Not Finn. His father, wearing clothes that mimicked his. In the low light, at a distance, it had been impossible to tell them apart.

Finn, Finn, where are you?

Finn, Finn, stay away.

Reed crouched in front of me, his face devoid of anything like Vincent's sneer. He looked almost apologetic as he bound my hands.

Cassel stood behind him, face white and nervous. A few of the others didn't look too happy about this, either, but the rest wore masks of indifference.

Vincent handed Cassel a note. "Deliver this to the village gates. Tell Clarisse if she wants to see her daughter alive, she needs to hand over her son."

"She won't do it!" I hissed into the palm still pressed against my mouth.

"Will she not?" Vincent's mouth twisted. "If she doesn't hand over the boy, her daughter dies. If she hands him over, both her children live. An easy choice for a mother to make, don't you think?"

A dark, bitter feeling gripped me, a cold realisation. Of course she'd do that. Of course she would. She'd despise herself for it, but she'd feel like she had no real choice.

"I hate you," I hissed at Vincent.

Vincent snorted. "Happily, I don't really care what you think of me."

A sharpness cracked across my cheek, so hard I thought my skin had split. Half of my face burned with pain.

My hands bound, I was yanked to my feet, still reeling from the blow, head aching, heart pounding. I didn't doubt his words, and we were too far away for screaming to do any good anyway. The only person who might hear me was Finn, and if he came...

He'd fight them. He'd fight them all. And I don't think most would think twice about killing him.

"Rowan will hate you too," I spat at Vincent. "He'll *despise* you. You want him as your heir? He won't be it. You took him from his family. He'll hate you as much as Finn does. He'll break away from you. He won't be yours. He won't ever be yours!"

Vincent laughed. "You think that's the first time I've heard words like that? Look how large my pack is, girl. They're all mine. They'll always *be* mine. Because in their hearts they know we're stronger together. That they'll never survive on their own."

"Finn has."

"So far."

"I don't understand," I turned to the others. "What do you owe him? He took you from your mothers—why would you follow him?"

No one spoke. No one even looked at me.

"Come on," said Vincent. "Let's get her away from here before someone spots us."

"Someone like me, you mean?"

The pack stopped, silence descending. They turned almost like one. Russell and his band of hunters stood behind them, weapons raised and ready.

"Interesting," said Vincent, no longer grinning, "I didn't hear you approach."

"I've spent almost a decade learning how to track your kind," Russell hissed. "A decade planning for this moment. You'll pay for what you've done, wolf."

Forrest frowned, staring at his father, confused no doubt as to what on earth was going on. He kept his crossbow steady.

Vincent grabbed me by the neck, drawing a dagger from his belt. "You come any closer, the girl dies."

"Really, Vincent? Your own child?"

"She isn't the one I'm here for."

At this, it was Russell's turn to frown. He cocked his gun.

"Father—" Forrest started.

"Don't worry, boy, I'm a steady shot."

"You can't—"

A white shape flung through the darkness, clamping onto Vincent's arm and slamming him towards the ground, away from me.

"Finn!" only it wasn't my cry, but Reed's.

Russell aimed his weapon. I launched forward, tripping over my half-bound feet. "Don't—"

A shot went off. There was a short, sharp yelp, and Finn hobbled off into the darkness.

"No!" I screamed, stumbling after, crawling. *No, no, no...*

Bolts soared overhead. The air grew thick with smoke and powder, crackling against the cold night air, ablaze with gunfire.

"Andie!"

Forrest battled forward, hauling me round and sawing through my bounds. Behind him, men erupted into wolves, charging at the hunters, scrambling and brawling in the snow. Some of the hunters' faces widened in confusion, but some already knew. They'd always known they were hunting men.

I hoped Cassel managed to break free.

Finn, Finn, Finn!

Forrest glanced about him. "Where did all these wolves come from?" He gaped, still cutting through the ropes.

I didn't explain. I couldn't. I didn't have time. I clambered upright as soon as I was free, racing into the woods.

"Andie! Andie, where are you going?"

For Finn to bolt like that, for him to forget about me, he must have been hurt. I could barely see anything in the dark under the dense canopy of trees, save tiny snatches below the slivers of moonlight. But I did not need to see. I could feel him, an ache against my chest. My shoulder twitched painfully, and I swore I could taste the coppery tang of blood in the air.

My eyes adjusted to the gloom, and a frail, inert shape spread out in front of me, a naked male sprawled on the ground.

Finn.

19
WOLF HUNT

"Finn, *Finn!*" I hovered over him, hands twitching over the wound in his shoulder, over his brow, almost as pale as the snow beneath. "Answer me!"

He murmured something beneath me, and I clutched his face.

"Open your eyes," I commanded, my voice hoarse. "Please."

He blinked, wearily and for a few seconds. "You're here."

"Of *course* I'm here, you stupid fool, I—" I wrestled with my skirts, tearing off the hem of my petticoat with my teeth and balling it into a fist over his wound. I wanted to spread my cloak over him, to offer him some protection from the cold, but I knew the danger that could invite. "It's not deep," I told him. "You're going to be fine."

"If you insist."

"I do. I do insist. I—"

But I needed to get him out of the cold and into the warm. I needed to stop the bleeding. I needed to—

I needed to calm down and think, because the alternative was too awful.

"Andesine!" A voice was calling through the trees. My heart lurched. Forrest.

"Here!" I screamed. "Forrest, here!"

Within seconds, he emerged at the top of the embankment, eyes widening at the scene below. "Great gods, what—"

"Your father shot him!" I hissed. "Help me get him to the hut." It was maybe not the safest of places, if the other wolves followed me, but the hunters were hot on their trail and I was probably a low priority. It was close, it was nearby, it was warm.

"My father shot a wolf."

"He's a person and his name is Finn and you have to help me save him!"

Forrest stood still as stone. For a moment, it looked like he would never answer at all. "Of course," he said eventually, and went to grab his arm.

Finn let out a groan of pain as we pulled him to his feet, barely any strength in him. He was as loose as a scarecrow. Either he'd lost more blood than I thought, or...

I didn't want to think about that.

We manoeuvred him into the hut and onto the cot.

"Get a cart," I barked at Forrest. I wasn't confident enough in my own remedies, or the safety of our location. I couldn't take him to the village. There was only one place we could go; the De Winter Chateau. Grandma would know how to fix him. She had to. "And if you tell anyone about this or lead anyone to us or do anything to hurt him ever again I swear I'll

—"

"What? What will you do?" Forrest snapped. "You've already done the worst thing to me."

"Forrest—"

"No," he said, shaking his head. "That wasn't fair of me. Don't apologise. And I won't tell anyone. Of that, I promise."

He was gone before I could thank him.

I crouched down by Finn's side, lighting a candle to fight the dark and holding it to his wound. "You're going to be fine," I repeated. "Barely a scratch."

"Bullet," he whispered.

"What?"

"Bullet. You need to… get it out…"

"I—"

"Andie," he coughed. "Please."

I had a pair of scissors, a dagger, and a large pair of tweezers at my disposal, not the sort to be used on flesh. I tried to get him to choke down willowbark for the pain before I began, but he retched most of it back up. He stuffed a bit of fabric into his mouth and told me to get it over with, bracing himself against the frame of the bed. If he'd had the strength, I fear he would have broken it as I snipped away at his flesh, stuck my fingers in the wound, and plunged my tweezers in, searching for the bullet.

He tried not to scream, but he did. He really did.

Pass out, pass out, just pass out, please…

It took far too long to find the bullet, far too long to grip hold of it, far too long until I finally wriggled it free of his flesh.

Finn turned on his side, retching again, while I crouched over him, still holding the bullet.

"Open it," he rasped.

"What?"

"Open the bullet."

With some difficulty, I prised open the back of the casing. There was only the faintest trace of gunpowder, the rest was packed with a fine, purplish herb.

"Wolfsbane," I whispered.

"I was afraid of that," Finn said, and slumped back against the cot, breathing hard, covered in a film of sweat.

My heart thumped against my ribcage. "It's all right," I told him. "Forrest has gone to get a cart. I'm taking you to my Grandma's. She'll have an antidote. It'll be fine."

"That's if your dear pal Forrest doesn't just summon the hunters instead."

"What?"

"He knows what I am."

I shook my head. "No, not Forrest. He wouldn't do that."

"He loves you."

"He likes me, and he's my friend, and *he wouldn't do that.* Are you honestly jealous of him right now?"

"He might... be a better... option."

"Idiot," I hissed, clasping his hand, the hand bound with a strand of my hair. "You're the only option I'm willing to consider. Mine, Finn, remember that."

I kissed his brow, tucking the bullet away inside a rag and stowing it inside my pocket. I didn't want to put it down and risk the dust of it going back into him. It was safer there. I fetched him some water, scrubbed the blood from my skin, and came back to dress the wound. Finn was burning up and quietly thrashing as I sponged the blood from his shoulder.

"Finn," I whispered, as he shivered underneath me, "I'm so sorry."

"You... didn't... shoot..."

"I... I could have stopped them, I could have—"

A white finger reached up and flicked a tear from my cheek. "It's all right. I'm fine."

"How can you say that?"

"You're here," he said, his voice ragged. "It's all fine... when you're here..." His eyes started to circle.

"Then stay with me," I rushed. "Because I need you here, too."

He slumped against the cot, leaving me to finish my work in agonising silence. I packed the wound with herbs and bandaged it tightly, wishing I had my grandma's skill with a needle and not daring to make it worse. I cleaned the sweat from his skin, rinsed my hands in the snow, and piled him with furs. I tried not to fixate on his laboured breaths or the ghostly pallor of his face.

"I'll hate you forever if you die," I hissed, hating the shredded sound of my voice. "I swear it. But if you live, Finn, if you live..." I took his hand, winding my fingers through his, brushing against his calloused palms and worn fingertips, like the rough pads of a dog. I traced the lines of his chest, his faded scars, the perfect slope of his nose. *Everything* about him was perfect, and I wished I was an artist, or a sculptor, or a wordsmith, had some way of rendering him into immortality, a way to express what he was to me, to give colour or shape to the ragged threads that bound my heart to the one pulsing weakly beneath his chest.

If you die, I will die. If you die, this muscled organ inside me will blacken like coal, shatter like glass in a fire. I will be less than a corpse. Living tissue. Everything will become nothing.

But if you live...

It was worse than when we were stuck in the pit, far worse. At least then, I knew he'd be all right, that we just had to endure until morning. Perhaps it should have been worse, perhaps I should have been more scared for myself, but I hadn't been.

I was more scared for myself, now. His death would be the end of me, a destruction far worse than anything else he could ever do.

"You'll be all right," I whispered. "If you love me, you have to be."

Forrest came back with the cart shortly afterwards. If maneuvering him into the hut was difficult before when he was conscious, it was worse the second time, but eventually we had him safely stowed on the back, covered under blankets. I held his head in my lap as we trundled down the dark round, shuddering at the sound of howling and shots. The air was ice and gunpowder.

Finn jerked in my arms, and I wondered how unconscious he really was.

Forrest was far more silent.

"Thank you," I said at one point.

"I think you owe me an explanation," he responded.

"Some of the wolves are men, too," I said.

"Right."

"Your father knows."

Even in the dark, I could sense his stiffening. "Why didn't you tell me?"

"Because I was afraid you might hurt Finn," I whispered, the tears inching down my face. "I had no way… I couldn't be sure…"

"I'm not in the habit of murdering *people,"* he hissed. "Why would you think—"

He turned to face me, but before he could ask the question or I could explain about what my father did to his mother, the horse came to a stop outside the gates, unable to go much further up the icy drive. It whinnied apprehensively, and within seconds my grandmother was streaming out of the house, wrapped up in a shawl against the cold.

"Andie, dearest, what are you thinking coming here at this hour with all the chaos in the woods—"

"It's Finn, Grandma," I sobbed, shuffling out of the back of the cart, "he's been hurt, wolfsbane—"

Grandma's face paled.

"Please tell me you have more antidote," I begged.

"I can make some," she said. "Let's get him in. Quickly now."

Together, the three of us brought him into the kitchen and laid him out on the table. The fire was already going. Grandma disappeared into the pantry to check her supplies, wittering under her breath.

"I'm never out of wolfsbane antidote, but I gave the last

of it to you… been meaning to top up my supplies… this damned weather…" She flung on a coat. "Can't be helped. I won't be too long. Unless someone shoots me."

"You're going out?" Forrest blanched.

"Herbs don't pick themselves, boy."

"I refuse to let you go out in the woods alone."

"Suit yourself. Don't slow me down." She grabbed her crossbow and basket and disappeared. Forrest cast one look at me, hovering beside Finn, and gave something like a nod before disappearing.

I sat down on the bench and took Finn's hand. His eyes fluttered open a few minutes later. "Where are we?" he asked, his voice rough.

"My grandma's. She's just popped out to get a few ingredients she needs for the antidote."

I stroked his forehead, damp with sweat, and he shivered underneath my touch.

"Your grandma… is out in the woods?"

"Nothing there is scarier than her, I assure you."

He coughed, hard and painful, a sound that hammered against my chest. He looked worse than Cassel. A lot worse. I wondered if the bullets were fresher than my grandmother's bolts, if the poison had lost part of its potency, or the severity of the wound was worse.

"Has she… been gone long?" he asked.

"A little while. No need to worry yet."

"*You're* worried."

I brushed his hair, and kissed the band on his finger. "It's my job to worry about you."

Finn swallowed, his chest heaving. I tried not to concentrate on it, tried to find somewhere else to look, but where else could my gaze possibly go but him?

"Do you think she was scared?"

"What?"

"My mother. Do you think she knew she was going to die? Do you think she was scared? Do you... do you think it hurt?"

Yes. Yes, I think it hurt. Neck snapping is quick, but Vincent is the type of person who would have found a way to make it hurt. He likes pain, likes being the cause of it. I think because that's the only time he feels anything at all.

Yes, I think she knew. But I think she knew there were worse things than death, like losing you.

"You're not going to die," I assured him.

"That doesn't answer my question." Finn shuddered and swallowed, painfully, sweat shivering from his skin. "I remember her sitting beside the fire as I was dragged away. I remember her not looking at me. But that didn't happen, did it? Vincent just made me think it did. She was already dead."

There was nothing I could say to that, nothing at all. I clutched his hand more tightly.

"He said he snapped her neck. How did people explain that? Did he make it look like a fall, do you think?"

He made it look like she'd taken her own life. There's only one way I can think of to make a broken neck look like a suicide.

Something in my face or the bond between us betrayed the words I could not speak.

"She was probably hanging from the rafters, wasn't she, when Vincent woke me? I screamed for her while she was hanging there."

"Finn, don't... please don't..."

"I can't stop thinking about it, Andie. It's stuck in my head. It's got claws and won't let go. She was my mother and she..."

"She loved you," I coughed, my throat hard. "She loved you, and I love you, and wherever else your mind goes, know that. I can't bring her back. I can't tear that image from your mind. But you're here now, and I need you here, and if you fall into that nightmare again, tell me, but know that I am always here to pull you back." I kissed his trembling fingers. "I'm here, Finn, and you are not allowed to go where I can't follow."

He murmured something that sounded like thanks, but his voice dribbled away from him. He was still conscious, so I got up and offered him some water, coming back with another cloth for his forehead.

"I never told you why I loved you, did I?"

Finn shook his head, unable to do much more.

"I love your heart," I told him. "I love that it's still so warm, that nothing anyone could do to you has stamped it out. I love that you laugh despite everything, truly laugh, and the sound is gold to me. I love how you can take a piece of wood and pull out beauty for the world to see. I love where your mind wanders, the way your voice goes when you tell a story, and if I could touch words I'd cling to them. I love how you've never called me weird or dark or different, how I feel more myself with you than ever. I love how neither of us feel alone when we're together, when we're together..." I swallowed, breathing carefully. "Even if magic wasn't real, I'd feel it with you. People must have souls, Finn, because I can feel yours next to mine."

I leant across and kissed him, lighter than a feather against the snow, and half crawled against him. I stayed there, close as I could get, keeping him as comfortable as I could and praying Grandma wouldn't be much longer. I wasn't sure how much longer I could bear to watch him that way.

Eventually, the sound of crunching snow and gravel sounded underfoot, and Grandma and Forrest burst back into the kitchen. "Got it!" Grandma declared, holding up a handful of herbs.

I leapt upright.

"What can I—"

"Boil some water, dear. I'll take care of the rest."

Boiling water didn't take nearly enough of my focus. I was back to hanging uselessly at the side while Grandma raced around the room, gathering ingredients, measuring them out, and grinding everything into a fine paste before mixing it with the water.

She poured it into an invalid cup and pressed it against Finn's mouth.

"Come on, boy, drink," she commanded. "Andie's waiting for you."

I clutched his head, pressing our foreheads together. Our sweat and breath mingled. "Please, Finn, come on. You'll feel better soon, you will, you just need to drink."

Finn murmured something weak and utterly imperceptible, but his mouth opened, and he took a slow sip. I held his head up to help him.

"That's it," Grandma said softly. "Keep going lad. You can do it."

He took it all, down to the dregs. "It's foul," he whispered.

Grandma laughed. "Didn't have time to add the honey, dear. But try to keep it in you. You'll be better in no time."

"If you insist…" he said, and slumped into unconsciousness.

I loosed a tight breath in my chest, and slid towards the floor. An age had passed before I moved again, before I had the strength to stand. Finn was sleeping soundly, colour brightening in his cheeks, and Grandma sat by the side of the fire in her rocking chair, smoking a pipe.

Forrest was nowhere to be seen.

I stepped outside. He leant against the side of the house, illuminated by the faint orange glow of the kitchen, his face white and drained of colour.

"Are you all right?" I asked him, which was a foolish question.

He shook his head. "Why him?" he asked. "Why not me?"

I was almost glad of this question, as it stopped me having to explain about my father, even though I knew I had to.

This first. "It's not *you,* Forrest," I told him, as gently as I could. "It's never been about you. You're fine. You're somebody else's wonderful. But you're not mine, and I'm not yours."

"Is it really that simple?"

"It is."

He sighed.

"Forrest?"

"Yes?"

"You really *are* somebody else's wonderful."

Forrest frowned at this, and I wasn't sure if I could spell it out anymore, if Daisy would want me to. Besides, this was hardly the moment.

I braced myself. "I... I have something else to tell you."

Something else took over Forrest's features. "My mother was killed by a wolf, wasn't she? One of... one of *those* wolves. A man."

I nodded, slowly.

"Not him though, right?" asked Forrest, jerking his head towards the kitchen, and the table where Finn lay.

I shook my head.

"Do you know who?"

Another nod, and painful, "Yes."

"Who, Andie?"

"I don't want you to hate me. Even though..." *Even though I've hurt you, even if I deserve it for having kept you in the dark...*

"Oh, Red." Forrest sighed. "Unless you killed her yourself, I don't think I could ever hate you. You are, first and always, my friend."

My chest hurt, raw and warm. "It was my father," I rushed. "My father killed your mother, because she tried to help mine keep my brother from him. Your mother died because she helped us."

"Your... your father?" Forrest stared at me.

"I'm so, so sorry, Forrest. I wanted to tell you, or at least, I didn't want to keep anything from you, but..."

Forrest sagged against the side of the house. I moved towards him, but before I could, the sound of whinnying and wheels clattered through the dark. A spot of amber jogged along the road, hurrying towards the gates. Unconsciously, I crept down the drive.

"Mama?" I said, when the driver's face came into view. "What are you—"

The cart came to an abrupt stop. Mama slid down, unbuckling the pony and patting it up the drive into relative safety. She glanced at us both, face ash-white. "You're all right," she said, coming forward to embrace me.

"What's going on?"

Daisy swung out of the back, helping Rowan down after her. He was bundled up and trembling, and raced straight into my arms.

"Daisy?" Forrest frowned, concern clouding his brow. "Would someone like to explain—"

The back door banged open. "Explain inside," hissed Grandma. "Get in!"

20
FIGHT OF THE WOLVES

“What were you thinking, bringing the boy in all this chaos?” Grandma hissed, barring the door behind us.

“Russell came back to the house. He was *crazy,* Mama! He realised Rowan was Vincent’s and that he could use him as bait. My son. My baby.”

“She hit him with a frying pan,” said Rowan, still attached to my side.

“I don’t think I hurt him, at least, not badly,” Mama added. She flashed a guilty look at Forrest. “He was still moving.”

“He wanted to use Rowan as *bait?*” Forrest looked sick. “I’m… I’m sorry, Clarisse. Truly.”

“You didn’t do anything,” she said, as softly as she could manage. She turned back to her mother. “Have you got any more mountain ash? We could put it at the windows and doors—”

“No,” said her mother sharply.

Mama’s face paled. “But you put it at the boundaries,

right?"

"Umm..."

"Mama!"

"It's in some places!"

"Once Vincent realises we aren't in the village—"

"I didn't bring him here!"

Rowan buried himself in my waist once more. "I don't want to go with that man, Andie."

"I know, darling, and you don't have to. I promise."

Finn, who'd been dozing silently on the table, shuffled upright. He smiled at me, and then frowned at the rest of the room. "What's going on?" he asked.

"Um..."

My mother's eyes narrowed. "Mother, why is there a naked man on your table?"

"Ask your daughter. He belongs to her."

"Grandma!"

Finn flushed a deep shade of scarlet, half residual fever, half embarrassment at the fact he was meeting my mother for the first time without a stitch on him.

"Andie?" Mama glanced at me. "What's going on?"

I barely had the energy to sigh. "This is Finn Whitethorn," I told her. "He was a wolf in Vincent's pack, but he broke free, and..."

"And?"

"We've been... seeing one another."

Daisy giggled.

"We're sort of... engaged."

"Sort of?" said Finn under his breath.

Mama stared at us for a full minute, her face a stark mask of bewilderment. Finally, she shook her head and sighed. "We'll talk later," she said. "*Much* later. Daisy, please take Rowan down to the cellar."

Surprisingly, Rowan didn't take much convincing. He seemed glad to get away from it all. Finn tried to stand up, but didn't get very far. I swooped under his arm and lowered him back down to the bench.

"Take it easy. You've just been poisoned."

"It's fine. I've had the antidote."

"You've also just been shot."

He waved his hand, as if this happened every other day.

"I'm going to find you some clothes," my mother declared, marching off into the rest of the house.

"Thank you," Finn called after her. "Nice to meet you, Madame De Winter!"

Mama gave a non-committal sound, the door closing behind her.

"Well, she seemed nice," said Finn sheepishly.

I kissed his cheek.

Daisy re-emerged from the cellar with a request for blankets to try and make Rowan a little more comfortable. She spied Forrest beside the fire, quiet and terse.

"Is he all right?" she asked me.

"Umm, well," I started, keeping my voice quiet, "I turned him down, his father tried to hurt a child, he's just found out wolves are men and that his mother was killed by one who's also my father."

"Damn," said Finn, "rough day. Poor Forrest."

"Because yours is going *so much* better."

"Oh," said Daisy, "oh, *oh.*"

Without another word, she went to Forrest's side. She whispered something I couldn't hear, and then he fell into her arms, eyes shut tight against her shoulder. It seemed like the safest, most natural place for him to be.

You're an idiot, Forrest. Whyever did you waste your time on me when you had Daisy beside you?

"We've got company," Grandma declared.

Forrest jerked back from Daisy and whipped out his pistol. Daisy grabbed Grandma's crossbow from the wall, loading it so deftly that Forrest smiled in bemused approval.

"It's your father," Grandma said, staring out the window. "Forrest's, that is. The less scary of the fathers we should be concerned about."

"That's well-spotted," Forrest said.

"I've got quite the eye."

They all bustled for the door. "Stay here," Grandma told me. "Grab a knife, defend your brother. Protect your mate."

"But—"

"Top drawer for knives, girl."

I wasn't in a hurry to leave Finn, who could barely stand, but leaving my friends and my grandma to face anything alone seemed wrong, too. I did as I was told, watching from the window.

"Andie, Daisy—" Rowan called from the cellar.

"Stay there, Ro. Keep your head down."

His little voice quietened. "All... all right." His shuffled back down the steps.

Finn sighed from the bench, hugging the furs to him. "I feel rather helpless."

"You and me both."

"Did your grandma just call me your mate?"

"I—"

"Forrest!" Russell called in the garden. "Son, what are you doing here?"

"I think the question should be what are *you* doing here, Pa?"

"It's difficult to explain, but I need to you to trust me—"

"I know that Mother was killed by Andie's father."

Russell tensed, and looked down at his feet. "I didn't know how to explain. I didn't want you to be afraid, or to look at the girl differently, or her mother. It wasn't their fault—"

"Of course it wasn't! But why wouldn't you tell me what we were *really* fighting?"

"I thought you might have reservations about killing men."

Forrest froze at this, because it was true, because hunter though he was, Forrest had never been a killer.

And for the first time, he realised that his father was. Russell was willing to kill for revenge, to kill others who had nothing to do with his mother's death. All wolves were one to him.

"I have reservations about using a child as bait," Forrest said instead.

Russell's jaw tightened. "I don't mean to hurt the boy."

"Pa, he's *terrified.*"

"It'll all be over soon. It's for the best, the boy will understand when he's older."

"You want to use him to kill his father. Do you realise how awful that is?"

Russell glared. "That man doesn't deserve to be anyone's father. He killed your mother, Forrest. Tore her to pieces... the undertaker had to stitch her back together to have something to bury—"

"Don't," said Daisy quietly, "please."

"I don't mean to upset you, Daisy."

"It's not me I'm worried about."

Forrest's entire body was tight and stiff as a nail. In the dark from this position, I could not make out his face, but my mind circled back to the boy beside the cart that day, and the bloodied body beneath the tarpaulin.

"The boy won't be hurt, son, I promise you," Russell continued.

"I think he's already hurt."

Russell shook his head, something more than rage brewing beneath him. "This is for your *mother!* It's for the greater good. The wolf needs to die—"

"Mother wouldn't want this."

"She never lived long enough for you to know what she would have wanted."

"That's enough," growled my grandmother. "You need to leave, Russell. You're not getting to my grandson. Get off my property."

Russell sneered. "You're not even armed, and they're not going to shoot me." He drew his dagger. I don't think he had any intention of using it, I think he just hoped to seem more desperate, more intimidating, to make them give him a wide berth as he barrelled towards the door. Daisy gave a shriek as the crossbow was pulled from her grip. Forrest reached out to catch his father's arm, and in the panic and confusion, fuelled by the sudden howling of wolves nearby, Russell slashed at him instinctively.

Daisy reacted instinctively too, trying to seize the knife before it reached him.

The blade sliced across her wrist, and her scream bolted through the air.

A silence fell over the party, over the wolves.

The smell of blood was almost tangible.

"Get inside!" hissed my grandmother, kicking Russell away. "Come here again and I'll kill you myself."

Russell didn't move. He was staring at the blood in the snow, at Daisy's wound, like he couldn't believe what he'd done, what he'd almost done. He'd not aimed for her. He'd aimed for his own son.

Mother wouldn't have wanted this.

I remembered little of Beatrice Carter, but I knew she'd been kind. I knew that she'd risked my father's wrath to help my mother escape from him. She had lost her life aiding her friend. She would have protected her family against anything.

Russell, in that moment, must have known it too.

I did not watch him leave.

21 DAUGHTER OF WOLVES

Forrest bundled Daisy inside and I raced forward to steer her towards the hearth, sitting her down and pressing a rag to the wound pulsing at her arm. It was deep, but not deadly. She'd scar, but it wasn't serious.

Grandma bolted the door. Mama arrived a minute later, her arms filled with clothes.

"What happened?" she asked, her eyes wide as she saw Daisy's wound.

Grandma filled her in. Mama swore. Forrest teased the rag from my hands, and took over. I went to help Finn dress, Mama too preoccupied with what had just transpired to mind that I was once more in close proximity to a naked man. I posted Finn's arms through the shirt and helped him wriggle into the trousers.

"You need a sling," I told him. "Keep the weight off your shoulder."

He shook his head. "I need to be able to fight."

The howling grew closer, and I looked around the room.

Finn was in no condition to fight. Grandma, for all her steel, was a poor shot, and it was dark. Daisy was injured, and I was no match for a wolf.

We'd be outnumbered. We'd be dead.

And Rowan…

Rowan would grow up like Finn. Alone, unloved, without us. Maybe one day, he'd manage to break free, but what would that matter if he had no home to come back to, if Vincent killed us here tonight?

Beside the hearth, Forrest tended to Daisy's wound.

"Daisy, Daisy," he said, with something between fear and affection, "why did you do that? What were you thinking?"

Daisy stared at him incredulously. "That I didn't want to see you get hurt?"

He sighed. "You're too good, Daisy."

"Yes," she said, and I wondered if Forrest could see the anger in her eyes, the flash of tears, of frustration quiet and bitter and brittle. "I *am* too good. I am too good for *you*. I shouldn't care that you've never noticed that. I shouldn't care that you've only ever had eyes for someone who didn't want you back. I am so kind and lovely that I could probably have almost any boy in the village. But I do care. I've never wanted them. I've never wanted anyone but you."

Forrest stared at her, silent and unblinking, as if, out of everything that had happened tonight, this was the most surprising. "Daisy—" he started.

"I know. I know. You're sorry. You don't want to hurt me."

"I…" He paused. "I would have dived in front of a dagger for you, too."

"Maybe," she said, looking up for a trembling moment. "But for the wrong reasons."

"They could become the right ones, one day."

"Don't do that. Don't dangle false hope in front of me. You don't know what it's been like all these years, how a single kind word from you could delight and crush me in equal measure."

"Oh, Daisy, I'm sorry, but I know exactly what that's like."

A silence stretched between the two of them.

"Permission to try and make up for being an oblivious fool by courting you appropriately when this is all over?"

"You..." Daisy stared at him, wide and unblinking, as if not daring to believe in his words. "You better do a really good job."

Grandma stood beside the window, staring out into the dark, her eyes as steely as a knife. "They're here," she said. "Get the wolf into the basement. Daisy, you too, dear."

"I can still fight—"

Grandma shook her head. "Let's not tempt them with fresh blood. The younger ones might find it hard to resist."

I wondered once more about my grandma knowing so much about wolves, but I didn't have time to push it. Forrest escorted Daisy awkwardly to the cellar door, and they shared a look they'd not shared before. They'd always hugged freely, but Daisy's confession was a weight between them. It would mean something different now.

Unwilling to do nothing, she stepped up and kissed his cheek. "Take care," she said.

"I will," Forrest replied, and then, quickly, "for you."

The weakest flicker of a smile flashed across her lips, and she disappeared beneath.

I put my arm around Finn and tried to guide him towards the cellar, but he jerked his head and pulled away.

"I'm not leaving you."

"You can barely stand."

"I'd rather fall beside you than let you fall alone."

At this, my chest cracked, because if the positions were reversed, I couldn't hide below, no matter what condition I was in. It would kill me.

So I had to let him stay.

"If you die…" I started, my throat tight.

"I know, I know, you'll never forgive me, I feel exactly the same."

I gathered his face in my hands and kissed him as deeply as I dared, crawling into that kiss, wishing pain could evaporate with touch, that true love was real, that I was a witch after all, capable of casting protection over those I loved.

But I did not have that kind of power.

I had none at all.

"Crossbow," said Grandma, flinging one in my direction. Mama brought out her pistol.

"Won't you need something?" she asked her mother.

"I have something else in mind."

I didn't ask what. Forrest hovered by the door, Mama moving to my side. Finn limped away from me, towards the window.

"Why didn't you tell me?" Mama asked, staring after him.

"That I was falling for a wolf? Gee, Ma, it's not like you'd not made it perfectly clear you hated them."

"I..." Her voice fell short. "I don't hate *all* wolves. I hate your father. I love your brother. I would have... I might have been a little cautious, but..." She shook her head. "I'm sorry for my secrets. I'm sorry you felt you couldn't come to me."

"I'm sorry too," I whispered.

"Never again," she said. "If we live through this, I promise. Never again."

There was a yelp from outside; one of Grandma's traps had worked. But the rest of the pack fast approached, tearing through the snow.

"Why, *why* didn't you ash the boundary?" Mama shrieked.

"That would have been foolish."

She frowned. "Mama?"

My grandma turned sharply towards Finn. "You, boy," she said. "You had the strength of will to tear away from your old pack. I'm hesitant to force you into another, but we can draw on each other's strength, if you're willing?"

Finn raised an eyebrow.

"I don't understand," I said.

"You will," said Grandma, and dropped to the floor.

Her hands balled against the snow, fingers twisting into claws. Thick, hairy ears sprouted at her head. Her nose elongated, her eyes bulged, and her teeth sharpened into long, fine points.

"Grandma," I gasped, "what big teeth you have!"

She gave something like a laugh, and there, in the space where Agatha De Winter had been, there was a huge, grey wolf.

She let out a monstrous howl.

No wonder she knew so much about wolves. No wonder she lived out here by herself. My eagle-eyed, sharp-eared grandmother was a wolf.

Her own alpha.

Finn shifted, returning her call, and bowed beneath her huge form. She howled again, and it almost seemed like he grew stronger, the wound in his shoulder less prominent.

One of the windows smashed. Glass splattered into the room. Forrest fired, his bullet striking the windowsill in a storm of splinters. A large brown wolf tumbled into the room.

Grandma lunged forward, striking him to the ground with a single massive paw. She chomped into his neck, flinging him to the corner for Finn to finish as another flew in through the second window.

I fired my own weapon, striking it in the shoulder. Forrest shot again, finishing it, but his eyes flashed as its form twisted, sliding back to a man.

He'd killed someone.

We'd killed someone.

There was a shout from outside; the hunters had arrived. The air was live with fangs and gunfire. The door held strong, but wolves streamed in through the windows, too many for us to fight.

Something hammered at the door. My bolts were no use against wood.

Thinking fast, I abandoned the room entirely, streaming up to the upper level and into the bedroom over the kitchen.

I flung open the window, firing into the dark. Three of the wolves had shifted back to men, hammering at the door with a broken trunk.

The solid oak held firm, but I could almost hear the creak of the bolts screwing the bar into place. It would not hold forever.

In the murky dark, the hunters fired, bullets and smoke pervading the air like a snowstorm, screams and howls merged together. Forrest appeared at my side, pistol cracking. Sometimes we hit, sometimes we didn't.

We lost count. We became killers, not feeling, not thinking.

Laurence appeared beside one of the men at the door, out of bullets. He raised a dagger to stop one, but it turned around in a flash and bit into his neck. Forrest cried out, and a scream ripped through my throat, unbidden.

Not thinking, I tumbled out of the window into the padded snow beneath, seizing a bolt from my belt and plunging it into the neck of the wolf. Forrest yelled behind me, but I could not hear his words.

The wolf downed, I crouched by Laurence's side. Blood pulsed at his throat, and I knew in an instant that he was beyond all care. His eyes stared up at me, live and vacant, and I held his hand in the seconds it took for him to trickle away.

He could not speak, but his mouth opened all the same, and I think he wanted to call for his mother.

Once upon a time, I hated him. I would have been glad to see him suffer.

But not like this, and not now.

"Andie!" Forrest screamed.

A wolf ploughed into me, but before he could sink his teeth into my flesh, a white shape sprung out of the dark and knocked him to his feet. Claws slashed across fur and eyeball, sending the wolf reeling and whimpering.

I scrambled to my feet, searching for my bolts scattered in the snow.

Three wolves circled round me.

A howl like a cry went up, and my grandmother's wolf came soaring through the air, striking one of them down. A bullet took out another. I streamed towards the house, my mother covering me from the window, but the blackest of shapes cut across me.

Vincent.

I had no bolts.

Finn darted out of the darkness, but a single swipe sent him reeling into the snow. Reed appeared, pinning him in place. He pressed against his son's chest, not drawing blood, not quite.

Grandma finished off the wolf and squared up to Vincent.

His gold eyes flickered, and I wondered if he knew who she was, if he'd always sensed it, the way Finn didn't seem surprised by her offer.

Agatha, his eyes seemed to say.

Vincent, she replied.

They lunged towards one another, fangs and flesh and fur, grey and brown meshed together. They were both so large, but Vincent was younger, fitter, the strength of the pack behind him. I grappled for my bolts, but I could not shoot; not without hitting Grandma.

I thought about shooting Reed, pinning Finn to the ground, but I wasn't sure I could trust my aim *not* to kill him.

I did not want Finn to lose a father, and another part of me, even in the chaos, knew that Finn was safer if I didn't free him.

I think Reed knew that too.

"Andie!"

My mother screamed for me, still in the house. I wanted to bolt for her, but as soon as I did, something clawed at my cloak, dragging me to the ground, and four massive paws stamped on my arms.

They kept me down, not hurting, not quite.

In the background, I saw a small brown wolf, cowering in the darkness, a wolf reluctant to fight.

Cassel. It must have been.

But he was as powerless as I was.

Vincent and my grandma still writhed in a circus of limbs, both torn and scratched and bleeding. The hunters ' numbers were thinning. The sound of gunfire had melted away like snowflakes in firelight. Many lay on the ground, bleeding or dead, the remaining wolves circling round the alphas.

I spared a thought for Forrest's father, wrong though he was, for Laurence dead in the snow, for anyone whose world had altered beyond all reckoning.

I prayed that I wouldn't join them.

Vincent struck another attack at my grandmother, smacking her to the ground. Before she could move, half a dozen wolves had set upon her, teeth gripping her limbs. She could not move.

He shifted back into his human form.

"Clarisse," he called. "I have your mother. I have our daughter. Let me come in, Clarisse. Let me have the boy. Let us have no more death tonight."

An awful, penetrating silence kicked at the night. I was sure Mama would refuse, that nothing in the world would ever convince her to give up her baby, but of course, I was her child too.

Lose one child, or keep both alive. What was she supposed to do?

"No, Mama," I whispered, although the claws on my back grew harder.

The bolts on the door unlatched. Half the wolves shifted back to human, and Vincent walked idly through the door.

I was brought, too, arms caught in vice-like grips. Reed shifted, dragging Finn forward. My heart prayed darkly for Forrest, but by the time we emerged in the kitchen, he had been snatched too, bloodier than the rest of us.

Vincent grinned, tearing open the cellar doors.

Daisy launched forwards, brandishing a knife, but he tore it out of her grip and threw her towards Forrest, too cut up to catch her. They grasped at each other, trembling and torn.

"Come on out, Rowan my boy. It is time to bid your mother and sister goodbye."

A part of me hoped that he'd managed to escape out the storm doors, but he hadn't, or that route had been cut off. It still took an age for him to emerge, white-faced, shaking.

"Don't hurt them," Rowan whispered. "Please, *please,* don't hurt them."

"I won't hurt anyone," Vincent assured him. "If you come with us. If you accept your role as my heir."

These words have meaning, I realised. He would be bound to him like the others. He would have no choice.

Rowan's lip trembled. "I'll do whatever you want," he said. "But don't hurt them."

No, Ro.

Vincent smiled. "Say that you're mine."

"I'm yours."

The pack let out a cheerful, delighted howl. It reverberated through the stone. Grandma hissed, still pinned, but back in human form.

"He's yours in name only, Vincent," she said. "His heart belongs with us."

Vincent snorted. "What care I for his heart?" His eyes fell to my mother and me, and he nodded at his underlings. They released us both, and all three of us snapped together.

"I'm sorry," Rowan wept in our arms. "I'm sorry, I'm sorry, I'm sorry."

Mama grabbed his face. "Don't be sorry, my dear, beautiful boy. You were brave."

"I don't want to go with him."

"I know, I know dear boy."

Vincent sighed. "You could have come with us, Andesine. You had the choice. But now I rather doubt that I could trust you. What is the worth of a woman to a wolf?"

I could think of nothing to say to this, but clung to my

brother. *I won't let go, I won't let go, I won't.*

Vincent clicked his fingers, and a few of the men walked into the pantry, bringing out a cask of ale and anything else they fancied, as if they'd won a game rather than a slaughter.

"Take heart, Clarisse. Your son will inherit a great pack. He'll be powerful beyond your comprehension. He'll want for nothing."

"He'll want for *us,*" she insisted, making Vincent's eyes flicker. She shook her head. "I know you're a wolf, but are you *that* devoid of humanity?"

Vincent said nothing, but his pack popped open the barrel.

Something weighty pressed against my lap. A tiny thing, a reminder.

"There's wine in the cellar," I said, my voice half numb.

Vincent frowned. "What's that?"

"Wine. There's better drink, below. Since this is such an occasion for you."

He snorted. "Why tell me that?"

I breathed carefully. "Take me with you."

Finn struggled, but another of the wolves—not his father—pressed against him.

Vincent laughed. "I think not."

"Hear me out," I said. "I'm a healer. I fixed one of your own already. And I have... other uses. Don't... don't let my little brother be alone. He'll behave better if I'm around. Take me on a trial basis, if you like. Give me until he changes. I'll do anything you ask. *Anything.*"

Vincent's smile changed. "I won't take the omega."

I cast my eyes towards the floor, ashamed to even glance in Finn's direction. "As long as you don't hurt him, I won't object."

He stroked his chin. "I will admit, you could certainly have your uses. And our numbers are thinner than I would like, especially after tonight. Repopulation isn't a bad idea..."

"No, Andie!" Mama yelled.

Vincent smacked her across her face with the back of her hand. My own cheek burned in memory. "Silence!" He turned back to me. "All right, daughter, let's see how you fare. Let's have that wine brought up."

There was another click and clatter, and the bottles were brought forth. I rose from beside my family to fetch the glasses, and poured my father the first measure.

"To our future," he declared, and drank a long, steady sip.

The rest of the pack followed.

Finn had shifted back into human form, and his father had dragged his shirt back over his head, but neither could quite meet my eyes. Reed did not look thrilled by the situation.

I wonder if he knew about Celine, if Vincent had ever told him. It seemed unlikely, somehow.

"The other women," I started, searching for some way to begin, to force him to explain. "When your pack makes mothers, let me speak to them. Let me prepare them. Let me stop anything like this slaughter from ever happening again."

"You are just *full* of ideas tonight, aren't you, daughter?"

"I want to spare lives," I told him. "I don't want you to

have to kill another, like you did Celine."

Vincent's eyebrow twitched, and I knew, in that moment, that he had not told this story to the others. Something almost like a whisper slid amongst them.

"Celine?" Reed frowned. "What... what happened with Celine?"

Vincent did not meet his gaze.

"She was still unwilling to give the boy up. The pack was small. We needed more numbers. When she tried to stop me from taking him..."

"You... you *killed* her?" Reed's face was white, eyes wide, incredulous, horrified.

"I didn't have a choice." Vincent downed the rest of his glass. "The pack must survive, Reed, you know this."

Reed fell silent, but the rest of the pack declared another toast. A half-hearted cheer went up.

Vincent stilled, and coughed. Lightly at first, and then again, harder. His hand went to his chest, and then his stomach. He doubled over in pain, sweat beading his brow. Blood trickled from his mouth.

"No..." he hissed. "No, no..."

I held up the empty wolfsbane bullet, the one I'd plucked from Finn's shoulder. "You said I'd never cut you again, Father," I told him, and flung the casing to his feet. "But you never said anything about poisoning you."

Vincent's body contorted. He glanced at his pack. "Antidote," he rasped.

"We... we used it all up before..." one stammered.

He turned towards Grandma. "You. You. Give me something. I'll give you anything..."

"Most unfortunately," she returned dryly, "I find myself completely out of stock... and ingesting wolfsbane? Well, even if I *had* the ingredients, I'd doubt you'd last long enough for me to brew them..."

Vincent howled, lunging towards me. Cassel dipped in between us, but he flung him aside, snarling him away. Cassel made no other move against him, but swiped at one of the wolves holding Finn, allowing him to tear free. He dived at Vincent as his hands went for my neck.

Vincent struggled against him, larger, stronger, but with blood dribbling down his beard. He clawed at Finn, halfway between man and wolf, squeezing at his wounded shoulder.

"I'll take you with me, boy, I swear it—"

Please work, I prayed to the poison, *please, please, please.*

Even if it took hours to kill him, he couldn't stay functional too much longer, alpha or no.

I searched for a weapon to speed up the process, to ensure his death, to protect Finn, but a black figure flew across the room.

A flash of claws. A bloodied chest.

Vincent sank to the floor. Still alive. Just. Barely. His eyes waned with ebbing horror, staring at the face that brought the final strike.

Reed.

"That is *my son,*" he snarled. "And Celine was *my mate.*"

A few moments later, Vincent's chest had stilled.

Finn stared at his father as if he couldn't quite believe what had just happened. The entire pack trembled before the scene, but his face was more shocked and surprised than any of them, as if he never expected Reed to defend him.

I scrambled towards Finn and launched into his arms, clinging to him like the rest of the world was a shapeless, intangible mess.

He grabbed me back, just as fiercely, and the spell of silence was broken.

Reed surveyed the rest of the pack.

"Vincent is dead," he declared. "I am the alpha now, and as such, I release all of you from your vows. If you wish to break from the pack and return to your families, you may do so with my blessing. If not, you may remain with me, but I make you a solemn vow; I shall never manipulate you against your will. I shall never force you to do something against your beliefs. You shall be my brothers, not my slaves."

A shuffling quiet descended upon the room as the wolves debated between themselves. It was Cassel that came forward first, kneeling beneath him, swearing his allegiance like a knight of old. After him came his father, then one by one, all the other men swore to Reed until every wolf but Finn—and my grandma—had done so. Finn gave his father a nod, and the ghost of a smile in Reed's cheeks suggested he treasured this action above all the others.

"Well," said Grandma, clapping her hands together, "that was lovely, but I think there are a fair few hunters bleeding out on my grounds, and I rather think they require our attention."

22 WHERE THE WOLVES WENT

We spent the next few hours tending to the wounded, setting them up on makeshift beds in the old dining room, and collecting the dead. The number was thankfully few. Vincent's desire had driven the other wolves towards the house, and they had not stopped to finish their foes once they were down.

Mama took Rowan upstairs to one of the bedrooms, and came back down to help with the wounded. Once Forrest had done everything he could, he took Daisy home along with the hunters who could travel, and Russell, who clearly wasn't welcome no matter how many apologies he uttered.

We lit a fire and left Vincent's body to burn. No grave, no mourners. No one stayed to watch him go, to speak soft words or utter peace. Anything he had he took with him.

I spared a thought for him as I went back into the house, only to question how I could feel glad that my father was gone, only to wonder if I should worry about how remorseless I was.

I decided I should not.

If Mama was surprised about what Grandma was, I didn't see her confront her. She busied herself with looking after the wounded and slipped away to bed as soon as all was quiet.

I found myself alone with Grandma, everyone asleep.

"Why didn't you tell us?" I asked her.

"I didn't want to."

"Did you think we would... I don't know, not see you as our grandma anymore?"

"Ha! No, dear, but I did sometimes worry you might enjoy it too much, try and sneak here on a full moon... you do rather court danger, you know."

"But—"

"We're allowed our secrets. Mine have kept me company many a year."

"And Rowan?"

"I suppose I would have told him, when the time came. Told you all. But I wanted to own my secrets a little longer. And your mother was *insistent* that he not know, that he not grow up afraid. I couldn't go against her wishes, there."

It seemed a poor excuse, but Grandma was Grandma, and I did not have the energy to be mad at her.

Finally, blissfully, I dismissed myself for the night, and made my way up to one of the spare bedrooms.

The door clicked open as I was getting undressed, but I didn't startle. I knew who it was, whether there was some imperceptible change in the air or simply by the sound of his footsteps.

He stopped as he entered, grinning at the sight of me

half-dressed.

I stopped, too. I stopped so that he could help me remove the rest of them.

His fingers came up to my cape—I'd kept it on whilst the wolves were around lest my scent agitated them—and it fell to the floor like a pool of red. Finn's pupils widened, and his face went immediately to my neck.

"You smell *divine,*" he murmured.

I lifted his shirt over his neck. "You're not bad yourself."

Finn smiled crookedly, catching my hand as it fell to his wound. "It doesn't hurt," he assured me.

"You're lying."

"Well, it doesn't hurt *too* much."

Layer by layer, we peeled each other free and inched towards the bed, kissing long and soft, blurred by exhaustion. We were too tired to do little more than hold each other and whisper in the dark, of fears and joys and promises. We sunk into heavy sleep, the most restful I had ever known, and when we woke…

I was pressed against Finn's good shoulder, his arm around my waist, his breath on my temple. He was half awake, stroking the bare skin of my back in long, lazy circles. He murmured 'morning' against me as I cradled his warmth.

"This is wonderful," I said, nuzzling closer.

"I want to wake up like this every day for the rest of my life."

"I think my mother might have something to say about that before we make it official…" I linked my fingers into his, our makeshift bands gleaming, and kissed his knuckles.

A soft, slow shiver tugged at Finn's skin, and I drew his mouth to mine. The hard panes of his chest flattened against the softness of my own, and he rolled over me, bracing against my hips, hands on my face, waist, thighs. A hotness grew between us, and ache inside that longed for him, and my hands grabbed his hair and tugged him closer, further, more.

"Will it always be like this?" I asked him, afterwards.

Finn shrugged, fingers playing with my hair. "I'm not sure. Can't say I'm in a hurry for it to change."

"We'll burn up."

"Bring on the flames."

We did not move from the bed until my mother came knocking at the door.

∞∞∞

The wolves left the following day, all healed from their wounds. Cassel hugged Finn fiercely and promised that it would not be so long, this time. He swore to write. Reed asked Finn to go with them, but in a way I think he was sure of his answer before he asked.

"My pack is here," Finn declared, glancing at me, and Reed smiled in approval.

"Take care of each other," he said, and then his face turned steely. "I have something for you."

Before Finn could ask what it was, he reached into his pocket and pulled out the carved totem of a woman. I knew, somehow, without ever having seen the face, exactly who she was.

Celine. Finn's mother.

Finn took the carving with trembling fingers, thumbing the smooth features. It was not a recent creation. It was worn in places, rubbed raw.

Finn stared down at the face I knew he had almost forgotten, and now remembered entirely. "You loved her," he said to his father.

"In another life, I would have spent all of mine beside her."

"Why didn't you go back for her?"

"I thought about it a hundred times, but I didn't think she wanted me to. Don't... don't make the mistakes I did. Be better. Stay—

"I will," said Finn, the resolution burning in his voice as he reached out to take my hand, lacing his fingers into mine. He had clung to me many times before, but there was something different about this grip, something that said, *I don't ever want to let you go... and I don't have to.*

"I was not good to her," Reed continued. "I was too afraid of losing myself to her, or losing the respect of the pack. I thought there was only one way to exist, only one life to live." He paused, as if struggling with the words. "I am happy you have found another way. A way I aim to emulate."

Finn nodded, his throat looking tight.

"I should have known," Reed continued, just as solemnly. "What Vincent did to her. I should have felt it. Perhaps he fiddled with my memories too. Perhaps I just fooled myself. I was already so torn up thinking she didn't want me anymore that I let it cloud everything else, including you. The father I should have been to you." He paused. "I'm sorry. For so much."

Finn swallowed. "Mother is gone."

Reed hung his head.

"But we're still here. There's still time, Father. There's time for a lot." He extended his hand. "Don't be a stranger."

Reed took his hand, but jerked him into his chest, clutching him tightly in his arms. It was not a brief hug, it was an embrace that spoke of a thousand others that had never happened, of other words that had yet to pass between them.

We watched the wolves leave together, Finn's hand tight in mine, his eyes misty. We stayed that way for a long time, until I was certain the snow might melt before we moved.

"I'd like children," he said eventually.

"I'm sorry?"

"Children. One day. I'd like them. I'm not sure if you would, and while I'm not sure there would be any kind of deal breakers at this point, I still want you to know where I stand. I'd like children. A few. A mini-pack of our own."

I stared at him.

"Unless… you don't want them?"

"I'm not the *biggest* fan of children," I admitted, "but I'd have yours, I think. As long as you were actually going to help raise them."

At this, Finn smiled crookedly. "Where else would I be?"

I flushed down to my bones, and we drew tightly against each other, our breath murmuring. I could feel the shimmer of change in the air around us, the promise of spring, of better times to come, of new life and love and adventure I had hardly dared to dream of. We would chase spring and weather tempests.

Together till the end of our days.

EPILOGUE

Finn returned to the cave only once to collect his belongings, and after that moved into the chateau where he helped Grandma fix up the roof and a handful of rooms in one of the wings that we could use as our own after the wedding. I visited every day, and if sometimes I snuck out of my room and down to the home Finn was making for us? No one ever mentioned it.

The week before the wedding, he refused to let me in, creeping into my chamber instead to keep it a "surprise" for after the big day.

It came within two months, by which time the first flowers of early spring were blooming beside the lake. The local priest married us there. We had a small wedding, my family, Daisy and Forrest the only ones in attendance. But that night, the wolves came to our reception at the Chateau, and howls became our wedding march.

Reed presented us with a great gold chalice as a wedding gift. "What?" he said at our surprise. "You never wondered where your father got that pretty dagger of yours? We've got treasure caches all over the place."

Finn blinked. "I really ought to have known that, shouldn't I?"

Reed laughed, clapped his back, and moved away to drink ale with my grandmother. "Spend it wisely!" he called over his back.

But better and more magnificent than the chalice was the bed that Finn had made for us, a creation of beauty. Each of the posts was made to resemble trees, the boughs arching over the centre, branches entwined. The headboard was carved with etchings of wolves running through forests, with the silhouette of a woman with a cape holding hands with a male figure at the centre.

"Finn... this is beautiful," I said, gaping. "You did this all yourself?"

"Forrest helped," he explained. "At least with the construction."

That confession was not as strange as it should have been. In the weeks beforehand, the two seemed to have become fast friends, and with Forrest courting Daisy in earnest, he did not seem in the least bit put out by my marriage.

My marriage. I was married to Finn. He was mine in another way, now, one everyone could understand.

I traced the carvings in the bed posts. "It'll be a shame to leave this behind when we go to Loussant."

Finn's hands slipped around my middle. "I assure you, we shall get plenty of use out of it..." He kissed my neck. "It's our first home, Andie. I wanted it to be special. And we'll come back plenty."

We moved to Loussant by spring's end, using the money from the chalice to purchase a little house and workshop, where Finn set up as a carpenter and I enrolled at the academy of healing. For years we lived in a narrow kind of contentment, happy with ourselves, our lives, each other, aware that this was not quite forever, that we would outgrow the city eventually, and that sometimes it was hard to conceal Finn's nature during the full moon.

We returned to Thornwood, of course, on occasion—to support Rowan through his first change, for Daisy and Forrest's wedding, for festivals and birthdays.

There was a slow shift in the village, borne partly from Russell's attempts to make amends for his actions against us, but also from Rowan himself. He was way more liked within the village than I ever was, and few did not see him as "one of them" even when they knew that he was a wolf beneath. He would shift and change for the village children like some kind of party game, thankfully after Grandma taught him how to keep his clothes on, a trick she also taught Finn before we moved to Loussant so he could disappear into the outskirts every full moon and not freeze before making it back home.

I still feared for him every time, feared he'd attack some farmer's chickens and they'd shoot him dead. So much so, that after a couple of close calls, and my training was complete, we decided to move somewhere more remote.

Eventually, our journey brought us back to Thornwood. Not to the village, which still felt like a stifling snow globe to me, but to the Chateau. So renowned were my services as a healer by that point, that Grandma had the idea of setting it up as a house of healing. The entire village came together to restore it to something like its former glory, with help from the wolves, who never seemed to stay away for long. Cassel spent so much time with us that he eventually fell in love with one of the young healers in my employ, and the two of them converted one of the disused outbuildings on the estate to use as their home.

By the time we returned to Thornwood, Forrest and Daisy were on their third child, a number that finally settled on six. We ourselves had four, three boys and a girl. All of them are wolves, and we now have quite the pack indeed, and I never fear the full moon again. I know they are safe in the woods, that in the morning they'll be back, traipsing mud or snow or grass into the kitchen. Their howls are ones of joy, wild and laughing, and no one fears their calls again.

When the wolves howl now, I howl back. I howl *come home, come home, there's food on the table* and with the seats filled once more, I forget that I was ever lonely. I look at Finn, a perpetual grin on his face, and find it hard to remember him as a lone wolf, hard to remember any time when he wasn't so completely and utterly a part of me.

Sometimes, when the children are all abed and their great-grandmother is safely watching over them, we sneak out to the woods again together, and remember other, less lonely days, times that feel easier compared to raising four children and running a healing house. Years blur any memory of pain and hardship.

Then we return to the house and watch the children sleep, and Finn sings them lullabies his mother once sang him, and we know, beyond all doubt, that we are exactly where we are supposed to be, and that now, the present, is the best time of all.

Happy ever after is utterly exhausting.

The End

If you enjoyed Finn and Andie's tale, please, *please*, consider leaving a review. Even a tiny, "really liked this!" boosts visibility that is vital to indie authors.

Many thanks for your custom. Please join my mailing list at katherinemacdonaldauthor.com to be notified of new releases and chances to secure free advanced copies!

Coming 21st June

Other Books by this Author:

The Phoenix Project Trilogy

Book I: Flight
Book II: Resurrection
Book III: Rebirth

∞∞∞

In the "Fairy Tale Retellings" series:

The Rose and the Thorn: A Beauty and the Beast Retelling
Kingdom of Thorns: A Sleeping Beauty Retelling
The Barnyard Princess: A Frog Prince Retelling
A Tale of Ice and Ash: A Snow White Retelling
A Song of Sea and Shore: A Little Mermaid Retelling
Heart of Thorns: A Beauty and the Beast Retelling

Coming Soon:

A Rose of Steel: Book One of the Mechanical Kingdoms Quartet

Acknowledgements

Thank you so much to my glorious alpha and beta readers, Alice, Lucy, Avalon, Natalie and Sydney. It really wouldn't be the same without you.

Particular thanks to Lydia, whose conversations inspired this story, and who came up with the name Andesine and created the fantastic cover. I hope there's an appropriate amount of whump in it for you.

And also, as always, to Kirsty, who is always ready to listen to every little idea and niggling plot point I have. You truly are a brilliant sister.

About The Author

Katherine Macdonald

Born and raised in Redditch, Worcestershire, to a couple of kick-ass parents, Katherine "Kate" Macdonald often bemoaned the fact that she would never be a successful author as "the key to good writing is an unhappy childhood".

Since her youth, Macdonald has always been a storyteller, inventing fantastically long and complicated tales to entertain her younger sister with on long drives. Some of these were written down, and others have been lost to the ethers of time somewhere along the A303.

With a degree in creative writing and six years of teaching English under her belt, Macd'onald thinks there's a slight possibility she might actually be able to write. She may be very wrong.

She currently lives in Devon with her manic toddler, in a cabin in the woods.

The Rose and the Thorn is her debut novel. A pseudo-prequel, "Kingdom of Thorns" was released in August 2020.

You can follow her at @KateMacAuthor.

Printed in Great Britain
by Amazon

66182389R00194